Return To The Dark Tower

Illustrated by Joseph Vargo

Written by Joseph Vargo and Joseph Iorillo
Monolith Graphics, USA

Published By Monolith Graphics
www.monolithgraphics.com

Cover and Interior Artwork by Joseph Vargo
Graphic Design by Christine Filipak

Publisher's Cataloging-in-Publication Data
Return To The Dark Tower / by Joseph Vargo and Joseph Iorillo
ISBN-13: 978-0982489932
ISBN-10: 0982489935
1. Fiction—Horror 2. Vampires
3. Ghost Stories I. Vargo, Joseph

First Edition
Printed and Published in the United States of America

Herein lie the dark legends scribed long ago, unearthed and translated from ancient scrolls and arcane tomes. These tragic tales of myth and forbidden lore chronicle a sinister legacy, as it unfolded in the forgotten past, and the curse that yet lurks within the shadow of The Dark Tower.

Contents

Guardian in Absentia

Joseph Vargo

Deep within the heart of the Dark Tower, two cloaked figures marched silently through the ancient realm of shadows and ghosts. Brom, the immortal lord and protector of the keep, led the way in sure steady strides as Lorand, the young man from the village, hurried to keep pace. With each step they took, the torchlight behind them grew dimmer and dimmer until they were nearly engulfed in total darkness, but as they turned a corner, a faint auburn glow in the distance ahead acted as a beacon, guiding them to their destination. The two came to a halt before the entrance to the Tower's chapel where a single votive candle burned, but as Lorand took a step toward the hallowed chamber, Brom turned to a shadowed archway on the opposite side of the hall. Here, winged skeletons adorned the supporting columns of the arch, standing guard on either side of a large oaken door. Lorand's eyes lingered upon three words deeply etched into the dark wood—*Sanvi, Sansavi, Semangelaf.* Brom laid his pale hand upon the inscription and the heavy door opened with the grinding rasp of wood on stone, revealing the Tower Lord's inner sanctum.

The windowless chamber was illuminated by a solitary candle that flickered near the verge of extinction. Tall shelves, thick with cobwebs, held artifacts from ancient eras nestled among books and scrolls arranged in neatly stacked rows. The stale smell of must and decay permeated the air within. Aside from the cluttered bookcases that lined the walls, the chamber was sparsely furnished, holding only a large table and a few cushioned chairs. The room's lone candle rested upon the central table amidst maps, parchments and more stacks of books. The far end of the chamber was dominated by a fireplace mantel inscribed with ornate filigree surrounding a stone hearth.

As soon as they entered the sanctum, Brom abruptly broke the silence. "Give me your cloak," he demanded.

Without question or hesitation, Lorand quickly removed the monk's robe that he wore and handed it to him.

Brom threw the cloak across his shoulders and fastened it at his throat. "I must go to the Priory on a mission of dire importance. You shall remain here in the Tower until I return. I trust you to guard the keep in my absence. No one must know that I have left."

An expression of bewilderment crossed Lorand's face.

"You will find water, bread and dried meat in the storeroom beyond the grand hall above," Brom continued. "I shall return in two nights, perhaps three... no longer." Brom pulled the cloak's thick hood over his head, concealing his face beneath the shadow of the cowl. "Bolt the Tower doors and do not open them—not for anyone—until my return. Do you understand?"

"Yes, but—" Lorand stammered.

"I have no time for questions." Brom held out a small leather-bound book, offering it to the boy. "This will shed light upon some of the secrets of the Tower and perhaps even aid you in my absence."

Lorand carefully took the book from Brom's hand.

The Tower Lord stepped to the hearth where an ornate sword hung hidden in the shadows above the mantel. "A storm is rising. Should this tempest strike during my leave, you will need to be prepared." Brom took the relic sword from the wall and ran his bone-white fingers across the blade's gleaming edge. He stood silent for a moment, keeping his eyes locked upon the sacred weapon, as if lost in deep reminiscence. "This blade is said to have been forged by the hand of the Almighty, its steel tempered in the fires of His wrath. It has prevailed in the hands of mortals where mere earthly weapons could not."

Brom held the sword by the blade and offered the hilt to Lorand, saying, "I rest my trust in you."

Lorand took hold of the sword, but Brom did not relinquish his grip. Instead he placed his other hand upon the boy's shoulder. "The fate of Vasaria rests with you as well," Brom said.

"I understand," Lorand whispered, taking the sword.

The Tower Lord escorted Lorand out of the chamber. Then, as if Brom had willed it to do so, the door slowly closed behind him, sealing the sanctum.

"Wait here until we have left," Brom said, "then secure the keep." With that, the Tower Lord strode back down the corridor and disappeared into the darkness.

Lorand waited in the fragile pool of light at the doorway to the chapel, the book of secrets in his hand and the sword of power beneath his belt. He looked at the steady flame of the votive candle and said a silent prayer. A few moments later, he heard the caw of ravens in the distance. As stealthily as possible, he made his way back along the corridor to the entrance hall. The great room stood empty. The two men who had escorted him to the Tower were gone, as was Lord Brom. Lorand crept to the castle doors and peered out into the night. Three shadowed figures mounted horses and began their trek down the mountain path. From the darkness of the doorway, Lorand watched the riders pass the gate ruins beneath the pallid light of the rising moon. When they were no longer in sight, he pressed his weight against the massive doors, slamming them shut, then slid the heavy bolt across the latch.

Within the ancient Tower, shadows held dominion. Lorand lit a candle and held it aloft, but its meager light struggled to illuminate more than a few yards ahead of him. The sound of ravens' wings fluttering above him drew his attention overhead. Peering into the darkness, his eyes began to focus on the gargoyles that lined the heights of the hall. Strangely, he had never taken notice of them before, but now he could not wrest his eyes from them. The grim sculptures stared down upon him in unblinking silence. With each step he took, shadows shifted across their faces, creating the sense that they were somehow alive, leering, grimacing, silently screaming into the endless dark. Lorand reached into his pocket and withdrew his mother's rosary, quickly placing it around his neck. He clutched the rosary's cross tightly in his hand, but the sacred relic had little effect in easing his dread. He tore his gaze from the monstrous sentinels of stone and hurried from the hall.

Lorand returned to the chapel, seeking shelter in the confines of the hallowed sanctuary. In the vast expanse of the keep, this was the sole place that afforded him some measure of comfort. He remembered the first time he had come to the Tower, many years ago. Lost in the night, he was rescued from the wolves of the forest only to awaken in the chapel, unaware of where he truly was. He had shared stories with Lord Brom, learning some of the Tower's history, and as the years passed he felt inexplicably compelled to return here.

The chapel was dim. The votive candle that hung suspended above the obsidian altar burned low. Lorand stepped forward along the twisting path of blue and red tiles that formed a labyrinth design upon the chapel floor, paying them little heed. Instead, his eyes were drawn upward to the stained glass windows that ran along the surrounding walls. Their artistry and craftsmanship were exquisite, while the subjects they depicted were sordid and grim. Turning his head from side to side, he beheld renderings of blood rituals, lewd women, beastly men, frenzied demonic fiends, and sacrificial offerings to unknown gods. He gazed in awe at the images, repulsed and intrigued by the sinister scenes they portrayed.

Stepping to the front of the chapel, Lorand took a seat upon an oaken bench. The sound of thunder rumbled in the distance, adding to his unease. He settled back against the hard wooden surface and closed his eyes. The hour was late and he was weary, but his mind flooded with thoughts of devils and spirits lurking in the surrounding darkness. At times, he heard strange noises—distant whispers that seemed to call to him, and a scratching noise, like the sound of an animal raking its claws against metal, that seemed to come from somewhere inside the chapel walls. He stirred restlessly throughout the night, drifting between short periods of sleep and wakefulness.

Unable to rest and curious to investigate the keep, Lorand rose with the first light of dawn. Leaving the chapel, he returned to the door of Brom's inner sanctum. He tested his weight against the heavy wooden slab that sealed the chamber, but it did not budge. Once more, his eyes fell upon the door's inscription. *Sanvi, Sansavi, Semangelaf.* He recalled similar engravings marking many of the doors in his village, and though he did not know the actual meaning of the words, he knew they were meant as a ward against evil. He ran his fingers over the carved letters and gazed upon the words with strange wonder.

Lorand had always been strangely drawn to the Dark Tower. All his life, it had been a place of mystery and intrigue, looming high above his village, but it had always been forbidden to venture there. Most obeyed the elder's decree out of fear. Only a brave and reckless few dared to learn for themselves the truth behind the whispered legends of ravenous beasts and restless spirits. Now, as Lorand stood on the threshold of discovering the Tower's secrets, an ominous chill crept over him. Lighting another candle, he drew a deep breath and set out to explore the castle.

The corridors in the lower regions of the keep remained black as night, but as he ventured to the higher levels, daylight penetrated the windows to offer scattered regions of illumination. Ascending the main staircase, Lorand entered a twin doorway to find himself in the grand hall. The room was vast. Rows of thick columns supported a vaulted ceiling, barely visible in the shadows overhead. Tattered remnants of ancient tapestries hung across tall windows, filtering beams of sunlight to a dim haze.

At the far end of the hall a stark throne chiseled from dark granite rested upon a tiered dais. Abandoned and neglected, the throne seemed to be the final vestige of some long-forgotten dynasty. Lorand could not imagine Brom sitting upon it. Instead, his mind conjured a vision of the Dark Queen seated here, her infernal legions bowing in worship before her, chanting her name and awaiting her command. Lorand warily crossed the great room, feeling an unearthly chill as he passed the tiered platform. A shaft of sunlight shone directly down upon the dais, but the light seemed to be absorbed by the ebon throne.

Discovering the storeroom beyond the hall, Lorand found food and water. After a hasty meal he resumed his investigation. Ascending the Tower stairs once more, he set forth to explore the rooms of the keep's upper regions. He had hoped that daylight would allow him to see his surroundings more clearly, but a dusty mist hung in the air and cobwebs draped the surrounding halls, casting a foreboding pall over the forsaken corridors. Lorand held his candle outstretched before him to disperse the murky gloom. At times, it seemed he could not trust his own eyes. Ghostly figures stirred in the periphery of his vision, yet each time he turned, he found nothing there. Every doorway and darkened corner appeared to be haunted by shadowy forms that danced and writhed in the flickering candlelight.

Cobweb-strewn statues and portraits of people long dead stared blankly as he passed by. Their lifeless eyes seemed to follow him, watching his every move. As he searched each chamber and hall, he sensed he was not alone. He passed doors he knew he had earlier left open only to find them shut. Unexplained footsteps, whispers and laughter echoed around him, yet there was no one to be seen. The Tower's history was strewn with tragedy and bloodshed, and it seemed it was indeed haunted by spirits of the restless dead.

Near the castle's highest floor, Lorand came upon a large bedchamber adorned with the lavish trappings of ancient royalty. Tall wardrobe cabinets of dark mahogany stood on each side of a plush canopy bed surrounded by tattered drapes of black velvet. On the wall opposite the bed, winged lions of stone supported the mantle of an immense hearth. The menacing statues faced outward, their fierce eyes watching over the abandoned chamber.

The wall directly ahead was dominated by an ornate mirror that rested between tall lancet windows. Lorand stepped toward the looking glass, curiously drawn by an alabaster mask that hung from its gilded frame. Lorand's eyes studied the mask. Its delicate features captured the essence of female beauty, much like the sculpted bust of a Greek goddess. In contrast to the flawless porcelain-white face, the eyes and brows were accented with heavy black lines. The lips were painted a deep scarlet shade, disturbingly reminiscent of fresh blood.

Lorand wiped the dust from the mirror. As he stared at his own reflection, he noticed several ghostly faces looming in the room behind him. He whirled round and held his candle out, illuminating the wall opposite the mirror. No grim specters or spirits of the dead awaited him in the shadows, but the scene before him was no less unsettling.

Dozens of masks hung upon the wall, partially concealed beneath a layer of cobwebs and dust. Lorand gazed with strange fascination upon the countenances of savage beasts, beautiful fairies, creatures of lore and ancient deities of the forest. The eerie faces were painted garish colors and decorated with feathers, beads and jewels. Some were stained with ruddy brown streaks as if they had been spattered with blood.

As Lorand stared in spellbound wonder at the masks, the sound of fluttering wings drew his attention to an open window. Just outside, a large raven had come to roost upon a ledge carved in the likeness of a mournful jester. The ebon bird held Lorand's gaze with cold, unblinking eyes that seemed to burn with a crimson glow. Lorand felt a sensation of breathlessness, as if an icy grip had tightened over his chest, constricting the air in his lungs. The raven let loose a shrill caw then flew off toward the forest. Lorand gasped for breath as the spell subsided. He quickly left the room, making sure to fasten the door tightly behind him.

The day passed swiftly. As darkness settled over the Tower once more, Lorand returned to the chapel. The sanctum was dark. The vigil light that burned above the altar was now extinguished. Statues of saints loomed in unlit alcoves, shrouded in ominous shadows. It seemed as though every trace of solace and hope the sanctuary offered had been consumed by the prevailing darkness. Lorand lit another candle and set it in the votive above the altar then sat upon a bench. His mind burdened, his body weary, the young man leaned back and closed his eyes, falling fast asleep.

After some time, the sound of a creaking door roused him from his slumber. Lorand opened his eyes and scanned the darkened room, noticing a passageway he had not seen before. A bronze door concealed in the wall behind the altar now stood fully open. As silently as possible, he stood and crept forward to investigate the secret passage. Beyond the opening, a narrow stone staircase led down into shadows. As he stared deep into the lightless void, a soft voice, barely more than a whisper, emanated from somewhere behind him.

"The abyss beckons," the voice said.

Lorand turned to see who was with him in the room and was startled to discover a woman draped in black looming before the altar. She seemed to float upon the air, and as she did, her velvet gown and raven-black tresses wavered behind her, fading off into the dark. Iron spikes rose from a crown upon her head, twisting upward like the horns of some ancient pagan goddess. As Lorand stood petrified, the shadow-clad form drifted closer, moving within the halo of candlelight, allowing him to gaze upon her face. Her flesh was pale and smooth, while her eyes were soulless pools of black. She was a creature of beauty, but her beauty was unearthly and sinister.

She spoke again. "Darkness holds many wonders, does it not? One need only peer into its black depths to behold countless mysteries." She gestured a clawed hand to the passageway behind Lorand. "What awaits in yonder shadows?

What lies buried far below?"

Her hypnotic voice held Lorand rapt, rendering him speechless.

"Are you not curious, child? Have you never wondered what treasures the Tower holds—what secret must be guarded so vigilantly?

At last Lorand found the power to speak. "A great evil is held here," he replied. "The Tower must be guarded, lest the darkness imprisoned within these walls be set loose to wreak havoc upon the world."

"This is not true," the dark woman said. "Evil resides within the hearts of men. No prison could ever contain it." She drifted closer, holding his gaze with her black eyes. "You speak of evil and darkness as if they were one, but this is not so. Darkness is not a thing to be feared. It is the ancient realm of shadows and night. It gives birth to dreams and grants safe haven for those who seek its refuge. It empowers all who embrace it, allowing them to bask in its eternal rapture."

She drifted closer still. Her eyes seemed to pierce the very core of his soul. "Your destiny is entwined in darkness, child. Allow me to guide you along the path of shadows."

Lorand found it nearly impossible to resist her seductive allure. He closed his eyes to break the spell and regained the will to speak once more. "Still your tongue, enchantress. I shall not be swayed by your charms." His voice wavered weakly as he spoke. "Your beauty is but a hollow husk—a spell to conceal the demon within, but I know what you truly are." He reopened his eyes to meet her cold stare. "You are Mara, the Dark Queen. The elders have warned me of your unholy magic."

Mara's blood-red lips formed a smile. "They are fools, blinded by their faith, refusing to see things as they truly are.

Lost in their own delusions, they seek to destroy all they do not understand. They fear me, for power such as mine can shape men's destinies. The blood that courses within me can transform mere peasants into warriors, even kings. If you were to taste such power, there would be no limit to the things you could attain. No dream would elude your grasp." The Dark Queen now hovered directly before Lorand. She stared deep into his eyes, penetrating his gaze and thoughts. She pressed herself to him, her lips brushing against his. "I can grant your every desire."

Leathery wings, like those of a bat, unfolded from the darkness behind her, stretching wide around Lorand, encompassing him in their unearthly embrace. "Come to me, child," Mara's voice purred seductively. "Release me," she whispered, "release me and I shall reward you with treasures untold." Her red lips drew back, exposing glistening fangs. Mara lowered her mouth to his throat.

Suddenly, it was as if the chapel had been struck by a bolt from the heavens. A brilliant light shot down from high above, setting the room ablaze with the sun's blinding radiance. The Dark Queen shrieked and recoiled, raising her arms to shield herself from the scorching rays. Then, as if yanked away by some unseen force, she flew backward toward the open passage and was swallowed by the shadows within. The door slammed shut with a resounding clang, sealing the abysmal portal and silencing Mara's screams.

Lorand awoke from his dream, his heart pounding madly. Vibrant colors filled the chapel as sunlight shone brightly through the stained glass windows. He turned his gaze upward, locking his eyes on a mural painted on the ceiling. High above him, three angels hovered within the chapel dome. The celestial beings were depicted as warriors with sleek ebon wings, clad in armor of lustrous black. Each held a gleaming sword, identical to the one Brom had bestowed upon him. Lorand rose to his feet and closed his eyes, tilting his head far back. Tears streaked his face as he basked in the sun's soothing warmth.

After a quick meal, Lorand resumed his investigation of the keep. His energy and curiosity rekindled, he raced up the Tower stairs, losing track of the levels he ascended. Eventually he emerged in the open air on the walkway surrounding the Tower's heights. Twin parapet walls framed the sides of the path that encircled the castle, joining the black spires that stretched upward from each of the keep's four corners. Lorand leaned against the parapet that crested the castle's facade and looked out over Vasaria far below, imagining Lord Brom surveying his domain. The meager village looked peaceful and inviting, offering no clue to the sinister secrets it harbored.

Lorand turned toward the towers that rose from the castle's corners. They soared high above the ancient fortress like black lances piercing the heavens. While three of the surrounding spires seemed to be no more than outlook posts, the fourth housed the keep's belfry. Lorand entered the base of the bell tower and climbed the stairs that wound upward toward the castle's lofty pinnacle. Reaching the belfry, he felt a strange sense of unease. The Tower bell hung motionless, undisturbed by the wind that whistled through the surrounding archways, but something stirred in the shadows overhead. Lorand slowly shifted his gaze above him. The rafters were filled with swarms of sleeping bats. The creatures were much larger than the bats he had seen in the forest. They clung to the wood and bricks with taloned feet and hung inverted as they slept. It seemed as though a legion of hellish demons had taken roost here, seeking haven from the light of day while awaiting night to fall. Making no sound or sudden movement to disturb their slumber, Lorand retreated back down the belfry stairs.

Again on the parapet, Lorand looked down upon the castle's small graveyard enclosed within the walls in a courtyard at the rear of the castle. From his lofty vantage point, the cemetery looked like a tranquil sea of mist. A thick fog shrouded the tombstones, covering all but the tallest trees and monuments. Statues of angels rose from the cloud-like haze, staring silently downward, as if keeping vigil over the hallowed ground. Lorand stared at the field of ancient graves, lost in an eerie sense of serenity.

Completing his search of the Tower's upper regions, Lorand made his way back down to the keep's ground level. The hours of daylight had quickly slipped away, leaving him little time to investigate the castle's last unexplored region. Shortly before dusk, he entered the Tower cemetery.

The pervading mist crept along the burial ground, steadily weaving its way between the weathered monuments. Skeletal branches of barren trees reached outward in all directions while twisted roots burrowed deep into the hallowed soil, causing the long-neglected headstones to lean at tilted angles. As Lorand walked amidst the forsaken graves and mourning statues a piercing sadness struck his heart. Here and there, ghostly figures seemed to rise from the mist, only to disappear into the cool autumn air. Lorand slowly wound his way throughout the field of tombstones, straining to read their age-worn inscriptions. He paused briefly before a mausoleum arch supported by graven angels of death. The stone crypt was sealed with iron bars and a large cross sanctified the gate. Lorand wondered if the sacred ward was there to keep some evil force from entering the tomb, or to contain it within.

At the furthest reaches of the burial ground, a simple headstone bore a solitary name—Rianna. Lorand reverently approached his mother's grave, the sadness inside of him increasing with every step. Though he had never known her, he had heard many stories of her beauty and kindness. She would have been a good mother, Lorand thought, had she not fallen victim to the Tower's curse. He laid his hand upon the cold stone and said a prayer for her soul. Before he could finish, darkness had begun its descent upon the Tower.

Lorand made his way back to the chapel. He entered warily, recalling his nightmare of the evening before. The memory still plagued him. The room that had once been his sanctuary of hope and comfort now held a sinister taint. He examined the bronze wall behind the altar, but could find no trace of a doorway or lock. He dreaded the thought of falling asleep for fear that the Dark Queen would invade his dreams once again. Nervously, he lit every candle in the chapel, surrounding himself in a protective circle of light.

Weary as he was after his long day, Lorand dared not even close his eyes. Remembering the journal that Brom had given him, he opened the book and began to read. The tales within chronicled the rise of Mara and her demise at the hand of the Baron, as well as the Baron's vigil, his sacrifices, his quest and his downfall. It related the mysteries of the Tower that Brom had discovered—the legend of the dark angels, their exile to the caverns deep below the Tower, and the secret crypt in the catacombs where Mara's body and undying spirit remained imprisoned. It also told of the warrior angels and the standing stones they set to mark the Dark Brood's earthly boundaries. Lorand took special interest in a passage describing how the angel's names were engraved as mystic barriers, creating wards that the dark ones could not cross.

He set the journal down and stared off at the door across the hall that sealed Brom's sanctum, realizing at last the true meaning of the three words inscribed there.

The cry of a solitary raven broke the still of the night. The bird's rasping croak echoed through the halls, sounding again and again, as if summoning Lorand from the sanctuary of the chapel back into the Tower's shadowy abyss. Taking candle and sword in hand, he followed the ghastly croaking to the entrance hall.

Upon entering the great room, the raven's call abruptly ceased, and Lorand found the hall silent and empty. He tested the Tower doors, pressing his full weight against them to affirm they remained securely bolted. Turning to leave, his eyes scanned the darkness overhead, peering deep into the shadows that concealed the hall's stone guardians. One by one, the nightmarish creatures surrounding the room became visible, as if they were slowly emerging from night's ebon shroud. As he gazed upon their faces, he was startled to see another figure staring down at him from the balcony above.

"Who goes there?" Lorand called, his voice quavering.

The intruder stared in silence.

"Answer me," Lorand demanded, but once more, the figure offered no reply.

Lorand held his sword out before him, trying to still his trembling hand, and ascended the staircase step by cautious step. At the top of the stair, he saw the intruder clearly. A bearded man, dressed in the robes of an ancient king stood on the balcony landing. A jeweled crown rested upon his head and his eyes held a look of dire sorrow. Lorand held his candle out toward the figure. The king's form cast no shadow and seemed to fade to nothingness as the light fell upon it. Fear gripped his heart as Lorand realized the thing that stood before him was no living person.

Without a word, the phantom turned and slowly ascended the stairs to the Tower's upper regions. Keeping a safe distance, Lorand followed the ghostly king to a balcony window overlooking the castle gate. The specter came to a halt beside a monstrous gargoyle and stood gazing out into the night. After a moment, the spirit turned to cast his hollow gaze upon Lorand one last time, then slowly faded from sight.

Lorand set his candle in a wall sconce and stepped forward onto the balcony. Finding no trace of the ghostly king, he turned to examine the fiendish statue perched upon the pedestal at his side. The sculpture captured the essence of nightmare, depicting a monstrous, horned demon with long, wolfish fangs and eyes of unfathomable menace. The stone beast seemed to howl with diabolic glee as it clutched a human skull in its claws. The creature glared outward over the landscape below, its thick muscles tensed as if ready to spring forth into the night.

Following the gargoyle's stare, Lorand looked down upon the gate ruins that stood beside the Tower path. A murder of ravens had taken roost atop the remnants of a pillared archway. The ebon birds sat deathly still, watching over the forest path as if awaiting some unseen prey to draw near. Suddenly, they began to stir from their roosts.

Below the ruins, a veil of fog spread across the ground, radiating a soft, unearthly glow. A swirling vapor slowly rose from the mist, taking the spectral form of a maiden shrouded in white. Her dark hair floated on the wind and seemed to shimmer beneath the light of the full moon. The ends of her gown trailed off into mist as she floated along the fog-covered ground. The beautiful spirit drifted beneath the open arch of the gate and stared off along the forest trail.

Peering out over the dark woodlands toward the village, Lorand spied the flicker of distant torchlight far down the mountainside, climbing the path to the Tower. A feeling of dread seized his heart. He looked toward the phantom once again, seeing that she had turned to face the castle. She tilted her head upward and cast her ghostly gaze directly upon him. Their eyes locked for a moment before the spirit faded from sight, returning to the mist from whence she came.

In the next instant, a chill swept over him and Lorand felt an icy caress upon his shoulder. Slowly, he turned to see a woman on the landing behind him. It was the same phantom he had just seen near the castle gate far below, now hovering before him, the wispy lengths of her gown brushing the floor of the landing.

Raising his sword, Lorand held it out between them in an attempt to keep the apparition at bay. "What do you want with me, spirit?" he demanded.

"Only to help you in your time of need." The beautiful specter spoke in a soft voice, yet her words echoed in Lorand's mind.

He peered deep into her eyes and his gaze was met with a tranquil stare. Sensing that she was no creature of darkness and finding no reason to doubt her words, Lorand lowered his blade. "Who are you?" he asked.

"In life, I was called Rianna."

Lorand's eyes grew wide. When he spoke, his voice was little more than a whisper. "You were... my mother."

"Yes," she said, "though our time together was short." The spirit's gaze fell upon the sword in Lorand's hand. A look of sadness filled her eyes as she recognized the instrument of her own death. "'Tis Lord Brom's sword you hold, is it not?"

"It is," Lorand replied. "He bestowed it upon me so that

I may guard the keep." Lorand drew the blade close, allowing it to slip beneath the cover of his cloak. "Is the tale he told me true? Were you slain by his hand?"

"He had little choice," the phantom said. "I was possessed of a vile spirit. Brom's actions thwarted the rise of the Dark Queen. I have watched him suffer with the consequences of his deeds. He remains here, in darkness, bound by moral duty and the promise of delivering salvation unto my soul."

"I have felt the ancient queen's power," Lorand said. "Her sway is irresistible. I can imagine nothing more difficult than the vigil he keeps. I cannot fathom how he has endured the years."

"His faith gives him strength."

Lorand noticed that Rianna's eyes had now come to rest upon the rosary that hung around his neck.

"The bond between you and the dark lord seems to run deep," Lorand said, "deeper than mere friendship."

"Yes," the spirit replied, "deeper than most could ever know."

"You loved him?"

"Yes."

"Is he then," Lorand stammered, "Lord Brom... is he... my true father?"

Rianna's eyes shone with love and sadness. "Yes," she replied. "The elders kept your true heritage secret for the sake of all. Lord Brom knew nothing of you until you came here the night of your guardian's death—until you yourself revealed the truth to him."

"Why did he not tell me?"

"Even with the revelation that you were my son—his son—he understood the danger that awaited you should your identity be known. You would have become a pawn in the Dark

Brood's plan, and ultimately, the instrument of his demise."

Lorand stood silent for a long moment as he contemplated her words. At last, he said, "I understand. Truly, I do."

The spirit drew closer and her voice dimmed to a whisper. "There is much that must be done this night, and little time left. Two convoys approach—one from the village, and one from afar. You must grant the emissaries from Vasaria passage to the Tower, before the others arrive."

"Lord Brom made me swear not to open the doors of the keep."

"He did not foresee how swiftly this storm was approaching, nor was he aware of its severity. You will need help to stand against the darkness that shall soon threaten the Tower."

"When shall he return?"

"Soon... fate willing," she replied. "His journey must unfold in due course. Until then, you must be strong." She reached out, laying her spectral hand upon his chest. "The fire in your heart cannot be extinguished by anything this world holds as long as you have faith in yourself."

Just then, a loud banging sound echoed through the keep, drawing Lorand's attention down toward the entrance hall. When he looked back to where his mother's spirit had been, she was gone.

Outside the keep, Talik, head of the elder council, pounded on the Tower doors then looked back at the three men waiting silently on the steps below. The men's eyes shifted nervously between the surrounding landscape and the black edifice looming before them as they waited to see who would answer their call.

Talik raised his torch to study the immense iron symbol that marked the Tower doors. His eyes scanned it intently as his mind struggled to decipher it. The ominous rune looked like some sort of ceremonial dagger or scepter crowned with talons. In the midst of the icon, serpentine spikes snaked outward from a central ring surrounding what seemed to be the skull of a horned beast. The true meaning of the ancient sigil had been lost over the centuries. It had now come to be known only as a symbol of darkness.

Talik raised his fist once more but before he could knock again he heard the sound of the latch-bolt being thrown. The old man stepped back as the Tower doors creaked open, splitting the ancient rune in two. A figure cloaked in black stood within the darkened entryway. As he stepped from the shadows, all eyes were drawn to the gleaming sword in his hand.

"Greetings, elder," Lorand said.

At first glance Talik thought it was Brom who stood before him. Beneath the moon's pale light, the boy looked enough like the Tower Lord to fool most, but the sound of his voice betrayed his true identity.

Talik stepped forth, holding his torch outward to see Lorand clearly. "So it is true," the elder said gruffly, "Lord Brom has left the Tower."

Lorand felt compelled to defend Brom's actions. "He has gone to the Priory of St. Sebastian to investigate a matter of great importance."

"Yes, Leonidas has told us of his mission. We have sent a rider to the monastery to retrieve him."

"Why have you come here?"

"Danger approaches." Talik's voice held a deathly solemn tone. "According to prophecy, the White Wolf has returned to stalk these lands once more. We believe he shall attempt to seize opportunity in the Tower Lord's absence. We have come to warn you, and help you stand against him."

Lorand took notice of the men who accompanied Talik, recognizing them as hunters from the village. Each carried an axe and sturdy bow, and their belts were weighted with an array of well-used knives. Though the men were a formidable lot, rugged and strong, their faces could not hide their unease. Talik nodded to the men and they entered the Tower, averting their eyes from Lorand as they passed.

Before entering the Tower, Talik grabbed Lorand's arm, holding him back. "I can think of nothing more important than guarding the keep in the Tower Lord's absence," the elder said. "Do you know why you were chosen for this task?"

Lorand looked directly into Talik's eyes, saying only, "Yes."

The old man held Lorand's gaze, studying his eyes for a long moment. At last he said, "The Tower Lord has protected us for many years. We rest our faith in him." Talik laid his hand upon Lorand's shoulder. "If he has chosen you to stand guard in his absence, we must abide by his wisdom."

The two men entered the keep and the great doors closed once more, meeting to form the ancient rune that marked the Tower as the realm of angels and demons.

The Company of Wolves

Joseph Vargo

The full moon hung low above the forest tree line, silhouetting the ancient tower that rose from the distant mountain summit. An eerie stillness gripped the woodlands, as if the forest had fallen beneath a spell of encompassing silence. The creatures of the timberlands remained quiet and still under the eaves of the wood, their watchful eyes fixed upon a grim procession of men and beasts steadily crossing an open field.

Four shadowy forms marched beneath the light of the rising moon. A tall figure led the way—a lean man clad in black, his flesh and hair white as bone. He was known in whispered legends as Dravek, the lord of wolves. His captive, Leonidas, venerable elder of Vasaria, labored behind him as they made their way toward the forest path that wove a serpentine route upward to the looming Tower. Two monstrous forms, more wolf than man, lumbered close behind, snarling and baring their fangs each time the old man's pace slackened.

Hidden from view at the edge of the woods, Falon watched and waited in silence as the wolfpack and their prisoner passed through the clearing. The young hunter knew that Dravek's caravan would be unable to take the perilous mountain trail due to the age of their captive. It would have been difficult for the old man to traverse the treacherous terrain in daylight, but it would be impossible in the dead of night, no matter how his captors tormented him. Weighing this, his only advantage, against the odds he faced, Falon quickly formed a desperate plan. He skirted the meadow just beneath the cover of the trees, racing to the edge of the forest path.

At the junction where the trail split, Falon swiftly embarked upon the mountain path, hoping to intercept Dravek's convoy before they reached the summit.

Leonidas struggled to keep pace with Dravek. The old man fought to catch his breath and sweat drenched his body and cloak. If not for the snapping jaws of the unholy creatures at his heels, his resolve to continue would have expired long ago. His heart pounded as if it were on the verge of bursting in his chest. Dravek stalked steadfastly forward, unmoved by the old man's gasps for breath.

Finally, Leonidas could bear no more. He fell to his knees, his hands clutching the ground. "I must rest," he gasped. "Please... I beg of you, stop... if only for a moment. I cannot continue."

Dravek slowed to a halt, then turned to consider his captive with a thoughtful gaze, as if weighing the old man's worth. "I am not without compassion, old one. I shall grant you a brief moment's rest."

Leonidas sat on the rough, rock-strewn soil while the wolves circled him, their glowing eyes gleaming like burning coals in the gloom. Leonidas shut his eyes in an attempt to ignore the fearsome creatures, but their low growls kept him aware of their menacing presence.

Dravek studied his prisoner with mild interest. "Where is your home, old one?"

"My village is called Vasaria," Leonidas replied. His voice was hoarse in the chilled air. "It lies beyond the mountain, beneath the shadow of the Dark Tower."

"Yes, I know it well. It was the village of my birth."

"You lived in our village?" Leonidas asked, feigning ignorance. "When?"

Dravek's eyes glistened, as if the recollection stirred vestiges of emotion from the distant past. He looked off toward the moon for a moment before his gaze fell upon Leonidas once more. "Many lifetimes ago," he said.

Leonidas peered deep into his captor's eyes. "Who are you?"

"I am Lord Dravek. I doubt my name has been forgotten, even after so many years."

Indeed, Leonidas recalled the tales of Dravek, the dreaded White Wolf, faithful servant of the Dark Queen. His name inspired fear among the villagers. Even the elders lowered their voices to hushed whispers when they spoke of him. He was thought to be long dead, yet here he stood in the realm of the living.

"How can this be?" Leonidas asked. "Our legends speak of your death at the hands of the Baron more than a century ago."

"The Baron," Dravek hissed, as if the name brought a foul taste to his lips.

At the risk of retribution from his captor, Leonidas continued to provoke him. "He reigned as the Tower Lord for many generations after slaying the Dark Queen. He—"

"He was no lord," Dravek interrupted, "merely a lowly priest—the weakest of the holy warriors we captured one fateful night." Dravek turned his gaze to the distant Tower and its tall black spires, lost in solemn reflection. "I remember that night all too clearly. Three crusaders dared to breach the Dark Queen's domain, and in turn, they sealed their own fates. We captured them at the Tower doors and brought them to stand before our queen, to face judgment by her decree. The priest pledged his loyalty to her, abandoning his god of light for a goddess of eternal darkness. He proved his devotion to her by mortally wounding one of his own comrades and my queen rewarded him by bestowing her dark gift upon him. He was bound to us by blood and initiated into our coven.

"But his actions were merely a deception and his allegiance was false. He used his newfound powers against his creator, murdering my queen in her throne and driving my kindred into the deadly sunlight. He banished me from the Tower and left me to die in the approaching light of day."

"How then did you survive?"

Dravek stepped close to Leonidas, looming over him. "I wrapped myself in the priest's own cloak to shield my flesh from the scorching rays of the sun. I often reflected upon this strange twist of fate—that this usurper's robe was the instrument of my salvation. I often wondered why I and I alone had been spared. For what purpose did I yet exist?

"Believing my queen to be dead, I fled the region, driven into exile by the slayers who hunted the remaining few of my kind. I lived among the wilds for more years than I can recall, running free with the wolves of the forest. More animal than man, living only for the hunt. For the kill. I know not how many generations of our pack I led as we hunted in the high mountains." Dravek closed his eyes and stood silent for a long moment, his stern face betraying a hint of a smile.

"But one night, after many decades in the wild, I heard my master's call. Her voice came to me as a siren's song upon the wind, summoning me to the Tower once more. But a new lord stood guard over the keep—an adversary much stronger and deadlier than the Baron. A true warrior. He silenced her voice that very night, yet in the few moments she called to me, my allegiance to her was rekindled. My true purpose in this life then became clear. I swore to avenge my queen and free her from the bonds that held her captive.

"I traveled east, to Castle Rankorr, laying siege to the keep, taking the fortress in one night. Though the king's guards were battle-hardened soldiers, experienced and strong, they had never faced an enemy such as I. During my siege, I released the prisoners of the dungeons who had been destined to meet their deaths. In exchange for their lives, the men swore their undying allegiance to me. I created an army, the Brotherhood of the Black Dawn, to wrest control of the Tower and free the Dark Queen. As more years passed, my legions grew in number."

Dravek's voice grew louder. "I have long waited for the time to strike, planning for this very night."

Leonidas stared at him curiously. "Why this night, after all these years?

"My oracle foresaw Lord Brom's departure from the Tower, assuring me the keep stood unguarded."

"Perhaps your oracle's vision could not penetrate the Shadow Lord's magic. He is a powerful sorcerer."

"We shall see, old one," Dravek said. "But it matters little. I am prepared for battle. My army awaits my command. If the Tower must be taken by force, my legions shall swarm this land." Dravek cast a pitiless gaze on the old man. "You have rested long enough."

Leonidas slowly rose to his feet. "Yes," he said. "The Shadow Lord awaits."

The convoy renewed their trek. The lowland trail was little more than a muddy path that meandered through thickets of brush and bramble, but as it wound its way upward through the foothills, the soil became rocky and the surrounding terrain grew dense with trees. Tall oaks and pines soon dominated the landscape, blocking the moonlight from the path. Dravek and his wolves continued relentlessly through the darkness, herding their captive along at a merciless pace. Leonidas felt his heart drumming in his chest and his legs grew sore and weak, yet somehow he forced himself to carry on.

Entering a clearing at the base of the mountain, they came upon an ancient monolith, forsaken and toppled long ago. Dravek stopped to survey the fallen monument that lay half-buried in a shallow gully beside the path. The weathered stone was covered in vines and a thick coat of moss, obscuring the runic inscription etched into its surface. Once a revered territorial landmark, it was now little more than a faded remnant of an era long past.

Dravek's black eyes glistened with delight as he ran his fingers along a large crack that ran through the stone. Turning his gaze to Leonidas, he said, "At the edge of Vasaria, near the mountain path, there once stood a monument such as this."

Leonidas studied the monolith at length, taking time to catch his breath. "Yes," he said at last, "I know it well."

"Tell me, old one, does the stone near your village also lay in ruin?"

"The stone you speak of marks the threshold of the Tower's domain," Leonidas said coldly. "It has never been toppled. It yet stands to designate the ancient boundary."

Dravek's jaw clenched. He turned away briskly, and stalked back to the path, resuming his trek at an angry pace. A slight smile crept across Leonidas' face as he followed close behind.

Falon emerged from the woods, reaching the crossroad where the mountain trail met the forest path. He took a moment to calm his heart and breath as he surveyed his surroundings. Jagged shards of moonlight broke through the tangle of branches to illuminate small patches of the ground along the path. He examined the trail, finding no trace of the wolfpack. But he knew he had little time before Dravek would reach this point. To the left of the path, the mountainside was sheer stone. A few trees jutted out here and there, but none that were large enough to support his weight or provide sufficient cover for him. He shifted his gaze to the opposite side of the path, over the edge of a craggy gorge. Far below, at the bottom of the ravine, the stream waters rushed by, crashing against the boulders to form churning rapids.

Taking his knife, Falon sliced a shallow gash along his forearm, letting the blood drip onto the ground at the cliff's edge. The crimson droplets appeared black beneath the moon's light. He climbed down to a small ledge and clambered onto a dead tree overhanging the ravine, finding a steady perch among its barren limbs. There, hidden from sight, he carefully withdrew an arrow from his quiver. He had specially prepared his arrowheads earlier that day, covering each of them in a fine coating of wolfsbane pollen, knowing its touch was poison to Dravek's monsters. He laid the arrow across his bow and waited, straining to listen to the noises of the forest against the low roar of the rapids that coursed through the ravine beneath him.

Dravek's convoy emerged from the shadows of the forest. After a long, slow ascent, the woodland trail had finally risen to join the steeper mountain path. Ahead, a moonlit clearing opened along a narrow cliff. Dravek slowed his pace and looked about warily, as if sensing something in the wind. The wolves began panting wildly as they caught the scent of human blood, following its trail toward the cliff's edge. Falon heard them and tensed, watching from the shadows below, waiting for the creatures to approach the brink of the ravine.

The snarling and growling of the wolves grew momentarily louder, and Falon used the noise as cover to draw his creaking bowstring back. He held it there, drawing in a deep breath. As the first wolf peered over the crest of the cliff, Falon raised the bow, steadying his aim on the creature for a brief moment before letting the arrow fly. It found its mark high in the wolf's chest, staggering the hulking beast. In two swift motions, Falon readied another arrow and fired again. The second arrow struck just below the first, delivering its deadly poison to the creature's heart. With a strangled, groaning gasp, the monstrous wolf fell. Its lifeless body toppled over the edge of the cliff, plummeting into the ravine where it was swallowed by the raging waters.

Leonidas turned a wild gaze to Dravek. "It is the Shadow Lord's magic. His reach is long, and his deadly grip is inescapable!"

"Silence, fool!" Dravek raised his head, sniffing the air like a hound, detecting Falon's scent in the wind. He stepped to the edge of the cliff and scanned the trees below. Falon let loose another arrow, this one intended for Dravek. With a swiftness that defied sight, Dravek caught the shaft, its deadly tip inches from his throat. He cast his piercing gaze down into the gorge, discovering Falon amidst the shadows.

Dravek shouted a command and the remaining wolf beast lunged down the cliff's rocky edge onto the tree, clawing its way up to Falon. Its monstrous jaws snapped wildly as it drew ever closer. But before it could reach him, Falon leapt to the river below, risking the chance of escape against certain death.

Dravek stood at the cliff's edge. He studied the arrow in his hand, then dropped it into the ravine and whispered,

"Wolfsbane."

Hearing this, Leonidas remembered the wolfsbane powder given to him by the sorceress Daria. He let his hand drop to his belt and found the pouch still securely tied there. But now was not the time. He struggled to keep his breathing under control. He saw the cruel embers of the wolf beast's eyes as the creature clawed its way back onto the mountain trail and took its place at its master's side.

Dravek stood at the cliff's edge, peering into the darkness below where moonlight glistened like black diamonds in the rushing water. "This was no magic, no dark power," he said, shaking his head, "no—merely a lone hunter lying in ambush." He turned to face Leonidas. "What other traps lie in wait for us? Tell me now, old man, or your wretched life shall end here, on this trail."

Leonidas kept his head bowed before Dravek. "I have told you all I know. I am merely a messenger, nothing more. The Shadow Lord commands us to do his bidding, and we must obey. We are powerless to defy him. Our wills are no longer our own."

Dravek clutched Leonidas by the jaw and forced his head back, his gaze boring deep into the old man's eyes. Leonidas felt his mind go numb. He could not move nor even breathe. The next sensation he experienced was the feeling of spidery legs, sharp and icy, crawling inside his head. Dravek's stare held Leonidas rapt as he peered into the elder's mind, probing his memories and thoughts. But the vision was faint and obscure, revealing only the vague form of a figure cloaked in black standing amidst the shadows of the Dark Tower.

Dravek looked away, releasing Leonidas from his spell, then addressed the old man once more. "If indeed this new Tower Lord truly exists and is as powerful as you have said, why does he not make himself known? He is no better than those who have reigned before him—mere shadow kings who sought the sanctuary of the Tower to claim dominion over the lowest of men."

Leonidas shook his head. "Those who have stood watch over the Tower have protected us and ruled over us wisely."

Dravek stepped closer, towering over the old man. "They are false lords, reigning over a tomb, keeping my queen imprisoned." Dravek's eyes were seething with rage. "I am the true heir to the Tower of Vasaria. And when my queen is restored to her throne, all men shall tremble beneath her power." He turned to face the mass of shadows comprising the Dark Tower and whispered, "Woe to those who dare stand against her."

Dravek's words chilled Leonidas to the bone, but the old man remained silent. He dared not risk angering his captor further for fear of incurring his wrath. But the seed had been planted in Dravek's mind. He now seemed to believe the story Leonidas had concocted about the mysterious new lord of the Dark Tower.

As they renewed their trek, Dravek led the way at a more cautious pace, alert to each rustling sound and wary of the slightest movement in the steep mountain forest. He scanned the dark woods on both sides of the path, his nocturnal vision granting him full view of whatever lay hidden in the surrounding shadows

Onward they traveled, ascending the mountain trail toward the stark citadel that loomed atop the summit. The moon had settled low in the night sky, barely staying above the treetops ahead. Mossy roots snaked across the path beneath their feet, while surrounding branches twisted menacingly outward, threatening to grasp travelers who strayed into the surrounding woods. Here and there, the distant cries of ravens echoed through the forest, breaking the stillness of the night.

The woodlands became more barren as they neared the mountaintop. Thick vines choked the trees, spiraling upward to wrap themselves around black branches thick with thorns. The path soon became little more than a tunnel that wound its way through a mesh of dead, tangled limbs. Far overhead, ravens filled the skeletal trees, peering down over the woodlands like grim, winged sentinels keeping vigil in the night. Leonidas marched sullenly along between the great wolf and its master, fearfully knowing they were nearing their destination.

At last, they crested the summit and came upon the ruins of the Tower gate. A creeping mist covered the ground in a ghostly haze that radiated an unearthly glow beneath the moon's pale light. As the convoy approached, the eerie fog began to stir. The wolf beast began to cower and growl, but Dravek stilled it with a cold glance. The mist rose in a swirling pillar that slowly softened into the form of a woman draped in a silken shroud. Her empty eyes stared upwards at the ravens perched upon the arch. After a moment her gaze slowly lowered, coming to rest upon the monstrous wolf.

"Wolves and ravens share the night." Her voice was soft, yet solemn. "'Tis a woeful omen indeed."

Dravek stood speechless, seemingly entranced by the beautiful phantom.

"You stand at the threshold of an ancient darkness," the spirit said. "Over the centuries, fate has lured many beyond these gates. Warriors and kings all sought their destinies within. Many have ventured to the Tower, yet few have returned. Countless souls have suffered beneath its curse. Beyond this barrier, misery and death lie in wait."

Dravek remained silent as his gaze shifted to the towering

keep looming just ahead. Distant memories of a life long-forgotten became clear once more. At last he said, "I have walked with misery all my life and I fear not death."

The specter's voice lowered to a grim whisper, saying, "The Tower holds fates far worse than death itself."

"We must turn back!" Leonidas pleaded.

Dravek cast a stern gaze upon the old man, saying, "Utter one word more and it shall be your last." Turning to face the spectral maiden once more, Dravek stepped closer. "I have long sought the destiny that awaits me in this Tower, and neither man nor specter shall thwart my quest. The words of the dead hold little sway with me. Be gone, spirit."

The phantom held Dravek's gaze a moment more then dissolved back into the mist. She was no more than a memory when Dravek stalked past the gate. The wolf beast scanned the depths of the forest then turned and followed his master, herding Leonidas along.

Dravek marched forward, stopping at the foot of the stairs that rose to the Tower's immense doors. Leonidas and the wolf remained a few steps behind. Dravek's eyes narrowed as he stared at the wrought iron design that formed the runic icon upon the centuries-old wood. The caw of ravens drew his attention upward. High above, among the gargoyles that lined the Tower's battlements, stood a lone figure draped in black. Scores of ravens roosted upon the monstrous statues, croaking shrill warning cries. Dravek stood in silence, keeping his eyes locked on the shadowy form. The figure remained motionless amidst the legion of macabre sentinels.

The wolf beast growled deep in its throat, low and rasping. In the distance beyond the Dark Tower, a scarlet glow had begun to form above the tree line.

"The dawn approaches," Leonidas said.

Dravek lowered his eyes to the horizon. When he looked back to the battlements, the figure was gone. Dravek's stare was met by the lifeless gazes of the gargoyles that clung to the stone walls. The ravens fell silent once more.

An icy breeze whistled and moaned over the stone parapet and through the limbs of the few sparse trees on the summit. Dravek surveyed the massive edifice towering above him once more before raising his deep voice in a commanding bellow. "Your messenger has delivered your warning, and I have now come to give my reply." The wind tossed his white hair like the banner of a conquering knight. "I have come to claim the Tower!"

He clutched Leonidas by the nape of his neck and drove the old man to his knees before him. Dravek's nails bit into the elder's flesh, drawing trickles of blood. "There is only one true master of this realm—only one rightful heir to the Tower!"

Dravek bared his fangs and lowered his mouth to the old man's throat.

The ravens erupted in an uproar of shrieks and caws, and the cold breeze rose to a howling wind. The Tower doors creaked open, as if the castle itself had granted them entry.

Dravek smiled and released Leonidas from his grip. He hoisted the old man to his feet and shoved him forward. The wolf beast stepped to his master's side, his eyes ablaze with the fires of Hell. The croaking of ravens announced their arrival as they ascended the steps to the Tower.

Blood of the Damned

JOSEPH VARGO AND JOSEPH IORILLO

Black pillars of smoke rose from the towering spires of Castle Rankorr, filling the morning sky with sparks and ash. In the keep below, fire devoured tapestries and engulfed wooden doors and beams, ravaging everything in its wake as it climbed through the castle. The ancient fortress that had withstood countless assaults and sieges throughout the centuries had been brought to the brink of destruction in a single night by a lone assailant.

The fire moved as if it had a mind all its own, spreading up along the castle's northern side, rising through the outermost chambers, leaving many of the keep's central halls untouched. Even so, dark smoke obstructed the passageways and the air raged with a sweltering heat, not unlike that of a furnace. Churning clouds of soot ran along the ceilings, escaping through windows to scatter in the open wind.

Within the castle, Serena led Brom along a smoky corridor as they rushed to escape the mounting blaze. A wall of stone crashed behind them and the floor they had just crossed gave way, collapsing down into the tumult below where the bricks and timbers were devoured by a whirlwind of howling flames. As the two reached the staircase that spiraled downward toward the great hall, the blaze erupted behind them, threatening to claim them in its fiery embrace. Serena looked back, half-expecting to see Brom gone or engulfed in flames, but there he stood, a black form against the burning rage, shielding her from the ensuing inferno.

Another danger now lay ahead. Brom held Serena back to take the lead as they descended the stair. Amidst the clamor and chaos, two castle sentries remained at their posts, standing guard at the base of the steps, their faces hidden beneath fearsome, wolfish helmets cast from blackest steel. They saw Brom when he was still a full flight of stairs above them, but before they could draw their swords, he was upon them, the razor edge of his nails tearing across their throats. Both men fell to their knees in a cascade of blood, their eyes gaping wide at the dark figure that now stood between them. Further down the hall, a group of guards who had witnessed their comrades' deadly encounter stood petrified with fear. They stared in horror at the shadow-clad figure that had effortlessly slain two well-armed warriors. The guards raised their weapons and prepared for attack, but as Brom's gaze fell upon them, they turned and fled through the smoky haze.

Brom looked past the clouded foyer toward the castle entrance. Though the doors stood open wide, the deadly rays of sunlight awaited just beyond, thwarting his escape. Serena grabbed hold of his arm and directed him back along the corridor and down a hidden staircase into her father's secret chamber. The fire had not yet breached the room's heavy stone walls, but the air inside was torrid and thin. The coals in the immense copper cauldron in the center of the room seemed to pulse and glow with unnatural life, as if channeling the inferno now consuming the castle. The light from the coals sent shadows dancing across a large tapestry upon which an armored knight drove a sword into a fearsome winged serpent. As the image writhed in the burning light, it reminded Brom of the vision he had seen through the oracle's dying eyes.

Serena took Brom's hand and led him to a far wall etched with ancient astrological symbols. As her eyes searched the wall, her fingers came to rest on a circle of runes that surrounded a five-star constellation. Serena's fingertips easily fit into the five indentations and she pushed firmly causing the stars to recede further into the design. A section of the wall, little more than a stone veneer mortared onto a wooden door, swung open on concealed hinges, revealing a narrow passage choked with forbidding darkness.

Serena led Brom inside and after a few moments they found themselves at a large iron door. The girl struggled to pull the heavy door toward her, but Brom gently pushed her aside and with one firm pull wrenched it open in a piercing squeal of rusted hinges. A rush of cool air swept past. Beyond the door was a low cavern braced with wooden beams and crude stone columns. Along the walls, the mouths of several tunnels stood open.

"This way," Serena said breathlessly, her voice raspy from the smoke. "The passageway we seek is marked with the sign of the serpent."

"I see it," Brom said. He guided Serena through the darkness to an archway inscribed with a coiled snake. He took the girl's hand and led her into the tunnel, which twisted and meandered in a gentle downward slope. At several junctures where the tunnel split into multiple directions, Serena did not hesitate but took the lead, guiding Brom into certain passageways as if knowing her way by heart. In time the tunnel ahead of them glowed dimly as it emptied into a large cave, and Brom heard the sounds of the forest. Beyond the ragged, half-collapsed cave entrance shafts of weak sunlight illuminated shrubs and fallen trees.

Serena stepped out into the gray light. A subtle, gauzy mist of smoke wended its way through the foliage like a specter.

Even so far below the mountaintop the burning castle was making its presence known.

The girl started forward toward the forest then looked back and saw that Brom still stood in the shadow of the cave.

"I cannot venture out into the sun's light," Brom said. "We must wait here till night falls." He turned and disappeared in the darkness.

Wrapped in his cloak, Brom crouched against the wall of the cave furthest from the entrance while Serena sat a few feet away, closer to the light. Around her neck hung a battered leather satchel from which she removed a handful of grapes and a crust of bread. She nibbled at the food but her body was wracked with painful fits of coughing. Her throat was raw from the smoke she had inhaled.

Brom moved closer to her and laid a hand on her shoulder. "You need water."

"There is a stream not far from here," she said, "along the forest path."

Brom gazed out at the smoky woodlands beyond the cave entrance. The bright sunlight filled him with an unease and dread that darkness inspired in ordinary mortals. "Go to the stream and return," he said. "Do not wander or stay too long."

Serena hurried from the cave, stepping over rotted logs and gnarled branches, heading westward where she knew the stream lay. The flowing water was a welcome sight to her as it glistened under the morning sunlight, and she knelt at the bank gulping handfuls of the cool water to slake her thirst, splashing it on her face as she drank. From her satchel she withdrew a wineskin, which she filled with water.

It was then that she heard the sound of rough male voices somewhere in the distance, followed by the dull clamor of horses' hooves. Through the latticework of tree branches Serena saw two riders moving toward her through the forest, one a tall, bearded man with a face ruined by a scar that had taken an eye, the other a stocky, hairless man. Both wore red tunics adorned with emblems of a black sun—the insignia of the Black Dawn.

Serena backed away from the water's edge, but the bald horseman saw her and leered with a predatory smile. The soldiers spurred their horses in her direction, and Serena turned to run for the safety of the cave.

The horses thundered closer, jumping the stream effortlessly. Serena raced through the trees, leaping over fallen logs and ducking beneath low branches. She could hear the men behind her, on foot now, their boots crushing their way through the woods. With their prey in sight, the warriors fast closed the distance. Serena crashed through the brush, seeing the cave entrance a short distance ahead, but before she could reach it, she felt a strong, rough hand catch her arm, yanking her back with brutal force.

The bearded man clutched Serena's arm tightly, twisting his grip as she struggled against him. He laughed and pulled her toward him by the laces of her bodice. "You run from us as if we were savage beasts," he said. "Tis rude to show us such disrespect." He put his face down close to hers, his beard coarse against her soft cheek. Serena began to weep.

"Release her," a calm voice called, a slight echo behind it.

The warriors turned and squinted at the cave. A dark figure stood in the shadows just inside the entrance. The taller of the brutes drew his sword, but kept it down by his side, expecting no battle. "Be gone, fool," he shouted, "lest you taste my steel."

"Release her," Brom said again, "and I shall reward you each."

The two men stepped forward, dragging the girl with them. The stocky warrior rested his axe on his shoulder, allowing Brom to see its blood-spattered blade. "And what could you offer us that we could not simply take?"

"That which you most desire..." Brom said.

The warriors tossed Serena aside and stepped into the cave, crossing the threshold of shadows.

Brom stood calmly before the hulking men and said, "... your lives."

The bearded man laughed heartily. Without warning, he swung his sword in a swift arc, delivering a blow intended to split Brom's skull. Brom caught his arm and thrust the blade deep into the other man's throat, nearly severing the warrior's head. The bearded man cried out in anguish as Brom's grip tightened, shattering the bones of his wrist. The sword dropped from his hand and the warrior fell to his knees, his eyes frozen in a terrified gaze. Without a word, Brom took hold of the man's head and twisted it fully around, snapping his neck. Seething rage filled Brom's eyes as he glared down upon the carnage he had wrought.

A short while later, Brom saw Serena making her way through the woods toward the cave entrance, leading two warhorses. In the blind heat of his anger he did not even notice her leave. As the horses neared the cave they stirred and stamped, smelling the blood of the warriors, but Serena spoke to them in a soft, consoling tone, gently stroking their manes, calming them beneath her soothing touch. As Brom watched her tender gestures, the fire within him subsided.

As the sun outside dropped past midday, Serena sat in the cave upon a flat boulder and ate. Brom sat beside her, solemn and deathly quiet. The wounds he had received in his battle with the monstrous bat creature in the dungeons of Castle Rankorr had swiftly healed, but the loss of blood had weakened him, putting him in a state of drowsy fatigue. He feared closing his eyes and not having the strength to open them again. He would be trapped between worlds, not alive but not quite dead. Brom nearly smiled, wondering if that fate would be so different from his current plight.

From the corner of his eye, Brom looked at Serena. She possessed a youthful beauty and innocence, yet her heart was strong, carrying a vitality and courage that surpassed her meager years. He and this girl were connected somehow, and not just by his oath to her father. When they met, she seemed to recognize him from her dreams, and in the short night they had known one another, her gentle spirit resonated within him.

Serena offered him a handful of grapes and a bit of dried meat. "Here," she said, "You will need your strength as well."

"Food offers me no nourishment," Brom said, turning his face away from her. "My desires are now far more savage. I do not eat as I did when I was mortal, yet I thirst. And though my thirst is maddening, I dare not succumb to it."

"Why?" Serena asked.

"There is but one substance that can silence my hunger."

"Tell me, what is it?" Serena asked, somewhat fearful of his answer.

"Blood," Brom replied coldly. "The blood of any creature can sustain me."

Serena contemplated his words. She held out her wrist, placing her dagger over her flesh, offering her own life's essence. Brom could sense the warm pulse of her blood flowing just beneath her skin, so close and so freely offered. The primal hunger rose in him. His muscles tensed as he fought back the urge, the yearning, the eternal thirst, fearing he might take her life and fall further into darkness.

"No," he said, moving the dagger away from her wrist. "Drinking the blood of humans strengthens my powers immensely. But it weakens my will to resist darker temptations."

Serena looked out toward the cave's entrance, where the bodies of the two soldiers lay dead. "The men you have slain—their blood is plentiful. Why do you not feed upon them?"

Brom shook his head. "Their hearts are dark, their minds vile and twisted. Their blood is venom to me."

"I fear you shall find the same blood in all of Lord Dravek's men."

Brom's eyes scanned the corpse of the bearded man that lay face up, coming to rest upon the sigil of the Black Dawn emblazoned on his tunic. "What can you tell me of Dravek?"

Fear glittered in Serena's eyes. "He is called the lord of wolves. He is a fiend who acts without mercy. He has no heart. I have witnessed his wrath. Dravek is a monster, far more fearsome and powerful than the dark creatures that serve him. He is cunning and sly—always planning several steps ahead before taking action.

"My father formed a plan as well. He told Dravek when you left the Tower of Vasaria, knowing he would seize the opportunity to strike your fortress. But my father's real intent was to send Dravek away from Rankorr. He foresaw your coming here, and he saw it as his only chance to save me."

"How many legions accompanied Dravek to the Tower?"

"He took only three others, his fiercest warriors—monstrous abominations in the guise of wolves. The creatures that accompany him are savage beasts, but they were once men. They are his most loyal minions. They are called the Volkodlak."

Brom knew the legends of the Volkodlak. They were a lesser form of wampior who served their masters as slaves. They were said to be ravenous beasts that hunted men and fed on human flesh.

"My father told me a tale once," Serena said. "About Dravek and his monsters. Perhaps it is only a grim fable, but I remember it, just as he told it to me, and I can tell it, if you care to listen."

Brom leaned back against the cave wall. "Tell me your story."

"Very well then," Serena said, and began to weave a vision in Brom's mind.

My tale begins with a sorceress, Estra, the Witch of the Black Woods. She was said to dwell in a cavernous lair deep in the midst of the forest, though few had ever ventured there. Her name was legend and her powers were feared by all. Though she had lived many lifetimes, her magic allowed her to hold fast to the beauty of her youth. Her allure was irresistible to mortal men.

One night, as the witch invoked spirits in her fiery cauldron, Dravek and three of his warriors came upon her lair. Estra's magic entranced the men, but her charms did not sway Dravek. The witch gazed into his black eyes and saw in him the demon wampior.

Knowing her magic was useless against him, she bargained for her life. She told him of a powerful talisman that would grant his darkest desires. The two struck a pact. If Estra would take him to where the artifact lay buried, Dravek would spare her life.

Dravek's eyes strayed throughout the witch's lair, seeing the pelts and bones of forest creatures.

"I take from the earth only what I need to survive," Estra said. "I kill only when I must."

Dravek's gaze lingered upon a fanged skull that rested on an oaken table amidst the skeletal remains of various animals. It was the skull of a wolf.

The sorceress was well aware of Dravek's feelings for the creatures. Long ago, before the siege of Castle Rankorr, he lived in the wild, running free among the wolves of the forest. He had more love for the beasts than he did for all of humankind. He detested those who hunted and trapped wolves for sport and regarded them with great contempt.

Estra's eyes revealed a trace of fear. "The beast set upon me. I had little choice."

Dravek picked up the skull and stared into its hollow eyes. "These creatures are magnificent. I find that I prefer their company to that of men. Wolves possess a purity and nobility that mankind shall never have. They are born hunters, swift and fierce, but there is much more to these wild beasts than their savage nature. Their ferocity is matched only by their loyalty to their pack."

Estra chose her words carefully before speaking again. At last she said, "The talisman you seek can grant you power over men and beasts." She opened a crude pine cabinet where rows of shelves held earthen jars etched with the markings of her craft. Her hand came to rest upon a jar engraved with five-pointed star. "Every part of my quarry is a vital ingredient to the magic I weave. Bones, teeth, flesh, fur—even blood. I let nothing waste."

She pried open the lid and allowed Dravek to view the contents within. As Dravek gazed upon the dark crimson liquid that filled the jar, he recognized the scent of wolf's blood.

The sorceress spoke again, her voice soft and hypnotic. "Do you know the legend of the Volkodlak? They are ancient creatures, born of dark magic—men who stalk the night as wolves." Estra slid her fingers along the fangs of the wolf skull, caressing them lightly. "Imagine an army of such creatures," she whispered. "Nothing would dare stand against you."

Dravek's eyes glistened. "Tell me more, witch. What is this talisman?"

"A mystical artifact—" she said, "a vial containing the essence of darkness. Its magic is strong—far more potent than any spell scrawled upon the Ebon Scrolls."

"If this is some lie, some ruse to deceive me, I shall wrest your heart from your chest."

"I would not dare lie to you, my lord."

"Very well," Dravek said, setting the wolf skull back on the table. "Once I possess the talisman's power, I shall release you from our pact."

Estra smiled. She sealed the jar once more and placed it in a large leather satchel along with a dagger and pewter goblet.

The witch led Dravek and his men out into the woodlands. As they set forth into the dark of night, the soldiers lit torches to guide them. They followed no path or trail as they traversed the forest deep into a canyon that narrowed to a craggy ravine. The twisting pass led them to a hidden cave at the base of a sheer rock cliff. Engravings of runic symbols surrounded the cave's entrance.

Estra studied the inscription, deciphering its forgotten meaning. "This region is known as the Forbidden Land. It was once the center of the Dark One's domain. Their ancient temple lies deep within the heart of this cavern. My kindred brought the talisman here, long ago, returning it to the gods from whence it came."

Dravek felt an eerie sense of menace as he peered into the depths of the cave, but he could see no threat within. "Lead on," he said.

With swords drawn, the men followed Estra deep into the winding passage. The light of their torches scattered sleeping bats and revealed mystic sigils covering the walls. The tunnel wove its way far beneath the earth before opening into an immense grotto. They emerged in the forgotten realm of the ancient ones. In the midst of the cavern stood the remains of a temple, magnificent and foreboding. Its towering walls had been hewn from the black stone of the surrounding earth.

Estra led them forth. They ascended a broad flight of crumbling steps to the temple entrance. The ruined cathedral was a monument to the macabre. Along the sides of the windowless chamber, immense stone guardians stood between rows of obsidian columns that stretched up into lofty shadows. The sound of bats echoed far above them. In the center of the chamber, a ritual altar stood, its ebon stone engraved with grooves to catch the blood of the victims who were sacrificed upon it. The graven channels twisted outward from the middle, like the legs of a spider reaching toward the altar's edge. A circle of crimson sigils was set into the black marble floor surrounding the sinister shrine.

Twin winged gargoyles had once clung to the columns on either side of the altar. Only one of the grim statues still stood, while the other lay in crumbled ruin. Dravek stepped forth, his eyes locked on the sculpted demon as he entered the mystic circle.

"The talisman rests within this sacred temple," Estra said, her whispered words echoing in the cavernous chamber. "My ancestors brought it here and left it as an offering to the Forest God so that he might protect them from the Dark Queen's power." She pointed to a sepulchre, chiseled in the likeness of a horned man. "What you seek lies buried there."

Dravek stepped toward the ancient sarcophagus, taking hold of its stone lid. He slid the heavy slab away and the sepulchre groaned open. Inside he found a darkly tarnished vial, crowned with the likeness of the head of a stag.

"Your men are loyal and fierce," the enchantress whispered, "but this can invoke the true beast within them."

The witch cast her gaze upon Dravek's soldiers and recited an incantation to enslave their wills. The men stared at her in spellbound silence. Their grips loosened and their swords and torches dropped to the ground. She gestured her hand, summoning them to her. The three men stepped forward and fell to their knees before the witch.

Estra reached into her satchel and withdrew the earthen jar and goblet. She poured the jar's contents into the chalice, filling it with the crimson nectar. She then handed the blood-filled goblet to Dravek, saying, "You need only desire it, and your wish shall be granted."

Dravek carefully lifted the stag head stopper from the vial, revealing a dark liquid within. He let a single black drop fall into the goblet to mingle with the wolf's blood, then sealed the vial again. He turned toward the kneeling men and delivered the unholy elixir unto them. Each drank their fill from the chalice of darkness. Within moments, they began to change. Their bodies convulsed and spasmed as their forms contorted into beastly shapes. Their bones crackled and stretched, and their flesh sprouted long, shaggy fur. Their teeth became fangs and their nails turned to sharp claws. Their eyes burned red with seething hellfire. The three creatures that had once been men now loomed before Dravek as monstrous wolves.

Estra said, "As I promised, my lord, the Volkodlak."

As Dravek stared at the hulking beasts, he realized another purpose for the power he now possessed. He stepped toward the fiendish sculpture that clutched the column beside the altar. Lifting the vial to the gargoyle's lips, he let an oily droplet fall into the statue's mouth. The black trickle slid across the statue's fangs, coming to rest upon its chiseled tongue. Dravek closed his eyes and focused his mind to summon the ancient god.

Black smoke spewed from the stone monster's mouth as

JOSEPH VARGO AND JOSEPH IORILLO 57

if something within it had been set ablaze. The statue's eyes took on the glow of seething embers as the creature slowly came to life. The demon's clawed hands broke free from the column and it lumbered forward, towering over Dravek.

Dravek stood in reverent silence before the living nightmare.

"Who wakes me from my slumber?" The creature's deep voice resounded through the chamber like the rumble of thunder.

"Forgive me, Dark One," Dravek said, bowing his head, "I stand before you, your humble servant."

"What is it you wish?"

"I desire nothing for myself. I act on behalf of my queen. She was murdered long ago and now lies in deathless slumber. My only purpose is to return her to this world and restore her to her rightful throne."

"You speak of Mara?"

"Yes, my lord. She is my master."

The demon's eyes burned brighter as they fell upon the vial in Dravek's hand. "The artifact you possess is a treasure most rare. It holds the blood of the fallen ones. For centuries men have sought this very power, waging wars in the attempt to attain merely a few drops of it. They spilled much of their own blood in their quest, knowing well the great sacrifice that must be made to wield and control it."

Estra stepped forward and chanted a string of words in a language unknown to Dravek. The demon cast its glowing eyes upon her. "You speak to me in the tongue of the ancients, child," the creature's deep voice bellowed.

"Yes," she replied, stepping closer. "My ancestors instructed me in the ways of old. I beseech you, Dark One, hearken to my call."

"I am not yours to command." The demon's voice filled with anger. "I bestowed this gift upon your kindred long ago and they cast it aside, returning it to me, heedless of its true worth." The creature gestured his clawed hand toward Dravek, leaving a trail of black smoke in its wake. "This one understands the immense power of such a gift. He serves the daughter of darkness." His molten gaze fell upon Dravek once more. "The blood you hold has the power to resurrect your queen," the demon said, "but as I have said, a great sacrifice must first be made."

Dravek's eyes shifted toward the witch. A look of terror swept over her as she realized his murderous intent. She took a step back and turned to flee, but the monstrous wolves blocked her path, snarling and baring their savage fangs. Dravek took hold of Estra's arm and dragged her to the sacrificial altar.

"No!" she shrieked. "You swore to spare me!"

"You promised me this power, witch. I can attain it no other way. You must now fulfill your bargain."

Dravek forced the witch onto the altar. She struggled to break free, but her power was no match for the wampior's strength. He swept a single claw across her neck, slicing it open. A rich scarlet stream pulsed from the wound to fill the altar's graven design. Dravek held her beneath him until the final beat of her heart. Her eyes stared blankly upward as her illusion of youth crumbled away. When at last she expired, the woman that lay dead upon the altar was little more than a withered crone.

Dravek lowered his lips to taste her blood.

"No," the Dark One roared. "Her blood is ours. Your offering must be untainted."

Dravek bowed his head reverently and backed away as the creature slowly returned to stone. Taking the talisman, Dravek left the forbidden temple in the cavern of the Dark

Ones, his three beastly minions following close behind.

Serena finished her tale. The garish images of Dravek and his abominable sacrifice in the subterranean temple lingered uncomfortably in Brom's mind.

"Perhaps it is simply a legend," Serena said. "A silly myth embellished over the years with every telling."

A faint smile touched Brom's lips. The girl's attempt to comfort him was endearing. He gently brushed her cheek with a finger. "Sleep," he said. "We shall leave at dusk."

They waited for darkness in the cave as the castle burned above them, spewing black smoke as thick as blood.

Serena slept through much of the day. When she awakened, she was startled to see Brom staring at her. "You stirred restlessly," he said.

"Yes," she said. "I dreamt, as I often do. Though the visions are vague, my dreams often reveal things that are yet to come—just as I dreamt of our meeting."

"Tell me what you saw."

"I dreamt of you," she whispered. "I stood witness to a ritual upon a black altar surrounded by crimson candles. Voices chanted incantations in an unknown tongue from the darkness around me. Beyond the altar, a robed figure held forth a goblet—a chalice filled with blood. His low voice joined in the chant, repeating the strange words over and over. The invocation cleansed the blood, purging all darkness from it. And then I saw that you were there, standing in the shadows. You stepped forward, taking the goblet and drinking deeply from it.

"A brilliant light shone down upon you, and you stood transformed in its luminous glow. You were no longer a man, and you were no longer as you are now. You had become a winged warrior and you reveled in the glory of the sun's radiant light."

"You say this arcane blood ritual will allow me to thrive in the daylight. How can this be?"

"I fear I can offer you no answers. I can tell you only what I saw. Perhaps it is nothing more than a meaningless dream."

"Perhaps," Brom said.

Dusk had finally arrived. As the sun disappeared from the horizon, Serena saddled the dead warriors' horses. Once darkness had settled over the land, Brom helped the girl mount one of the steeds and he mounted the other. Their horses waded the stream and they took the road westward toward Vasaria.

As they crested a small rise, Brom looked back and could see the castle looming in the distance, still ablaze beneath the cold light of the full moon, just as the seer had prophesied. Brom turned and they rode down into a valley, the trees closing in upon the road behind them, and the ruin that was Castle Rankorr was lost from view.

After several hours, the land sloped ever more sharply downward, and the forest thinned. They found themselves slowly navigating a treacherous mountain path that careened perilously close to the cliff's edge. Loose rocks tumbled down the mountainside beneath their horses' hooves. They slowed their steeds to a careful walk. Brom rode in the lead, lost in bleak thought. He knew his soul hung in a delicate balance between the forces of good and evil and he dared not slip further into darkness. He reflected upon the final vision the seer revealed to him.

As the trail widened, Serena pulled her horse alongside Brom's. She seemed to sense his discomfort. "What troubles you, my lord?"

"The vision I saw through your father's eyes. The memory yet lingers to haunt me."

"What did you see?"

"I saw myself as an emerging beast, a great dragon rising from the fires of Hell. Darkness spread across the land beneath the shadow of my wings, engulfing all light in its path."

Serena pondered his words, then said, "You speak of a clash between darkness and light. Surely both forces rest inside your heart, as they do with all men. Perhaps the beast you saw was nothing more than the savage, frenzied rage you released during your battle with Ramiel. But the darkness within you has subsided. You are no longer possessed of the beast's fury. You called upon its strength to battle your foes, and it served you in your time of need." She leaned close to him and gently took his hand, whispering, "You are its master."

Brom's hand slipped from her grasp and he looked away. "The ancient prophecy foretells of the rise of the dark one, the destroyer of life..."

"There is more... much more. I wish to tell you all I know, but..." Her words trailed off.

"I know of the oath you swore to your father. I made a vow to him as well. No harm shall come to you while you are in my care." Brom lifted her chin with his fingers, and the girl offered a smile through teary eyes. "I have sworn to deliver you to safety. You can reveal the full prophecy to me when we reach Vasaria."

He spurred his horse into a gallop as the road plunged again toward the forest and Serena followed quickly behind. The full moon shone brightly upon the woodlands, suspended in a sea of blackness. The radiant orb hovered above the distant tower, gazing down from the starless heavens like an ever-watchful eye.

When they neared the base of the mountain, Brom

reigned in his horse, slowing it to a steady trot. "The village of Vasaria lies through the forest," he said. "We shall arrive there before dawn." He steered his horse from the trail and into the woods.

As the forest grew thicker, the riders dismounted and walked their horses between the twisting trees. The surrounding darkness was filled with eyes that glittered in the moonlight, revealing nocturnal creatures in search of prey. A low growl, barely more than a breath, drew Brom's attention to the shadows beyond Serena. He caught the flicker of movement behind the trees, a dark shape coming quickly toward them. As it left the cover of the forest, Brom recognized the form of a wolf, bounding toward the girl. Swift as an arrow, Brom leapt between the beast and its intended prey. He caught the wolf by the throat, snapping its neck instantly. With a strangled yelp, its body fell limp. Brom held the dying wolf in his arms, watching the life fade from its eyes.

Before the creature expired, Brom raised the wolf's throat to his lips. Brom's gaze turned wild and fierce, as if he were possessed by some diabolic force. His mouth opened wide, exposing long, gleaming fangs, then he bit into the wolf's neck, tearing into its flesh like a ravenous demon. He drank deeply from the dying beast, quenching his thirst upon its essence. Serena gazed upon Brom's blood-soaked visage and took a step back, aghast at what she had witnessed. The savage look faded from Brom's eyes as he set the wolf down. He stood before Serena, calm and revitalized.

Brom wiped the blood from his lips. "I fear I shall need to summon the beast that dwells within me once more. I must call upon its strength and fury to battle what awaits in the Tower," he said softly. "It is as you have said, I am its master, though the struggle to control the darkness that resides in my heart becomes more difficult each time I surrender to it."

They resumed their trek through the forest, winding around the southern base of the mountain, continuing westward toward Vasaria. They soon spied the soft glow of firelight in the distance. Within moments, the silhouettes of crude huts and hovels appeared in a mist-shrouded clearing ahead. The surrounding silence was broken by a clamoring sound as the chill autumn air suddenly rang with the tolling of the Tower bell.

Brom looked off in the direction of the Dark Tower, its outline distinct against the dawning sky. He turned his gaze back toward the village and pointed toward a dwelling at the edge of the forest. "Seek one named Daria there. Tell her all you know. You will be safe with her." In one motion he mounted his horse again and took the reins.

Serena's eyes widened in alarm. She ran to him. "Wait! I must tell you the prophecy!"

But she spoke to shadows. Without another word Brom had vanished into the engulfing darkness as he sped along a path that twisted toward the mountain. High above upon the ominous summit, the Tower bell continued its summoning toll.

Dark Dominion

Joseph Vargo

The massive doors of the Dark Tower gaped open wide, like the maw of some hellish behemoth. Dravek stepped boldly forward, undaunted by the looming darkness or whatever dangers lurked within. He entered the keep, followed by Leonidas and the savage wolf-beast that drove the old man forward and kept him from fleeing. Memories flooded Dravek's mind, taking him back through the lost decades to the first time he set foot inside the Tower. He had been young then, a mere mortal boy, curious to explore the Tower's looming mysteries, yet fearful of its sinister legends. Even now, all these years later, being inside the castle still filled him with a sense of unease. He felt as if he had entered an immense spider's web.

Dravek ventured forth into the entrance hall, ever wary of his surroundings. Beams of moonlight broke through narrow windows overhead, bathing the chamber in an eerie, otherworldly glow. In the shadows high above, a legion of stone sentinels kept their unending vigil over the cavernous hall. Dravek circumvented the center of the chamber, mindfully stepping around the crimson rune emblazoned upon the floor—the ancient sigil that marked the keep as the earthly arena for the forces of light and darkness.

Leonidas staggered to the middle of the hall and fell to his knees upon the sigil, crying out to the darkness above.

"Shadow Lord, I beg of you, be merciful, for I have done as you commanded! I have delivered your message, but the White Wolf was heedless of your warning! He has accompanied me to the Tower so that he may face you. He stands here with his last minion—"

"Silence!" Dravek's command echoed throughout the heights of the chamber. He stood scanning the court of gargoyles that peered down from their shadowy perches. Their chiseled faces revealed no signs of life. "Show yourself!" he demanded.

The sound of distant laughter rose from the depths of the keep, drawing Dravek's attention to the archway beneath the balcony. He stepped forward, now more cautious than before. With a slight gesture of his hand, Dravek signaled his minion to follow. The beast growled and snarled, baring its monstrous fangs at Leonidas, herding the old man along.

Descending the staircase beneath the arch, Dravek followed the twisting corridor to the chapel entrance, but his attention was drawn to a sealed doorway on the opposite side of the hall. Three words were etched into the dark, knotted wood. Dravek studied the inscription with great curiosity, as if he had not seen it before. He pushed against the heavy door, and instantly a burning pain shot through him. He drew back from the searing heat and stared in dismay at his palms, their bone-white flesh smoldering, as if they had been immersed in fire.

Again, the sound of laughter echoed around him, now seeming to come from the chapel. Dravek stepped toward the doorway, but hesitated before entering the sanctuary. Every candelabra and votive blazed with a harsh light that nearly blinded him. Dravek's eyes narrowed as he scanned his surroundings. He whispered a single word in an language known only to those who practiced the black arts, and as if by his command, the air in the room began to stir. An unearthly wind swept through the chapel, encircling the sanctuary in a swirling gust, extinguishing the candelabras one by one. As quickly as it rose, the wind subsided, leaving the room cloaked in shadows. Only the crimson votive suspended above the altar remained lit.

Dravek entered the sanctuary, leaving Leonidas and the great wolf at the room's threshold. As he walked amidst the statues of saints and angels, his face twisted into a scowl. He felt a profound disdain for those who worshiped the god of light. He regarded them as little more than hapless slaves who groveled before a vengeful master, begging forgiveness for their petty trespasses. Their fear of his almighty wrath kept them from quenching their primal desires and living their lives freely. They sought to be righteous, yet they were spiteful and intolerant, judgmental and vindictive. Their cruelty had caused Dravek to seek solace in the Dark Queen's embrace—to discover a life where no temptation was forbidden and sin was unknown.

Dravek made his way toward the obsidian altar that consecrated the sanctuary. He withdrew an ornate key from the pocket of his cloak and began to step toward a wall of graven bronze behind the altar. Just then, the tower bell sounded, splitting the silence with a thunderous clang that reverberated throughout the chapel. Dravek stopped and looked overhead. Slipping the key back into the pocket of his cloak, he turned to follow the summoning toll. Before leaving the sanctuary, he looked back again, whispering his invocation once more. A powerful gust swept straight through the room, dousing the flame of the vigil light, leaving the chapel in total darkness.

Dravek strode swiftly past Leonidas and the wolf-beast, giving neither even a glance. "Come," he barked, and they both quickly followed.

Led by the bell's clamor, the three came to a stairwell

that spiraled upward to the castle's heights. As they made their way up the stairs, the tolling continued, resounding throughout the keep in long, steady intervals. Leonidas struggled to keep pace with his captors, stumbling more than once in his climb. After ascending several flights, the old man fell to his hands and knees upon the stone stairs, coughing and panting for breath.

"I cannot continue," Leonidas gasped. "Do with me as you will—end my life, if you must—but I can climb no further."

Dravek's patience with the old man had neared its end. Without a word of warning, he took hold of Leonidas, clutching him by the cloak at his chest. He hoisted the old man from his feet, holding him out over the deep stairwell. Dravek's black eyes were pools of seething rage. Leonidas met the fiend's glower with an empty stare.

"No," Dravek said, setting Leonidas back onto the landing. "You shall not meet your death yet, old one. You shall witness my conquest of the Tower and its Shadow Lord, and you shall chronicle my victory for all to know of it."

Dravek dragged the old man behind him up the last few flights until at last they reached the parapet landing. As Dravek pulled open the door to the parapet walk, the tolling ceased. Torches crackled on both sides of the walkway that circled the perimeter of the castle's heights. Casting his gaze upward, Dravek watched as scores of bats fluttered toward the bell tower, returning to their roosts after their night's hunt. At the tower's peak, the great bell hung silent and still, its last tone yet lingering in the chill air. The sky beyond held a dark grey hue, but a crimson glow above the eastern hills warned that dawn was soon approaching.

Dravek stepped out into the waning darkness, throwing Leonidas aside to lie exhausted and panting against the castle wall. The Volkodlak followed its master, sniffing the air and the flagstones beneath its feet, detecting a scent upon the walkway path. The creature followed the trail toward the bell tower. As it approached the door, it emitted a menacing growl, guttural and low.

Without warning, an arrow whistled down from the tower above, striking the beast in the back. Another and then another hit in rapid succession, lodging in the creature's shoulder and side, causing the beast to howl in rage. Two more arrows sailed down from the adjacent watchtower and hissed toward Dravek. He dodged the first, but the second arrow struck him in the chest.

Amidst the chaotic rain of arrows, Dravek heard a sound from somewhere behind him. The creak of the stairwell door betrayed its closing. Dravek leapt to the archway, catching the heavy door inches before it slammed shut. He shoved the door back open, toppling Talik who stood behind it, trying to push it closed. Dravek dragged the old man out into the torchlit night and the torrent of arrows ceased.

Dravek yanked the arrow from his chest and tossed it aside as if he felt nothing. Heedless of his wound, he stared at the bell tower, locking his gaze on the archer hiding amidst the shadows. Lifting an arm, Dravek gestured his skeletal hand toward the belfry. The giant bats that roosted there erupted in a violent frenzy, swarming the bowman. The man flailed and screamed as the winged creatures tore at his flesh with their talons and fangs. The hunter toppled over the belfry rail and plummeted to the ground far below. The bats abandoned him along his descent, returning to the sanctuary of the belltower as their victim crashed to his doom.

The Volkodlak had swiftly scaled the other watchtower and forced the other archer down from his ambush perch, dragging him from the tower by the leg. As the huntsman reached for a knife in his belt, the beast's jaws snapped shut, biting clean through the bone, severing the man's leg below the knee. The hunter shrieked and convulsed as his life's blood pulsed out, covering the flagstones in a gush of crimson. His cries faded and ceased as death quickly claimed him.

Lorand sprang from cover and ran toward the monster, the relic sword raised overhead. The beast leapt upon him, driving the breath from him and pinning him to the ground. Its jaws yawned wide for the killing strike, but Dravek shouted a command and the creature halted, its fangs a mere breath away from Lorand's face.

The final huntsman leapt from the shadows and sprinted toward Dravek with axe in hand, ready to strike, but Dravek caught the man's eyes with his stare. The hunter came to an instant halt and stood petrified beneath the wampior's gaze.

Drooling and snarling, the Volkodlak crawled off Lorand and let him get to his feet. Dravek shoved Talik forward to stand with the others then surveyed the scene before him. The foes he faced were merely men, frail and mortal. He had been led to believe a great adversary awaited him in the Tower—a dreaded sorcerer who commanded not only men and beasts, but the forces of darkness as well. The old one had lied to him.

Dravek's soulless eyes fell upon Leonidas. "Did you think me a fool? Your grim fables may frighten the children of your village, but fear has no place in my heart. Your ruse is finished, old one. Your Shadow Lord is vanquished."

Dravek turned to face his conquered foes. "You dared conspire against me—to lure me here, to the Tower's heights and trap me like a caged animal—to perish in the breaking dawn beneath the sun's infernal rays." He stepped beside his monstrous minion and plucked the arrows one by one from the creature's back, snapping each of them between his fingers like brittle twigs. "Your axes and arrows cannot harm us."

Dravek's eyes came to rest upon the sword in Lorand's hand, recognizing the sacred blade from his encounter with the Baron, more than a century ago. "Ah, but I see one among you holds a true warrior's blade." Dravek stepped toward Lorand. "And what would you do with such a weapon, boy?"

"I have sworn to defend the Tower," Lorand said, "with my life, if need be."

"How valiant," Dravek said, a mocking tone to his voice. "It seems our paths were duly destined to cross. The sword in your hand holds the power to slay those of my immortal bloodline. If you would use it to strike me down, then do so." Dravek held his arms out to his sides.

Lorand lunged toward him but Dravek merely leaned away, dodging his attack. With the swiftness of a striking snake Dravek grabbed the sword by the blade and turned it toward himself, setting its sharp tip against his own chest. "Pierce my heart, boy," Dravek taunted. "Kill me, or feel my wrath."

Lorand thrust the sword forward with all his might, but it did not move in the fiend's grasp.

Dravek's lips twisted to a smile. He wrenched the sword from Lorand's grip and stood admiring the blade's sleek dark beauty as it reflected the torchlight's fiery glow. "Such a fine weapon," he said. "'Tis a pity you possess neither the strength nor skill to wield it. Had it not been for this sword, my queen would still reign over these lands." His voice lowered to a gravelly whisper. "But all shall be set right soon... very soon."

Dravek's dark eyes rose to meet the somber stares of the men before him. "How little has changed after all these years," he said. "Vasaria's outcast son has returned, only to be spurned once more by the wretched lot who dwell here. Tis a fitting welcome, indeed." He turned to look out toward the village where smoke plumed upward from the chimneys of several small hovels. "Ah, Vasaria—" he hissed, "the bane of my youth. I shall revel in its conquest and destruction. The villagers shall become my minions and I shall slake my thirsts upon the blood of their children."

"You cannot enter the village." Talik's raspy voice held a tone of confidence. "The final standing stone yet marks the ancient boundary of the Dark Brood's domain. Do you not remember what happened the last time your legions ventured beyond it? It marked the end of Mara's reign. In all the years since you fled the Tower, you never once ventured westward, past the ancient landmark. You dared not incur the wrath of the celestial sentinels that enforce the Lord's will."

Dravek's mind reflected back upon that fateful night more than a century ago, recalling how Mara's reckless choice to cross the sacred threshold led to her eventual downfall. "Then you shall topple it," he said, "to allow me free passage. Do as I command and I shall grant you mercy."

Talik shook his head. "We shall do no such thing. We do not heed the commands of devils."

Dravek's eyes narrowed. "Then you shall all meet your deaths here this night. If this is your wish, I will gladly make it so, but I assure you, your suffering will be beyond anything your simple minds can fathom and the end will not come swiftly."

"Do what you will," Talik said. "Slay us all. We shall welcome our deaths knowing that we have thwarted your plan."

"You are brave, old fool, but your life is near its natural end. The threat of death holds little sway with one so old. Azrael's icy grasp encircles you, drawing you closer to your mortal demise with each passing day. Perhaps those who have their full lives ahead of them would not sacrifice themselves so willingly."

Dravek shifted his eyes between his beastly minion and the final huntsman, and the creature obeyed his master's silent command. It sprang upon the man, driving him to the ground before he could lift his axe. The wolf's fangs hovered above the hunter's throat. "You need only bow before me and I shall show you mercy. Obey my commands and I shall spare your lives."

"You are a demon!" Talik shouted. "We shall never bow before you... or your queen. We will die first!"

"So be it," Dravek said. With that, the wolf dug its fangs deep into the man's throat, clamping its jaws around his neck. The creature shook its head violently, ripping flesh from bone in a spurting fountain of blood that soon drained the man's life.

Leonidas let his hand fall to the pouch at his side and fumbled for the wolfsbane powder within.

"Bow before me! Now!" Dravek screamed. "Spare yourselves a wretched death!"

Talik stepped forward and stood defiant before Dravek.

Dravek clutched Talik by his hair and forced him to his knees. He raised the relic sword and placed the flat of the blade against the side of the elder's head, resting its razor-sharp edge on top of his ear.

"If you cannot hear the reason of my words, then it would seem your ears serve no useful purpose. You shall hardly miss them." Dravek swiftly drew the sword down toward him, slicing the old man's ear cleanly off. Talik winced, but fought the urge to cry out in pain. His trembling hand reached up to press against the wound, but he was unable to stop the blood that seeped between his fingers.

Still clutching the old man's hair, Dravek held the sword's tip before Talik's eye. "Or are you are blind to the events that have unfolded this night?" Dravek's voice was perversely calm. "If your eyes fail to see who holds dominion here, perhaps I should pluck them from their sockets."

Talik stared at him, remaining defiantly silent. Dravek's grip tightened as he readied to plunge the blade forward and the old man clenched his jaw in anticipation of the forthcoming agony. The wind rose to a tumultuous howl, reaching a crescendo that sounded like the roar of a demonic legion.

"Enough!" a deep voice bellowed.

All heads turned toward the entrance to the Tower stairwell. Brom stood in the doorway, his cape billowing in the wind behind him like a writhing cloud of black smoke. His eyes held a bestial ferocity as he glared at Dravek. The wind dropped away and a hush befell the scene as the two foes remained locked in a deadly stare. Though each had heard tales of the other, this marked the first time they had come face to face.

"Release them, now," Brom demanded, "or meet your death."

A sinister smile crept across Dravek's lips. He whispered a command to his minion and the great wolf bounded toward Brom, leaping upon him and driving him back against the stone battlements. The Tower Lord caught the creature's throat and held its snapping jaws away from him, twisting its monstrous head back.

Dravek followed with his own fierce assault, swinging his sword down at Brom's head. The Tower Lord ducked the blow and the blade bit deep into the stone of the castle wall in a hail of sparks. Brom flung the wolf aside to face Dravek's violent onslaught.

Brom grabbed hold of Dravek's sword arm with one hand and clutched his neck with the other. But Dravek's strength matched Brom's own. His free hand clamped around Brom's throat and tightened to a crushing grip. The two remained entangled in their deadly struggle as they smashed against the parapet. Dravek wrenched his sword arm free and raised it to strike again. Brom pushed him away, leaping backward as Dravek lashed out. The sword hissed through the air, slicing Brom's cape, narrowly missing his throat.

The Volkodlak scrambled to its feet and readied to lunge again, but before it could, Leonidas cast a handful of wolfsbane dust into its face. The creature howled in agony, thrashing and convulsing as its flesh blistered beneath the powder's poisonous touch. The wounded beast gagged and choked, spewing forth a spray of blood, then stood upright like a man. The monster's face appeared horribly scalded, its left eye glazed and dead. Its anatomy was no longer fully that of a wolf. Its countenance and form seemed almost human and its paws had contorted into clawed hands and feet.

The beast turned its good eye toward Brom and leapt at him again. Brom wrested a torch from its sconce and swung it down toward the beast's oncoming charge. The torch smashed against the creature's head in an explosion of sparks and fiery embers. Brom seized the dazed monster, wrapping his arms around its neck. Grabbing the beast's jaws in his hands, he wrenched them apart with a bone-shattering crackle. The monstrous wolf yelped in agony. In one violent twist,

Brom snapped the creature's neck. The Volkodlak's lifeless body slumped to the ground.

As Brom turned to face Dravek, a searing pain shot through his body. Dravek stood before him, the hilt of his sword pressed against Brom's abdomen. The blade had pierced him below his ribcage, running clean and swift through his torso, protruding through his back and cape. Dravek's black eyes stared at him coldly and his lips formed a fiendish smile as he twisted the sword in his hand. Brom took a step back, freeing himself from the impaling blade, and dropped to his knees. A stream of crimson flowed from the wound.

In all the years he had ruled the Tower, Brom had not known mortal pain. Now it shot through him like cold fire. He tried to stand, but his strength waned and his legs collapsed beneath him. Finding a grip on the ledge, he strained once more to pull himself to his feet, but once more, he could not. He fell to the ground and slumped back against the parapet wall.

Dravek stepped forth, dragging Lorand by his hair. "Your reign has ended, Lord Brom. You shall not emerge the victor on this night."

Brom knew it was true. He could not defeat such a powerful foe in his wounded and weakened state. In order to match Dravek's strength, he would have to nourish himself with human blood, as Dravek had for long years. But this would lead to surrendering to the darkness within, corrupting his soul and destroying his last shreds of humanity.

Dravek held Lorand's neck before Brom's face. "Join us," Dravek whispered.

Brom's lips drew back in a feral snarl, revealing long white fangs. His eyes held the look of a savage beast. Brom's mind flooded with desperate thoughts as he weighed the risk of saving himself against the horror of sacrificing his only son.

"Never," Brom said.

"Then your vigil shall end here." Dravek cast Lorand aside and raised the relic sword high above his head, clutching it with both hands. "In Mara's name," Dravek shouted, "I claim the Tower as mine!"

But before Dravek could strike the fatal blow, Talik leapt across the parapet in one final desperate act, tackling Dravek at the waist, driving him over the edge of the battlements. The two bodies plummeted toward the ground, vanishing into the mists of the graveyard below.

A frenzied look overcame Leonidas as he picked up the dead huntsman's axe. Letting loose a primal scream, the old man swung the blade in a wild arc, burying it deep in the wolf-beast's skull. Lorand helped Brom to his feet. Tears welled in Leonidas' eyes as he looked down into the mist-shrouded cemetery.

As sunlight crested the forest, they ushered Brom inside the keep. The two men helped him down the Tower stairs and left him to rest upon a bench in the chapel.

By the time they reached the graveyard Dravek was gone. Talik's broken body lay atop a granite monument, his empty eyes staring upward into the dawning sky. A stone angel stood over him, gazing down upon his body as if delivering a prayer for his soul. Talik's throat was torn open, and his flesh was devoid of all color. His blood had been drained.

Leonidas gently closed his dead friend's eyes and stood in silence beside him. After a moment he said, "His body must be burned, before night arrives to ensure the demon does not seize his soul."

Brom remained in the shadows of the chapel arch and watched his grieving friend. As the dawn cast a blood-red glow across the sky, Leonidas and Lorand returned to the sanctuary.

Brom laid a consoling hand upon his friend's shoulder. "His sacrifice shall not be forgotten," he said softly.

Leonidas pulled away. "You abandoned your vigil," he said gruffly, "and we have paid dearly."

Brom's eyes revealed his sorrow. He shared Leonidas' grief and feelings of despair, but could find no words to ease his friend's pain.

"The darkness has returned to the Tower," the old man continued, his voice rising with anger. "How many more shall suffer because of your reckless act? How many more shall die?"

Leonidas awaited an answer, but Brom's attention was drawn to something beyond the altar. The secret passage in the chapel wall now stood open and a key remained in the lock. Brom limped to the bronze door and slammed it shut, locking it with a twist of the key. He reached into his pocket and withdrew a matching artifact. As he stared at the twin keys in his hand, an ominous dread seized his heart.

Brom slumped back against a chapel bench, saying, "The avatar of evil shall soon be awakened. I can do nothing to stop it." He lifted his blood-drenched hand from the gash in his side revealing a sanguine stream that continued to seep from the wound. "I must regain my strength to face this demon," he said, a somber tremor to his voice, "for once it is unleashed, it shall surely emerge from the depths to seek vengeance upon us all."

Lost in endless night
Wounded and alone,

Surrounded by shadows of despair,

And haunted by demons of fear,

I am thus plagued, yet I endure—

Your memory renews my faith,

Rekindling the fire within my heart,

Restoring my strength and courage,

Giving me the will to carry on

In my darkest hours—

Nightmare

JOSEPH VARGO

Brom stared at the wall of bronze that loomed behind the obsidian altar, his eyes frozen in a desolate gaze. The rays of the dawning sun shone through the chapel windows, catching the colors of the stained glass to bathe the wall in a macabre crimson glow. Brom's eyes slowly shifted to the two men who stood in the sanctuary before him. Lorand and Leonidas remained silent as they returned his woeful stare.

"We have little time before the darkness returns." Brom's voice was deathly solemn, full of quiet resolve. "I ventured into the catacombs beneath the Tower and was nearly lost within the labyrinth. The caverns are an endless maze of winding tunnels. If Dravek returns this way, it shall not be soon, but there is much we must do."

Leonidas looked toward the bronze wall that concealed the catacombs' hidden entrance. "We must take action to ensure his path is blocked."

Brom slowly rose from his seat, his hand firmly pressed against the wound in his side. Ignoring the pain that coursed through his body, he stepped to the sealed passage beyond the altar, keeping his cloaked back to the sunlight. He set a sharp claw to the metal and scrawled three words into the bronze door. *Sanvi, Sansavi, Semangelaf.*

Leonidas squinted at the graven names. "The sacred

inscription is a powerful ward against the forces of darkness."

"Yes," the Tower Lord said. "The evil must be contained by all means available. We cannot allow it to break free of this realm." Brom paused for a moment as his mind recalled another legend from the Tower's history. "The ancient standing stones must be set right once more as well."

The old man's expression remained grim as he nodded his head. All the elders of Vasaria knew the legend of the standing stones. It was said that angels set three monuments around the mountain to act as mystic barriers, marking the boundaries of the Dark Brood's domain. One yet stood between the mountain and the village, but the others lay in ruin, toppled long ago by ignorant men. Should Mara rise again, restoring the ancient markers would constrict her freedom, confining her to the Tower and mountain woodlands.

Brom scanned the statues of saints and angels that stood in the shadowed recesses of the chapel before turning his gaze to the unholy images depicted in the surrounding windows. The sinister figures in the stained glass seemed to pulse with life, while the sacred statues remained sorrowfully still, seemingly lost in the engulfing darkness.

The Tower Lord turned to Lorand, taking hold of his arm. Even in his wounded condition, Brom's grip was like iron. "I entrusted you in my leave to maintain my vigil and guard the keep against intruders. What possessed you to open the Tower doors?"

"I was visited by a spirit—the ghost of my mother. She sought to protect me. She warned me of the approaching danger and told me I would need help to stand against it. When Elder Talik and his hunting party arrived, I allowed them to enter—to help me defend the keep."

Brom's grip loosened. He stared deep into Lorand's eyes,

seeing a look that plumbed the depths of sorrow and fear.

Leonidas now turned to the boy. "Why then did you allow Dravek to enter the Tower?"

"Talik said the Tower doors would do little to thwart the White Wolf. Instead we set a trap and lured him inside. Had we not granted him entrance, Dravek would surely have killed you."

A trace of a smile touched Leonidas' weathered face as he reflected upon the memory of his dead friend. Beneath his words of wisdom, Talik was a man of action. He was a born warrior, not one to stand idly by as an enemy threatened his home. Even to the end he acted bravely and without fear. Had he not, Dravek would have slain the Tower Lord on the parapet before dawn and all would have been lost.

Lorand felt the need to further explain Talik's reasoning. "The elder's plan was to lure the enemy to the Tower's heights and trap them in the sun's dawning light. Had we been successful, Dravek and his monster would have perished."

"But the White Wolf yet lives," Leonidas said, turning to Brom, "while good men have fallen."

Brom ignored the elder's chastising gaze. "There is a girl in the village," he said. "Her name is Serena. I left her in Daria's care. I am in her debt. Allow no harm to come to her. Rest and regain your strength, then return here with her before sunset." Brom lifted his hand from the gash in his side. Blood dripped from his fingers and continued to seep from the wound. "Bring the witch as well," he whispered.

Brom steadied himself against the corridor walls as he escorted Lorand and the elder to the Tower doors.

Leonidas stepped out into the sunlit day, then turned to face Brom. "I will send men to retrieve the bodies of our fallen comrades."

Without a word, Brom receded back into the shadows,

leaving the massive doors open. The Tower Lord followed his own bloodstained trail back to the chapel. His strength and hope waning, he stumbled to the center of the sanctum. Casting his eyes upward, Brom looked upon the mural encircling the chapel dome where a trio of angels depicted as sacred knights hovered amidst a backdrop of silvery clouds. He recalled a time long ago, when one of the celestial warriors came to counsel him during his darkest hour. But in all the years since, through all Brom's struggles, the angelic knight never appeared again.

His spirit devastated, Brom fell to his knees, as if burdened by a crushing weight. Beyond the verge of despair, he cried out, "Why have you abandoned me?" His words echoed throughout the empty chapel like the forlorn tolling of a bell.

Brom slowly forced himself to his feet and turned to leave the sanctuary. As he neared the chapel doors, a gust of wind rushed past from behind him, sending his cloak and hair swirling up around him. A chill trembled along his spine, and he became aware of another presence in the room. Brom turned and looked back.

A warrior in dark armor stood before the altar. An ebon crown crested his head and raven-black wings rose from his back. His face held a majestic beauty and luster, as if his flawless features had been hewn from polished marble. Though darkly robed, the angelic guardian radiated with an unearthly light.

"Thou hast not been forsaken, brother." The angel's voice, though soft, resounded beneath the chapel dome, surrounded by others in distant harmony. "We have followed thy plight with yearning, but we cannot interfere with thy destiny here in this earthly arena."

"My destiny?"

"Yes—thy vigil to protect this realm from the forces of darkness."

"Tis an endless struggle."

"No," the angel said. "The ancient conflict shall soon be settled for all time—the fate of man resting with the victor."

Brom stepped toward the angelic knight. "If my foes are triumphant, they will surely bring mankind to their doom. I beseech you—aid me to combat this evil."

"We cannot fight alongside thee. Thou must vanquish Mara and her minion alone. We can bring neither aid nor harm to those born of mortal blood."

"Then arm me," Brom said, lifting a bloodied hand. "Lend me your sword as you did long ago for the mortals who stood against the Dark Queen."

The angel's eyes glistened with light. "The sword thou speakest of was bestowed upon the crusaders only after Mara's legions trespassed beyond our sacred boundary, crossing the threshold of the last remaining standing stone. The Dark Brood is free to do as they will within the borders of their earthly domain—such are the laws of the ancient pact. But Mara heedlessly sent her armies forth to trod upon forbidden ground. For this, she suffered dire consequences."

Brom lowered his head. "Then hope is lost. Can you offer me nothing?"

"Heed my words. The Dark Brood were once our brethren, but their pride led them to their downfall. They now wallow in vice. They are powerful and wise, yet their wisdom is tainted by their lust for indulgence. Their greed leaves them blind and vulnerable to many things. They shall try to deceive and sway you by any means, tempting you with earthly desires to lead your heart astray. The course of victory lies in unwavering strength of will."

A halo of light surrounded the angel, engulfing him in a shimmering glow until at last he vanished from sight. Brom stood alone in the chapel once more.

The Tower Lord retreated to his inner sanctum, closing the heavy door behind him. He staggered across the chamber, steadying himself against the bookshelves that lined the walls. In a far corner of the room he came to a cabinet filled with tall bottles. Each held the blood of a slaughtered animal. Brom selected a bottle from the rack and sliced open the wax seal with a claw. The scent of blood roused the dark hunger within him. He lifted the bottle to his lips and drank deeply. He soon felt its power spreading through him, restoring some measure of stamina and balance. But though the blood replenished his strength, it could not heal the wound inflicted by the sacred blade, nor could it relieve his suffering. He felt as if the sword were still within him, twisting in his flesh.

Taking a seat at his table, Brom closed his eyes, hoping to free his mind in reverie where he might escape his pain. He soon drifted into the realm of dreams.

Brom opened his eyes to find himself in the Tower's grand hall, alone in the darkness, standing before the ebon throne. An eerie stillness gripped the air, creating an unsettling aura much like the calm before a storm. The surrounding silence was interrupted by a roar from the depths of the earth. A tremor shook the ground beneath his feet, sending an immense crack through the floor, splitting the great hall in two. Dark smoke issued forth from the gaping fissure and rose to take the shape of a human figure draped in black. The shadow lifted its crowned head, revealing a deathly white face, fearsome yet beautiful. Eyes black as sin held Brom in their cold gaze and lips parting around glistening fangs formed a hungry smile. It was Mara, the Dark Queen.

She raised her taloned hand and the outside sky erupted with lightning. A violent thunderbolt shot down from the heavens, striking the Tower and shattering the ancient bricks that formed the castle walls. The keep crumbled away around Mara, filling the air with a shower of stones. Its great towers crashed down into the mountaintop, smashing to pieces on the jagged rocks below. The Dark Queen had unleashed the fury of Hell upon the keep, destroying the ancient fortress that had long held her bound. At last she was free of her prison.

As Mara hovered before Brom, an ebon mist swirled beneath her, forming a stallion of writhing shadows. The spectral horse was black as pitch, save for its eyes, which held a burning fire. The demon steed reared and leapt into the sky, carrying the Dark Queen up into the moonless night. Lightning slashed across the horizon as the storm raged around her. Mara soared amidst the tumultuous heavens, and in her wake the clouds billowed and churned, sending swarms of bats and winged demons to descend upon the earth below.

Brom stood frozen in place as he watched the nightmarish scene unfold. Suddenly a burning pain overwhelmed him, as if his body had been gripped by fire. He turned to see Dravek standing behind him, the relic sword in his hand. A stream of blood ran from the blade, forming a crimson rune upon the ground between them. The symbol was all too familiar to Brom—it was the icon of the Dark Tower.

Slowly, shadows began to stir and rise from the bloodstained soil. A legion of cloaked forms, twisted and distorted, reached out with skeletal hands to claw at Brom's flesh, clutching him in their sinister grip, dragging him down into the black abyss. Brom struggled with all his power against the swarming shadows, but he was soon swallowed by the lightless void.

Brom plummeted downward till at last he found himself at the bottom of a deep chasm. In the fathomless dark he could see that he was surrounded by spirits of the dead, looming silent and still. He recognized the faces of many of the phantoms, gazing in horror upon the forlorn countenances of Victor and Gabriella, Maeve and the Baron, the ancient king of the Tower, and countless others who fell victim to the Dark Queen's wrath. The grim specters stood motionless and stared at him with hollow eyes. Brom felt their grief, knowing he had become one of them—yet another cursed soul, forever trapped between the realms of the living and the dead. He turned his gaze upward where the chasm walls closed in, sealing him in the forgotten depths of the underworld. Brom screamed in anguish, but his voice was soon silenced by the suffocating darkness that consumed him.

As Leonidas and Lorand hiked along the mountain path that snaked downward toward Vasaria, neither spoke a word. Their minds were lost in deep thought as they reflected upon the staggering events of the past few days. They had survived their ordeal with Dravek, either by luck or the grace of fate, but now a greater threat loomed ahead. There was much to do and little time. Leonidas knew that every hour was of the essence, but he and Lorand had not slept for more than a day and they both languished beneath the spell of weariness. The journey from the Tower had never taken so long.

As the morning sun crested the mountain behind them, they emerged from the forest trail. Vasaria stood before them in the bleak light, a cluster of hovels in a clearing carved from the vast forest that dominated the land. Never had Leonidas thought it so meager, so fragile. A crowd of villagers gathered along the path, just beyond the great standing stone. Men, women and children waited in silence, their eyes filled with fear.

Kasmarak the elder stepped forward to address Leonidas. "We woke to the tolling of the Tower bell. What has happened?"

"The keep was under siege," Leonidas said. "The Tower Lord has protected us, as he always does, but he did not vanquish the darkness. An evil force now dwells in our midst. We must prepare for what is to come."

"What of Talik and the others?" Kasmarak asked in a harsh whisper.

Leonidas shook his head. "We alone survived," he said quietly.

Leonidas sent the women and children to their homes, assuring them they would be safe there. The elder then addressed the remaining men, assigning them to various missions. Two groups of workers were dispatched to right the toppled standing stones, while a third group was sent to the Tower to retrieve the bodies of Talik and the fallen huntsmen. The men set about their tasks without delay, fully understanding the urgency of completing their work before nightfall.

Before entering the village, Leonidas and Lorand parted ways. The boy returned to his home to rest, while Leonidas followed a trail into the woods toward Daria's dwelling. The young witch met him at her door, her face fraught with dire concern. Her eyes brimmed with tears as she wrapped her arms around her dear friend. She held him for a long moment before inviting him inside.

Daria's abode was cluttered with the implements of her craft. Feathers and animal bones, braided together with dried herbs, hung from the ceiling throughout the hut. On every wall earthen jars shared shelves with twisting roots, exotic flowering plants and a variety of unusual trinkets fashioned from twine and polished gemstones. A jawless skull inscribed with mystic sigils and an hourglass filled with black sand rested upon a table strewn with scrolls and crystals.

Several cats had made the hut their home. Two wove

deftly between the collection of strange artifacts scattered across her table. One large black cat nestled in Daria's lap as soon as she sat. Leonidas took a seat across from her and recounted his tale, telling her of all that had transpired between Dravek and the Tower Lord.

The elder's eyes scanned the room, seemingly searching for something in the shadows. "Brom said he left a girl in your care."

"Her name is Serena." Daria kept her voice to a soft whisper. "She is asleep, sharing Annika's bed." She glanced at a door at the back of the hut. "She will be safe here. You must rest as well. It will take me some time to gather the things I need."

Leonidas nodded, struggling to keep his heavy eyelids open. His mind and body suffered the strains of fatigue and he could no longer stave off the effects. He leaned back in the chair and fell fast asleep. After what felt like moments, he awoke with a start. The light in the hut had strangely shifted and the shadows were longer. He realized that hours had passed. Daria stood at his side, her hand resting gently on his shoulder.

"You have a visitor," she said.

A cloaked man stood in the doorway. As Leonidas regained his focus, he recognized the face of Brother Adrian.

Leonidas greeted his old friend with a cold stare as he slowly rose to his feet. "Why have you returned to Vasaria?"

Adrian hesitantly stepped inside the doorway. "When your emissary delivered word of the danger that threatened the village, I came as swiftly as possible. I returned here hoping to repay my debt to Lord Brom and aid him in his time of need."

"Your debt?" Leonidas narrowed an eye.

Adrian nodded timidly. "Lord Brom was of great service to us. He ended our plight in the monastery, resolving our mystery and banishing the dark spirit that plagued us. He left two nights ago, destined for Castle Rankorr."

A look of rage flashed across the elder's face. "His duty lay here! He should never have left the Tower. At the very least, he should have returned here without delay. Because of his flagrant recklessness, we are all in peril. The White Wolf has returned to resurrect the Dark Queen from her grave. Once she is free, the armies of the night shall rise once more to serve her."

"No," a young voice said.

Leonidas turned to see Serena in the doorway behind him. Though she was young, she carried herself with authority as she stepped into the room.

"The legions of the Black Dawn shall never march upon this land," she said. "Lord Brom laid ruin to their plan. He destroyed their stronghold and scattered the Dark Queen's followers. And after he did this, he honored his promise to deliver me to safety, though his most dire concern was returning here to protect Vasaria and vanquish the evil that plagues the Tower.

"We were both bound to a pact, an oath we swore to my dying father who had aided Lord Brom's quest. My father possessed the gift of second sight. He was enslaved by Dravek and forced to serve the Black Dawn. But he acted against his captors, seeking to save my life." The girl's eyes were wet with tears, but she fought them off and continued resolutely. "He translated an ancient scroll for Lord Brom and made him vow to protect me in return. With his last words, my father revealed the scroll's contents to me and made me promise to keep them secret until I was free of Dravek's grasp."

The girl's words bore down upon Leonidas like a landslide. They had all made great sacrifices, willingly risking their own lives for the sake of the greater good. But Brom had fearlessly ventured where none other dared, into the dragon's lair to vanquish the beast before it could rise. The Brotherhood of the Black Dawn was no more. All that remained was Mara's undying spirit and her ever-faithful servant.

Adrian rested a consoling hand on his friend's shoulder.

Leonidas shook his head sorrowfully. "I cursed Brom for abandoning the Tower, thinking he left the keep vulnerable to siege, when in truth, his absence lured Dravek away from his own fortress, allowing Brom to lay waste to the Black Dawn's infernal legions. The price we have paid here is naught compared to the horror Brom has spared us."

Adrian turned to Serena. "You spoke of a scroll?"

"Lord Brom brought it to my father to translate its ancient text. It contained a prophecy."

"Where is it now?"

"Lost—destroyed in the fires of Castle Rankorr."

Adrian stepped to the girl's side. "What message did it hold?"

"I... cannot say. When we reached the edge of Vasaria, Brom was summoned away by the tolling of the Tower bell. He ventured to the castle before I could relate the scroll's contents. I cannot reveal the message to anyone other than Lord Brom."

"Very well," Leonidas said. "Lord Brom instructed us to bring you to him. We shall take you to the Tower, and you may tell him all you know."

Later in the day Falon returned to the village, bloody and hobbling, but very much alive. Leonidas told him of his father's brave death, and the young man grieved in silence. The elder instructed Falon to remain in the village, entrusting him to protect Vasaria while Leonidas returned to the Tower. Though the fires of vengeance smoldered within him, Falon accepted his duty. Shortly thereafter, the wagon returned from the keep with the bodies of Talik and the fallen huntsmen. The villagers constructed a funeral pyre in the center of town and Talik's body was laid reverently upon it. In the hours before sunset, the people of Vasaria gathered to mourn the death of their honored sage. Brother Adrian presided over the ceremony, delivering a blessing to purge Talik's soul of all darkness.

As the dying sun burned low on the horizon, Leonidas and Lorand saddled horses and made their way back to Daria's hut. They arrived to see the witch crouching beside her daughter, Annika. The young girl cast a handful of bones to the ground and gazed upon the scattered fragments.

"What do you see?" Daria asked.

"A white wolf hearkens to its master," the girl whispered calmly. She tossed the skeletal remnants down once more and stared at the pattern that lay in the dirt, saying, "The bite of twin serpents shall deliver a mortal wound." The girl cast the bones a final time. She stared at the strewn array then looked up toward the road where Leonidas and Lorand sat upon their horses in the dying sunlight. Turning back toward her mother, the girl whispered, "The dark lord requires sacrifice. Only blood shall thwart the shadow of death."

Daria listened with great interest to the omens foretold. She hugged her daughter and said goodbye, leaving her in the care of the village midwife.

Daria called to Serena and the young woman emerged from the hut carrying a large woven satchel. The two mounted horses, sharing saddles with the men. Daria rode with Leonidas while Serena rode with Lorand. Serena cast her gaze above the treeline where the Tower loomed ominously over the forest, the sunset gilding its black edges with crimson. Her eyes held a look of fear as she stared off toward their grim destination. Lorand offered soft, soothing words, coaxing her to rest her worries in his care. She returned his tender gesture with a sweet smile.

In Vasaria behind them, the villagers lit the funeral pyre and joined voices in a song to honor their fallen elder. The haunting melody echoed through the woodlands as the party ascended the path to the Tower. The slow rhythm of the song pulsed like the beat of a giant heart, setting a somber pace for their journey. As they neared the mountaintop, the low, mournful singing was accented by the harsh ring of ravens' cries.

The air held an icy chill. A gray mist clung between the barren trees, giving them the appearance of dark wraiths lurking in the gloom, reaching out with long, bony arms. The riders ventured forward, undaunted by their sinister surroundings. The mist parted as they arrived at the summit and Leonidas and Lorand looked toward the ruins beside the path, hoping to see the beautiful spirit that haunted the gate, but their gazes were met only by the rising moon.

They rode to the base of the Tower stairs and dismounted. The castle's black walls cast a stark silhouette against the scarlet remnants of sunset. Black on black, ravens lined the ledges above the Tower doors, watching the visitors in silence. As Lorand tethered their horses, a cloaked rider swiftly approached from the forest path. The horseman brought his steed to a halt before them, then drew back his hood, revealing the familiar face of Brother Adrian.

"Why have you followed us?" Leonidas demanded.

"My debt to Lord Brom remains unpaid," Adrian said breathlessly. "I could not sit idle in the village while this unholy terror lurks here." He stared up at the Tower looming high above them. "It is as if I were summoned here by an inner voice. I could not ignore the call."

Leonidas stared at the priest for a long moment, locking his eyes upon the chained crucifix that Adrian wore around his neck. At last he said, "Very well."

They ascended the castle steps and peered between the gaping doors into nothing. The scant light that crept through the entryway was quickly consumed by the chamber's oppressive darkness. Leonidas lit a torch and led the way. As they entered the keep, their eyes beheld a grim sight. At the center of the hall, Brom lay lifeless on the floor, sprawled over the runic sigil. The ancient icon seemed to clutch him in its grasp. Blood pooled beneath his body, covering the black marble floor in a scarlet stain. Leonidas rushed to Brom, lifting his head and calling his name. The fallen Tower Lord strained to open his eyes, but they soon drifted closed. He tried to speak but could form no words.

The men carried Brom to his sanctum and laid him on the central table. Daria had Lorand light a fire in the great fireplace. Adrian blessed himself and waved his hand over Brom, casting the sign of the cross upon him.

Leonidas looked down upon the Tower Lord, a sorrowful cast to his eyes. "The girl told us of your ordeal in the fortress of the Black Dawn," he said quietly. "No words can express our gratitude for what you have done. Forgive me."

Brom lay motionless and unresponsive.

"Leave us," Daria said.

Leonidas ushered the others out of the chamber and the witch quickly set about her work. Stripping off Brom's blood-soaked tunic, she found two wounds in his flesh, jagged and torn where Dravek had twisted the relic sword. Opening her satchel, she withdrew several earthen jars, a silver dagger, shafts of incense and a bronze bowl. Daria stepped to the hearth and laid the blade of her dagger over the flames. She then lit the incense and recited a rhythmic chant in a tongue long forgotten by all but her kind, all the while moving her hands lightly over Brom's body. Taking the dagger from the fire, Daria set its red-hot blade against Brom's wounds, searing them shut. She then opened the jars, revealing moss and healing herbs, and mixed the contents in her bowl. When her concoction began to congeal, the witch smeared the ruddy paste over Brom's scars, whispering more mystic words.

Brom's eyes slowly opened. He tried to rise but did not possess the strength.

"Be still," Daria said, turning away from him. She busied herself for a moment then turned back holding a wooden goblet. She tilted his head forward and pressed the cup to his lips.

Brom hesitated, staring helplessly into Daria's eyes.

"Lamb's blood," she whispered.

Brom closed his eyes and drank till the goblet was empty. The burning fire that coursed through his veins slowly subsided and he could feel his strength return. As his eyes regained their focus, he saw that Daria's face was pale white. He took hold of her arm and noticed her wrist was wrapped with a bloodstained cloth.

"What have you done, witch?" Brom demanded.

"It was the only way," Daria said. "Only human blood can heal such a wound." She rested her hand over his heart. "Have no fear. I gave this gift willingly and cleansed it of all impurity. It holds no taint or poison."

Brom released her from his grip and slowly rose to his feet. He felt neither pain nor weakness. The witch had freed him from Death's grasp.

"Where is Serena?" Brom asked.

"She is here. She waits outside with the others. She told us of the prophecy, but she will only reveal it to you."

Brom stared at the empty goblet. "She had a dream—a vision of an arcane ceremony. She described a blood ritual that enabled me to thrive in daylight once more." He turned to Daria and asked, "Tell me, does such a spell exist?"

"I know of no such ritual that would allow you to withstand the sun's rays, but the girl's dream may hold some undiscovered secret. If her father was truly a seer, I believe she may possess the gift of foresight as well. There is much more to her than a mere pretty face."

Brom nodded.

"She rode here with the boy, Lorand," Daria said. "Their interest in one another is plain to see."

Brom studied her. "And what do you know of the boy?"

The witch smiled. "Vasaria has few secrets that have remained hidden from me."

Brom's eyes narrowed. "Then you know what he means to me."

"Yes," Daria said. "I will do all I can to keep him safe from harm."

"Then I shall be even further in your debt." Brom stared off toward the hearth where firelight flickered weakly. "Should my enemies discover the truth about him, I fear his life would be in danger."

"Such a discovery could be perilous for you as well, my lord."

"How so?" Brom asked.

"Ancestral blood is a powerful ingredient for many potions and spells. It can be used to control and destroy anyone born of the same bloodline. Bones ground to dust can be used in the same manner—even to cause harm to..." She paused, choosing her words delicately. "To one such as yourself, Lord Brom."

Daria turned to her satchel and retrieved a thick, worm-eaten book. She set the tome on the table and began leafing through the age-worn pages. Etchings of strange symbols adorned the scribed parchment. At last she stopped at a passage of ancient script above a diagram of a skull within a circle of mystic sigils.

"Here," she said, laying her finger on the tattered page. Her eyes darted back and forth across the runic letters until at last she said, "The earthly essence of kindred—one of your own mortal bloodline—can be used to bind undead spirits to the mortal realm."

Brom contemplated Daria's words in silence for a long moment. At last he spoke again. "Mara was slain by the Baron, but her immortal spirit yet lives. If her soul were bound to the mortal realm by such a spell, could she then be destroyed for all time?"

"I believe so. She is an ancient creature. If her essence were bound to her mortal body, time would be her undoing. The years would reclaim her flesh. If the life is driven from her body in such a way, her spirit would die as well."

Brom studied the page intently, lost in deep thought.

Daria removed a pendant necklace and held it out for Brom to see. "Here," she said. An amulet of silver hung suspended from a thin leather braid. "Do you remember the tale I once told you—the tale of Mara's mother, Endora?"

"Yes."

"This amulet holds her heart's blood. The crones seized it upon Endora's death, perhaps as a precaution against Mara. My ancestors passed the amulet from one generation to the next, until my mother bestowed it upon me."

Brom held the pendant in his gaze. "You also spoke of another talisman, a vial, crested with the head of a stag."

"Yes. It contains the blood of Leshii, the Dark Lord of the Forest. But it was lost long ago."

"No more," Brom's voice grew somber. "I fear Dravek possesses it. He means to use it to resurrect Mara."

"If this is true, the Dark Queen will rise again."

Brom clenched his jaw tightly and gazed into the dying

fire of the hearth.

Daria rested a hand on his shoulder. "Your enemies grow stronger, but you are no longer alone in this war." The witch turned and stepped to the doorway. "Come," she said. "The others await."

Daria led Brom out into the hall where Leonidas and Lorand paced nervously. Relief filled their faces as they beheld Brom well and walking. Beyond the hall, Serena and Adrian waited in the chapel. The girl wept softly as she read from a book of psalms while the monk knelt before the altar, his head bowed in prayer.

Brom entered the hallowed sanctuary. "It seems our paths were destined to cross yet again," he said.

Adrian lifted his head and smiled.

Serena ran to Brom, throwing her arms around him. "I thought death had come for you," she whispered.

"Death has beckoned me many times, but I have yet to accept his invitation. I must speak with you alone."

Serena followed Brom back across the hall to his inner sanctum. The massive door creaked shut behind them, sealing them inside.

Daria stepped into the chapel. Her eyes wandered throughout the sanctuary, lingering upon the sacred effigies graven in stone and etched in stained glass. She made her way toward the altar where Adrian knelt. "Your house of worship honors many idols," she said. The witch turned to a plaque on the wall depicting angels and winged demons locked in a deathly struggle. "Yet your faith reduces the vast trials of life to a sole principle—the eternal clash between the forces of good and evil..." She ran her fingers over the plaque, caressing the graven faces of a heavenly king and a diabolic horned monster. "...the battle between your god and his nemesis, the Devil."

Adrian raised his head, saying, "God created all things, even the Fallen Ones. The Prince of Darkness is not the Lord's nemesis, for God can have no equal. Satan is not his foe, but his fallen son—a lost child who chose the path of vice and defied his almighty father. For this, he was banished from the virtuous order of the heavenly kingdom to the earthly realm where chaos is free to reign. Those who follow him into darkness are damned for all time."

Daria smiled. "Do not confuse good and evil with light and darkness. According to your own beliefs, the creator gave birth to all the known realms, not just the world of light. Those who follow only one path are unaware of the full spectrum of beauty, for both light and darkness are blinding in their extremes. Those who can see no beauty in darkness are just as lost as those who see none in light. Yet many men are compelled to find inspiration in only one of these domains, holding their chosen path in the highest esteem while condemning all others. This narrow vision of the world leads to conflicts among men. It is the basis of hatred, violence and war."

Adrian stood and turned to face Daria. "From whence do your powers of sorcery come?" he asked.

Again, the witch smiled. "All magic comes from one source. The magic of my kindred is the magic of the Old Ways, taught to us by the Ancient Ones—the Watchers—the angelic emissaries of the very god you worship." She ran her fingers over the crucifix that hung from the chain around Adrian's neck. "Though pious lords dictate that our religions must be opposed, that none but their own faith may be accepted, our beliefs are very much the same. We both value order above chaos, wisdom over ignorance, and the good of mankind above all. We condemn those who want only to do harm. Yet there are those whose minds are unwilling to accept this. They are blind to the truth. They persecute anything they do not understand, deeming it unholy and evil, merely because it does not align with the strict teachings of their faith."

Adrian nodded. "I have read and witnessed many things that have made me question much of ancient scripture. In my studies, I have sought knowledge based in fact instead of superstition and myth. The books of the monastery library granted me access to numerous religions and philosophies of the world. I found much truth and wisdom among faiths other than my own."

Daria stared at him in wonder. "I would not expect such words from a priest. Your mind is open and tolerant, reaching far beyond the limits of most holy men. You may be of help after all."

A slight smile touched Adrian's lips.

The creak of the sanctum door announced Brom's return. A moment later, the Tower Lord stood at the chapel entrance with Serena at his side. "It seems we each hold keys to unlocking this mystery," he said.

Stepping to the altar, Brom lit the vigil light that hung suspended overhead. He looked down upon the others, like a high priest delivering mass, and said, "The fates have drawn us together for a solitary purpose—" He raised Daria's silver dagger, allowing it to catch the candlelight's gleam. "To vanquish the Dark Queen for all time."

As if in answer to Brom's proclamation, a mournful wail rose, echoing beneath the chapel dome. The lamenting moan surrounded the sanctuary, as if it were coming from somewhere within the walls. A chill gripped the air as the sound grew louder, rising to fill the room with an ominous howl, like the cry of a wolf closing in on its prey.

Dark forces infest the Tower like air thick with plague. Concealed in shadows, they lie in wait to rise and claim the ancient keep. Though I carry their vile blood in my veins, I am sworn to defend against them.

This accursed place is both prison and battleground. I stand here alone, keeping watch at the gateway between the realms of the living and the dead.

Loneliness and despair wear against my spirit as a river wears against stone, eroding my will to carry on. Time is my enemy. No matter how steadfast my resolve, with each new day my existence becomes more difficult to endure. Yet, I cannot fail in my task, for if I do, mankind shall be forever lost.

Rise of the Dark Queen

JOSEPH VARGO

Dravek heard the thunderous echo of the chapel door as it slammed shut far behind him, sealing the entrance to the catacombs. He knew he was now trapped inside the kingdom of the dead—the vast underworld beneath the Dark Tower—but it mattered little to him. His plan to seize the castle had come undone at every turn, yet fate could not thwart or deter him from his mission. He drew closer to his ultimate goal with each step he took.

Reaching into the pocket of his cloak, he withdrew a black vial crowned with the sculpted head of a stag. Dravek gazed upon the ancient artifact reverently, knowing his queen's salvation rested within. Placing the talisman back in his pocket, he continued on his way.

No light had shone in these Stygian tunnels for uncounted years and their darkness was absolute, but the absence of light was no obstacle. Dravek's unearthly vision allowed him to see clearly in the pitch-black maze. His eyes pierced the surrounding gloom, revealing the grim path ahead in shades of blue. The tunnels were laden with skeletal remains, presenting a gruesome tableau that would have stricken most men with mortal fear. Human bones lined the walls, fitted together in long, precise rows, forming a macabre shrine to those who had died here over the centuries. Their hollow skulls, now stacked in piles, stared emptily into the lightless void. Countless denizens of the realm had met with grisly, anguished deaths beneath the Dark Queen's merciless reign. Many had been slain by Dravek's own hand. Their lives were taken without pity or remorse as he quenched his thirst upon their blood.

As Dravek made his way through the network of passageways, the hushed breath of whispers hissed around him and he caught glimpses of spectral forms rising and sinking back into the surrounding shadows. He had entered a haunted realm—a desolate place inhabited by wandering, accursed spirits. They were lost and restless souls, condemned to an eternity of suffering, doomed to oblivion here in the labyrinth. Their ghostly presence was seldom detected by the living, but Dravek's mortal life had ended long ago, enabling him to see beyond the veil of death.

Dravek marched along at an unrelenting pace. Rats scurried around his boots, fleeing his trampling footsteps. The air had turned colder, but this too made little impression on him. He passed through a region of the catacombs reserved for the Tower's royalty, where iron bars sealed vaulted crypts. Ornate sepulchres rested within each burial chamber, their marble lids chiseled in the likeness of the knights and noblemen who lay entombed beneath them. Dravek paid them little heed. His queen was not buried here, nor had she been laid to rest in any dignified manner. Mara's remains had been interred with blasphemous disrespect by those who feared her wrath. Her body and spirit were banished to the deepest pits of the labyrinth, imprisoned there in the dark abyss to be forever forgotten by mankind, erased from the book of time. But Dravek had never forgotten.

As he ventured further into the catacombs, Dravek's course grew increasingly difficult. The twisting tunnels wove back and forth, intersecting one another at irregular angles, splitting again and again to form new paths that spiraled deeper and deeper into the mountain. He wandered in circles, searching for direction in the endless network of passageways, but there was none to be found. At various intervals along the walls, he saw crude crosses etched into the cornerstones of intersections, but Dravek's mind could not fathom whatever path they were meant to mark.

A shrill scream split the surrounding silence. Quickening his pace, Dravek followed the sound down a narrow passageway lined entirely with skulls. Shattered bones lay strewn throughout the tunnel, as if it were the den of some ghoulish beast. After some distance the corridor ended in a solid wall. The air held an unnatural coldness, like the icy chill of the grave.

Dravek turned to leave but found that the path behind him was now blocked by a wall of skulls. A young woman stood before the barrier, her eyes sunken and hollow, the skin taut across the bones of her face. The tattered dress that clung to her frail form was drenched in blood. Her throat had been savagely torn open, as if she were the victim of ravenous wolves. Her sad, porcelain-white face seemed remotely familiar to Dravek, stirring a vague recollection from the distant past, but he had long since lost count of the lives he had taken. His victims were faded memories, their faces forgotten.

The phantom reached out toward him. Though flesh still clung to her bloody hands, her arms had been gnawed to the bone. The grisly specter moved her lips as if to speak, but she could form no words. Though Dravek could not remember her, it seemed she had not forgotten the fiend who ended her life. Her spirit now sought vengeance.

As the apparition stepped closer, something stirred amidst the death's heads behind her. Swarms of spiders crept from the skulls' hollow sockets, crawling across the decayed bones, forming a writhing mass upon the surrounding walls. In mere moments, the spiders scurried to weave a layer of silken webs, forming ghastly faces upon the skulls. Dravek stood transfixed as he gazed upon the emerging countenances of men and women, their expressions twisted and distorted in deathly torment, their mouths gaping in anguished screams.

The girl took another step forward and stood directly before Dravek. Her eyes were pools of blood spilling over their rims in long scarlet tears and her lips curled up over her teeth in a grotesque smile. Dravek drew his sword and swung it out toward the phantom, but the blade slashed through empty air as the grim spirit faded to darkness. The passageway stood open once more and the surrounding skulls stared out from their resting places in lifeless silence.

Dravek continued on his way, unmoved by his eerie encounter but more disoriented than before. He had lost all sense of direction and was unsure of which paths he had already followed. Each time he felt as if he had advanced to some new area, he found himself doubling back across his own trail. He had spent far more time wandering the maze than he would have thought possible. The corridors unraveled before him, seemingly without end.

At times he heard the murmur of voices surrounding him and more than once he felt the icy caress of fingers upon his skin. But each time he turned to discover who was with him, he found only empty darkness. He could not trust his own senses. The ghosts that ruled this dark kingdom were perversely mischievous, teasing him, taunting him, leading him in circles. They seemed to revel in his torment.

Dravek was lost. His mind wrestled with the limitless choices that the labyrinth held. He could not be certain which barriers were real and which were illusions conjured by the vengeful dead. He would rather wage battle against an army of living men than contend with the unseen forces that thwarted his path.

A distant sound drew his attention to a dark passage ahead. He halted in place to hear it more clearly. As the echo of his footsteps receded, the sound came again. Though the noise was faint, it sounded like the dull jingle of bells. Dravek crept forward to discover a figure waiting at an intersection ahead—a lean man dressed in the patchwork costume of a court jester. Round bells adorned his tunic and hung from the horns of his headpiece. His skeletal face was painted in the garish mockery of a smile. The harlequin burst into a fit of maniacal laughter then disappeared around a corner. Dravek gave chase but found no one there. The corridor came to an abrupt end at yet another wall of piled bones. Laughter echoed around him—an unnerving childish giggle. Dravek pressed his weight against the wall and the bones came crashing down, revealing a passageway behind them. He ventured forth to explore the region that lay hidden beyond the barrier. The walls here were bare stone, chiseled from the very rock of the mountain itself. He was certain he had not visited this part of the labyrinth before.

Dravek had long since lost track of time, but he knew more than a day had passed since he entered the catacombs. He felt his vigor fading as thirst settled upon him. He had been deprived of blood too long and he could feel the hunger rising within him. He knew the desire would soon consume him, filling his mind with nothing other than the need to slake his thirst. He struggled with the urge, but he was helpless in the face of his bloodlust. It was his master, and he was forever its slave.

He could do nothing to suppress his dark desires. He could only resolve to carry on.

The tunnels fell deathly silent once more, allowing Dravek a moment of solitude. His mind lingered upon the memory of his queen and savior, Mara. She was an enchanting vision—a dark goddess whose beauty was unmatched by mortal women. Dravek had fallen under her bewitching spell the first moment his eyes beheld her. Though it had been more than a century since he last gazed upon her, her image remained firmly etched in his mind. He envisioned her before him—her flesh soft and pale, her crimson lips supple and full, her black eyes full of mystery and promise. The flames of desire burned within him as he recalled every curve and delicate nuance of her body. How he had longed for her touch over the years. He had been apart from her too long. Their worlds remained separated by an ocean of sorrows, but they would soon be together once more. Dravek would not rest until he completed his mission. He had vowed to free Mara from her deathly prison and restore her to her throne at any cost. The Dark Queen would rise from the shadows to claim all that was rightfully hers. Her time of reckoning was drawing near.

Fighting back the mad thirst welling within him, Dravek marched on. As he rounded a bend in the tunnel, he caught sight of a shadowy form in the distance ahead. The figure stood motionless before him, blocking his path. It was cloaked in the robes of a monk, a black velvet hood covering its head.

Dravek slowed his pace as he approached the figure, saying, "Be gone, phantom."

The shadow gave no response.

Dravek withdrew the sword from his belt and stepped warily closer.

The dark monk lifted its head, exposing eyes of burning

fire. "Welcome, brother," he whispered.

Dravek peered into the shadows of the monk's hood to glimpse the creature's face. He saw only writhing smoke behind its glowing eyes, as if the figure were formed of living shadows.

Dravek raised the relic sword and held it between them. "What are you?"

"I am the guardian of the necropolis." From beneath its cloak, the figure slowly withdrew a sword, identical to the one Dravek held. "We are kindred spirits, Lord Dravek." A face took form beneath the monk's cowl—a chiseled countenance, ominous and majestic, seemingly sculpted from solid obsidian. The dark creature smiled, revealing glistening fangs.

Dravek slid his sword back into his belt. "You know my name?"

"I know many things. I know of your devotion to your master and I know of the quest that brought you here. I have watched your toils with great interest. Your journey has been fraught with misfortune and loss, yet you carry on, steadfast in your mission."

"The fates have plagued me," Dravek said. "My minions are dead—slain by the wretched lot who sought to guard the Tower. But I have wounded their champion, Brom. He proved to be a worthy foe, but his vigil is near its end."

"Brom is a formidable warrior indeed. I would not dismiss him so easily."

"I left him at death's threshold."

"True," the guardian said, "but now circumstance lies in his favor. He regains his powers, while yours wane here in the labyrinth."

"He shall meet his end when I emerge from this place with my queen. The Black Dawn shall swarm this land like a ravaging tide."

"Your vision is but a broken dream. Much more has come to pass since you ventured here. In your absence, fate led Brom to Castle Rankorr. The fates do indeed plague you. Your forces have been vanquished."

"How can this be?" A tremor of anger rose beneath Dravek's voice.

"Your stronghold has fallen. Your fortress lies in ruin."

Dravek's eyes held a look of disbelief. "What of Ramiel... and my army?"

"Your warlord is dead. Your legions are lost—scattered to the wind." The dark monk's voice grew more somber. "Lord Brom has laid waste to your plan. The Black Dawn is no more. All that remains is your queen, and she lies in a deathly state."

Dravek's head sunk. "I seek her tomb," he said, "but the spirits that haunt this place hunger for vengeance. They plague me, obstructing my path at every turn."

"They cannot harm you. They can only hinder your way. They are mere whispers in the dark—the echoes of voices silenced long ago. Pay them no heed." The creature turned its burning gaze toward the passageway ahead. "I cannot guide you through the labyrinth. I can only reveal that which eludes your notice." The dark monk gestured to the earth beneath their feet.

Dravek studied the ground, detecting traces of footsteps in the dust. "Someone else has passed this way."

"Yes," the guardian said. "The Tower Lord wandered this maze, lost and searching for countless days until at last he came upon Mara's tomb. A hunter such as yourself should be able to follow his trail with little trouble." The creature's voice dropped to a deep whisper, saying, "When you draw near your queen, you will hear her call. Her voice shall summon you to her."

Dravek peered deep into the guardian's crimson gaze. "Nothing shall stand in my way."

"Go, now," the creature's voice rumbled. "Your queen awaits."

His resolve rekindled, Dravek set off down the passageway following the trail of footprints. He looked back to the grim guardian once more, seeing two more cloaked forms standing beside it. Their molten eyes grew dim as the sinister shadows receded into the dark.

The trail twisted and wound its way downward into newfound realms deep in the heart of the mountain. Dravek marched relentlessly forward, ignoring the apparitions and sounds that manifested around him. Vengeful wraiths howled and shrieked, reaching out with skeletal hands as Dravek stalked heedlessly past. He would not be deterred from his goal. He continued along the trail as it plummeted further into the Tower's forgotten underworld, knowing his salvation lay at the path's end.

As he ventured onward, the roughly hewn tunnel gradually became a smooth, round bore. Dravek felt as if he had entered the lair of some gigantic serpent that had made its nest far below the Tower. He envisioned the great wyrm, its scaly skin, white and hardened from centuries beneath the earth, burrowing its path deeper and deeper into the mountain, its monstrous teeth gnawing at the solid stone before it.

The passageways soon grew wider and taller and the architecture of the tunnels became more refined. The walls and supporting columns were adorned with intricate engravings. Mystic sigils and unknown hieroglyphs ornamented the black stone, inscribed long ago by some forgotten race. Dravek paused for a moment to study his surroundings. The encompassing darkness was silent and still. No spirits tormented him here. He had left the kingdom of the dead and entered the ancient realm of the Fallen.

Dravek noticed the path held two sets of footprints—one leading forward and one leading back—both made by identical boots. Brom had come and gone this same way. As Dravek followed the trail further he saw that both sets of prints stayed the same course without falter, never once wandering into any intersecting corridors. He realized he was nearing his journey's end.

Dravek continued his trek at an invigorated pace, ever wary of his surroundings. His eyes searched the stone corridors for traces of Mara's crypt, finding nothing hidden among the shadows. But he knew she was near. He could sense her aura of divine darkness. It enveloped him like the exotic fragrance of a night-blooming flower. A noise rose in the distance, ghostly and faint, like a voice mingled with a raven's cry. Dravek stopped to listen and the sound came again. This time he recognized a single word. It seemed to whisper his name. He hurried along the corridors, following the beckoning call.

At the furthest reaches of the labyrinth, he came to a corridor flanked by macabre sentinels of stone. Columns sculpted in the likeness of winged skeletons ran along the walls. The grim statues stood with their heads reverently bowed to watch over the unhallowed hall. A solitary crypt rested at the corridor's end. Twin angels of death adorned the pillars supporting the tomb's arched entrance, keeping silent vigil on either side of the burial vault. An inscription above the archway held a single name—Lilith. It was a name of the ancient demon queen, engraved here to warn mortals of the dark goddess entombed within. At last he had reached Mara's resting place.

Dravek ran toward the crypt, hurling his body against the masonry blocks that sealed the archway. He met the stones with a violent crash, sending cracks through the ancient wall. He dug his sharp nails into the crumbled mortar and tore away the loosened bricks, one by one. Other blocks dropped away as the opening widened until the breach was large enough to enter. But now he faced another barricade. Beyond the bricks stood a wall of solid stone.

Dravek pressed against the heavy slab that sealed the burial vault but found it immovable. Had the tomb been sealed with iron gates, he would have wrested them from their hinges, but the barrier he faced was solid granite. He pounded his fists against the stone, delivering furious, smashing blows, but the wall remained intact.

Dravek felt the crushing weight of despair. Destiny had led him here, within arm's length of his queen, only to prevent him from reaching her with this final, impenetrable obstacle. The fates mocked him. He had sacrificed everything for this moment, and now his existence seemed to be for naught. For a brief instant he thought to retreat to the Tower—to meet his end at Brom's hand or beneath the sun's scalding rays. But he could not turn back. He had waited too long and come too far to be denied his goal.

Dravek fell to his knees, screaming, "No!" His voice echoed through the crypt like the howl of a wounded beast. He knelt in the dust, his body bent, his eyes closed, his mind and heart empty.

Suddenly, he felt the sensation of another presence nearby. The silence of the catacombs was broken by a dripping sound. Dravek slowly turned and scanned the corridor, searching for the source of the noise. His eyes came to rest on the ground beneath one of the guardian skeletons where a dark puddle had formed. Looking up, Dravek saw an oily stream trickling from the statue's eye sockets. It ran down along the skull's cheekbones, as if the sculpture were crying tears of murky blood. Dravek turned and saw that the same thing was true for every grim statue along the corridor. Blood, black as pitch, ran from their hollow eyes.

Slowly, then, a distant wail began to rise. The mournful sound was joined by shrieking voices, as if all the souls trapped in the catacombs were crying out for release. The ghostly cries reached a deafening crescendo, forcing Dravek to cover his ears.

He closed his eyes, crying out, "I have come for you, my queen!"

With that, the sound subsided. But now a new noise emerged from the darkness. The sound of crumbling stone drew his attention to one of the winged skeletons that stood beside the crypt. Dravek watched spellbound as the statue broke free of the chiseled column. The stone sentinel stepped from the broken pillar and stood before Dravek, spreading its dark wings across the tomb entrance.

Dravek drew his sword and held it out before him. The skeletal guardian took hold of the weapon, clamping its bony fingers around the blade and wrenching it from Dravek's grip. The grim angel turned and struck the sword against the granite slab sealing Mara's crypt, shattering the stone, leaving a gaping hole beneath the archway.

There inside was Mara. A black velvet gown clung to her figure like the sleek feathers of a raven and a crown of twisting spikes rested upon her head. Her white flesh was smooth as polished alabaster and her eyes glistened like dark jewels. She hovered before him in all her sinister glory. But as Dravek reached toward her, the scene slowly faded to black.

The vision vanished before Dravek's eyes. The tomb and its skeletal guardians remained in place, and silence prevailed in the crypt once more. He slid the relic blade from his belt and stared at it in wonder. Even in the darkness, the blade held a gleaming shimmer. Dravek lifted the sword overhead with both hands and tightened his grip. He swung the weapon downward with all his strength. The blade bit deep into the stone sealing the tomb, shattering the rock and sending shards in all directions. Dravek lashed out again and again, crumbling more of the rock with each strike, until at last he had breached the tomb door.

A howling breeze rushed past, as if the crypt itself had gasped for breath. Dravek stepped inside the vault. A stone sarcophagus, crudely graven in the form of a female devil, rested within. He cast the lid aside as if it were weightless and gazed upon his queen in horror.

Mara was no longer the flawless beauty that lived in Dravek's memory. The body that lay lifeless before him was little more than a skeleton wrapped in charred, rotted flesh. Long strands of dark hair lay tangled beneath a crown of rusted spikes. The thing's jaw hung open, forever frozen in a deathly scream, revealing beastly fangs.

Dravek reached into the pocket of his cloak and withdrew the tarnished vial. His hands trembled as he opened the stopper and poured the vial's contents into the corpse's gaping mouth. The skeleton's tongue began to wriggle and squirm as the thing swallowed the black blood. A serpentine tendril of smoke slithered from Mara's mouth and crept over her body. Her skeletal fingers twitched and Mara's black eyes opened.

The clawed hands reached up and gripped the edge of the sarcophagus and the monstrous lich pulled herself up. Black smoke slowly flowed from her body, cloaking her form in a veil of writhing darkness. "You have come for me at last." Mara's voice—barely more than a whisper—sounded like the raspy croak of an ancient crone. "How long have I slumbered?"

It took a long moment for Dravek to find his own voice. "It has been more than nine generations, my queen. Much has

transpired over the long years."

"Yes," she hissed. "Though I was unable to leave the confines of this tomb, I dreamt, and in my visions, I saw many things as they came to pass." Mara's eyes stared off toward the crypt's jagged opening before returning to Dravek. "All the while, my faith in you never faltered. I knew you would find your way to my side once more. Tell me, what army has accompanied you?"

Dravek lowered his gaze, averting his eyes from Mara's ghastly visage. "For years I waited, silent and patient, amassing my forces and forming my plan to reclaim the keep until at last the hour of reckoning had come. I breached the Tower, but my minions were slain during the siege. I fear my legions lie vanquished. I have endured many losses and overcome countless obstacles to reach you. But I am now alone."

Mara's eyes narrowed. "And what of the infidel who doomed me to this prison? Have you avenged my murder?"

"The priest who took your life is long dead—slain by the hand of the new Tower Lord, Brom."

"Yes," Mara rasped, "I know of him. More than once I held him within my grasp, but his will was too strong to claim. He is a mighty adversary, but once I fully regain my strength and powers, he shall fall beneath me. After the sentinel is vanquished, I shall spread my shadow over the land. None shall escape my wrath. The Black Dawn shall rise once more, and all who dare stand against me shall be trampled beneath my armies."

Dravek smiled as the thought lingered in his mind. "What do you desire of me?"

"I hunger," Mara's voice screeched.

"Take me, my queen." Dravek held forth his wrist, bowing his head. "My blood is yours."

Mara's black eyes glistened with desire, but she resisted

the impulse to feed. Her skeletal fingers gently stroked his wrist, then Dravek's white hair. "Your offering pleases me, but I am in need of your strength. You are far too vital to be sacrificed."

The creature rose from her tomb, floating like a dark mist above the ground. Dravek turned to escort her out through the shattered opening in the stone that sealed the crypt.

"No," Mara croaked, "surely the Tower Lord has sealed our exit." She pointed a clawed finger to the opposite wall. "This way."

Dravek stepped to the wall, seeing only solid bricks sealed with mortar. He raised his sword, then looked back toward Mara. The creature nodded her head, signaling him to proceed. Dravek swung the blade downward, striking the wall with a thunderous blow. The bricks shattered, crumbling to rubble, revealing a narrow passageway with steps that twisted upward.

Mara closed her eyes and a slow, exultant smile touched her withered lips. "I have waited so long," she whispered. "So very long."

"This is now the hour of your triumph," Dravek said, his voice choked with emotion.

Mara drifted past Dravek, leaving a trail of billowing smoke in her wake. "Come," she commanded.

Dravek followed his dark master like a faithful dog as she led him out of the tomb. Together they ascended the shadowed path to claim the Tower above.

Intruders hath trespassed upon my domain once more—foolish men in search of fortune. I quenched my hunger upon their lives. But before they died, they told me their tale. They said they had come to the Tower in pursuit of an enemy—a wounded knight, a crusader.

I can sense him in the village, his body and spirit regaining their strength. I know he can sense me as well, as surely as I know he shall come for me, seeking his destiny in the Tower.

It seems my successor has arrived—the worthy heir to my legacy, the one who shall release me from my torment.

At long last, my vigil is nearing its end, and his shall soon begin. May God have mercy upon him.

Necromancer

Joseph Vargo

Night's ebon cloak had long settled over the land, wrapping the Tower in its bleak embrace. Inside the keep, Brom and Adrian strode warily through the castle's shadowed halls, keeping vigilant guard during the hours that darkness held dominion. While Adrian carried a candle to illuminate the path ahead, Brom needed no such light to see. The Tower Lord's immortal eyes were well-accustomed to the dark. He thrived in the unhallowed blackness of night's abyss.

The two men marched along, watchful and alert, searching the chambers and corridors of the keep's upper floors for any indication of intruders. Their footfalls were the only sound other than the distant moan of the wind. Though all around them seemed tranquil and quiet, Brom found no solace in the eerie calm. He knew a terrible storm would soon be upon them—an unstoppable tempest that would unleash its raging fury to destroy everything in its path.

A sudden chill descended over them, turning the still air frigid and stale. Adrian shuddered and his breath turned to frost as the icy cold clutched him in its grasp. A tinge of fear entered his heart, causing him to slow his pace. The monk began to lag behind as Brom continued heedlessly forward, undaunted by the bitter chill. The Tower Lord was familiar with the cold caress of the dead, knowing full well there were spirits lurking unseen in every corner of the ancient keep. Some were merely harmless, wayward souls, while others fed like vicious predators upon the fear and sorrow of the living. The oppressive aura of evil that loomed over the region was strongest here in the Tower, its unholy place of origin.

The surrounding silence was broken by a distant voice— barely a whisper that echoed along the hall like a call from the grave. The two men stopped to listen and the voice came again, louder this time. *"Follow,"* it seemed to say.

As they ventured in the direction of the ghostly summons, Brom took notice of a shadow moving along the wall ahead. The lightless form seemed to taunt them as they quickened their pace, matching their speed to elude them, staying just beyond reach of the candlelight's flickering glow.

Losing sight of the shadow near an intersection, the two men stopped to survey the adjoining halls. Along one of the side corridors, a hooded figure, slight of stature, stood waiting in the darkness. Adrian took a step toward the mysterious shadow, but Brom laid a firm hand across the monk's chest, halting his approach.

The Tower Lord moved cautiously closer, asking, "Who goes there?"

The shadow gave no answer. It turned and drifted around a bend in the hall, disappearing from sight. Brom rushed forth in pursuit, but rounding the corner he found no one there. The empty corridor came to an end at a sealed doorway. Brom stepped to the door and tested the latch, finding it locked and frozen with rust. Heaving his weight against the wood, he smashed the door open, breaching its threshold to a small room beyond.

Adrian thrust his candle forth to illuminate the dim chamber. All that waited within were a few neglected remnants from a time long past—an empty bookcase covered in cobwebs, a simple wooden chair, and a table piled with debris.

A biting wind swept through an open window on the southern wall, creating a low, droning howl that circled the room. Adrian stepped to the window and looked down onto the rocky cliffs and forest far below, seeing no possible means of escape. "The spirits taunt us," he said.

"The Tower is home to many," Brom replied, a solemn reverence to his voice. His eyes scanned the dark chamber, searching for another exit, but there was none to be found. "The dead wander these halls, restless and hungry for vengeance and redemption. They are cursed to remain here as long as Mara's vile essence exists."

"Yes," Adrian said quietly, "I remember the tales from my youth. The Dark Queen's sordid legacy is one of blood and damnation. Throughout the years, many have sought their destinies here, only to meet cruel fates beneath the Tower's shadow."

Brom nodded. "Indeed, many have died within these walls—violently murdered," he paused, then added, "some by my own hand."

Upon the central table, a tangle of straw and twigs formed what seemed to be a large nest. Several long feathers, sleek and black as night, rested inside. Brom lifted one of the ebon quills, rolling its bare tip between his fingers.

Adrian squinted at the feather. "The ravens have made this place their roost."

"So it would seem," the Tower Lord said.

Brom's eyes fell upon a vellum scroll that lay half-buried beneath the nest's twisted branches. He pulled it free and carefully unrolled it. A simple map had been scrawled across the yellowed parchment. The diagram depicted the forest surrounding Vasaria, marking the location of the Dark Tower and the ancient standing stones. The three megaliths formed a triangle around the keep and surrounding woodlands. In the heart of the forest, near the triangle's southernmost corner, the map depicted a clearing marked by a drawing of a black bird, its wings outstretched.

Beneath the map, a poem had been written in a delicate hand. Adrian drew his candle close and read the verse aloud.

"*Our bones rest here, 'neath sacred earth,*
Our essence dwells midst forest trees,
Our blood lives on through daughter's birth,
Our spirits dance upon the breeze—

"What does this mean?" Adrian's eyes searched the tattered vellum for more clues, but his efforts were in vain. "Surely, we were guided here by some unknown spirit, but for what purpose?"

Brom shook his head. "The voices of the dead are but distant murmurs, often cryptic and vague. Their intent is seldom clear."

Brom stepped to the window and peered out over the forest, his eyes piercing the dark. His vision stretched far into the night, seeing a distant clearing deep within the southern wilds. He looked back at the parchment in his hand, realizing that the window overlooked the same landmark depicted on the map. He then noticed an engraving on the window ledge, two words roughly etched into the stone.

"This window and map point to the same place," Brom said, running his fingers over the age-worn letters. "Raven's Hollow."

Adrian held his candle over the crude inscription, seeing it now for the first time. "What lies there?"

Brom returned his gaze to the distant hollow. "Daria

once told me of it. It is a ritual site, sacred to those who worship the gods of old. I know little else about it."

"Perhaps the witch can tell us more—if only to enlighten us to its history."

"Yes." Brom rolled the parchment and tucked it away inside his cloak. "I shall consult her."

The two left the room and made their way back down through the keep, returning to the chapel where they found Leonidas kneeling before the altar, lost in prayer. Hearing Brom and Adrian's approach, the elder blessed himself and rose to greet them.

"What have you found?" Leonidas asked.

"The Tower is secure," Brom said. "All remains quiet."

"Save for the stir of ghosts and ravens," Adrian added.

"Ghosts?" The elder's voice wavered with unease.

"Merely whispers in the wind—tis nothing of concern." Brom's eyes darted around the chapel, searching for the others, finding only the statues of martyred saints. "Where is Daria?"

"I last saw her in the graveyard. Why do you ask?"

Brom peered toward an open door that led to the cemetery, seeing no one in the burial grounds beyond. "I need to speak with her. Find her and bring her to me in the sanctum." Saying no more, the Tower Lord turned and strode away, his black cape flowing behind him like a shadow.

Adrian followed him out of the chapel and across the hall to a door framed by columns carved in the likeness of winged skeletons. The macabre statues seemed to mark some grim threshold, as if designating the entrance to the domain of the dead. Three words had been carved deep into the wood of the door—*Sanvi, Sansavi, Semangelaf.* Adrian recognized the inscription as the names of angels believed to watch over the realm of men, protecting them from evil.

Brom laid his hand upon the graven words and the door ground open across the stone threshold with a groaning rasp. He entered the sanctum but abruptly stopped, raising his hand to signal Adrian to remain silent and still. The Tower Lord looked about slowly, as if sensing a disturbance in the room or detecting some unseen presence lingering nearby. His eyes settled upon the far wall of the chamber where one of the heavy oaken panels that lined the room stood open like a door. Brom stepped warily forward to investigate the scene, discovering an opening in the wall behind the hinged panel.

Adrian followed a few paces behind, stopping at Brom's side. The monk held his candle forth, illuminating the threshold of a corridor that faded off into unknown darkness. "A hidden passage," he whispered. "But where does it lead?"

The Tower Lord peered curiously into the tunnel, his eyes scanning its depths. "Let us find out," he said, stepping through the opening.

Brom led the way along a narrow corridor of roughly hewn stone. The mildewed walls trapped the musty scent of ancient decay. Ages of cobwebs hung draped throughout the passage, forming a series of tattered silken veils that stretched across their path. The webbing caressed their faces as they passed beneath its low reaches. After a short way, the corridor opened into another chamber.

The air grew bitterly cold as the two entered the room. Adrian held his candle aloft, allowing him to see his surroundings clearly. The chamber was much smaller than the sanctum, no more than a half dozen strides in either direction with no windows or doors. Walls of black brick rose to support a vaulted ceiling high above. The flagstones that formed the floor were etched with a ring of mystic symbols that held an arcane flourish. In the midst of the circle, at the room's center, the candlelight settled upon a stone altar that held a display of bones, neatly laid out and arranged to form a human skeleton.

Beyond the grisly shrine, a cloaked form stood amidst the shadows, looming motionless, as if awaiting their arrival. The figure was draped in a hooded robe of deep green velvet that shimmered softly in the flickering light. At first, Adrian thought he was in the presence of yet another of the Tower's ghosts, but in the candle's dim glow, he could discern the traces of Daria's face beneath the hood's shadowy folds.

"Daria?" Adrian's words rang clear, but she gave no response.

Brom peered through the gloom to gaze into Daria's eyes, seeing a distant and unfamiliar spirit looming behind them. "Why are you here?" he asked.

She lowered her head, concealing the top of her face beneath her velvet cowl. "This place holds many secrets." Her quiet voice carried a soothing tone. "I have come to bring them to light."

"How so?" Adrian kept his eyes firmly fixed upon her, wary of her slightest move.

"By telling a tale that has been lost in time—a tale of forgotten lore that has remained buried beneath the Tower's shadow since Mara's fall." Her words were trailed by whispers that leapt from wall to wall.

Brom stepped cautiously forward. "How did you know of this place? This chamber has remained hidden for countless years. It was unknown even to myself."

"I know this place all too well. I have long awaited you to discover it and all it holds. At long last, the time has come to unveil this mystery."

Adrian leaned close to Brom. "She is bewitched," he whispered, "some foreign power has possessed her and holds her in its grasp, claiming her mind, perhaps even her soul. She is now a slave to whatever unearthly force has overcome her."

"Perhaps," Brom said quietly, "Of a certainty, there is sorcery at work here, but to what purpose?" Brom glanced down at the array of bones and then back up at the cloaked figure beyond. He seemed to study her intently as if weighing the merit of her words. He had come to trust Daria, but something was not right. Still, he owed the witch a great debt and was curious as to what mystery the secret room held. "Tell us your tale," he said at last.

She kept her head bowed toward the skeletal remains on the altar before her, as if in reverence for the soul that once inhabited them. "Death comes for us all, swiftly and without mercy, upon wings black as night." Her voice now carried a somber chill, like the whisper of the winter wind. "Azrael's icy grasp brings our hearts to a final halt and the blood in our veins ceases to flow. Flesh withers, bones decay, and in time we return to the dust from whence we came. All that we ever were fades like the sun at dusk, till at last we become nothing more than distant memories—ghostly shadows to haunt the living. Thus, my tale begins, for it is a tale of the living and the dead... and the restless souls that inhabit the realm between.

"Long ago, during the reign of he whom men called the Baron, there lived a witch named Elisandra. She was known by all, yet few had ever seen her, for she dwelled in the deepest shadows of the forest where she practiced her ancient craft far from the eyes of men. The village elders oft sought her council, for she possessed not only the lost wisdom of the dark arts, but the gift of second sight as well. Knowing the Tower Lord suffered beneath the Dark Queen's curse, the elders feared that the Baron might in time succumb to the savage hungers that welled within him. They summoned the witch and confided

their fears to her, hoping she might know a way to free the Baron from Mara's spell.

"Elisandra stood before the elders and cast the bones of ravens to foresee what was yet to come. The witch read the relics and, with heavy heart, told them there was nothing that could be done to help him—this outlander priest who sacrificed his life and soul to save their village and children from the grasp of the demon queen. Though Elisandra's words filled the elders with sorrow and dread, they accepted them as truth.

"As Elisandra returned to her home, she felt compelled to somehow aid the Baron in his mission, for she was one of the remaining few that knew the sinister origins of the curse that plagued him. She cast the bones to reveal her own future, discovering that her destiny lay within the Dark Tower.

"One moonless night, during the autumn harvest, the witch ventured to the Tower, seeking an audience with the Baron. The Tower Lord granted her request, whether out of curiosity to discover the region's history, or out of mere loneliness for the company of others, none can truly say. Though he was devout in his faith, the Baron listened with an open mind as Elisandra relayed the realm's legacy of dark sorcery and described her own worship of the gods of old—the pagan gods, as the Baron called them.

"She told him the legends of the Dark Brood, the ancient creatures of shadow that were said to slumber deep within the mountain. She related the tale of Leshii, the Forest Lord, and his pact with her ancestors, the crones, the three witches who raised the infant Mara. The Baron listened with great interest as Elisandra spoke long into the night, revealing the details of her arcane faith.

"She told him of Raven's Hollow, a clearing that lay south through the forest wilds, where a circle of graven standing stones marked the site of ancient rituals. It was here that her ancestors presented sacrifices to summon and appease the woodland deities. 'Twas also the witches' sacred burial ground. As Elisandra explained, when death claimed one of her coven, the body of the deceased would be brought to the hollow at dusk where it was left upon the altar as an offering to the forest. There, ravens flocked to the ancient stones surrounding the altar and descended upon the body in droves to feast upon the witch's flesh, thus claiming her earthly core. The ritual bestowed the witch with immortality, enabling her essence to live on in the forest among the spirits of her ancestors. The witch's bones were then buried within the ring of standing stones—returned to the earth where they rested alongside those of her kin.

"As the Baron heard more, his curiosity grew to obsession. He yearned to discover the secrets of the sinister forces that ruled the Tower. He bade the witch to instruct him in the ways of her craft so that he might better understand the dark magic that opposed him. Elisandra was hesitant to share the sacred knowledge of her ancestors, but the Baron was unyielding in his demand, and the witch knew that if Vasaria was ever to be free of the curse that plagued it, she could not refuse.

"Elisandra returned to the keep again and again, beneath the darkness of each new moon, to teach the Tower Lord the magic of the Old Ways. This strange alliance was kept secret from all. Even the village elders were unaware of what transpired deep within the shadows of the Tower on moonless nights. The Baron himself told no one, nor did he chronicle their meetings in any of his journals.

"As time went on, the Tower Lord was drawn further and further into the forbidden realms of sorcery. He soon became well-versed in the black arts. And though his powers grew, he held fast to his beliefs, never ceasing his prayers, never relinquishing his faith in his own god.

"The Baron was also curious of things yet to come. Though Elisandra possessed the power of foresight, it was a gift she had inherited, not a skill that could be taught. Even so, she cast the raven bones and told him all they revealed. The bones foretold a grim future for the Baron, showing that his vigil would be long and trying and that his life would end in the Tower. The Baron accepted his fate without remorse.

"Months passed and winter claimed the realm. The snow and harsh cold kept Elisandra from venturing to the Tower. When spring thawed the forest, she returned to the Baron with joyous news. She told him she was with child, carrying the seed of her gypsy love. The Tower Lord gave her his blessing and wished her well. The witch took her leave, vowing to resume her visits the following year.

"Elisandra returned to the Tower after the birth of her daughter, but she no longer possessed her gift of second sight. Though she had lost the ability to see what the future held, Elisandra imparted one final secret to allow the Baron to peer into the past. She instructed him in the ways of necromancy, showing him how to commune with the spirit realm, channeling the dead through their mortal remains.

"The Baron constructed a ritual chamber within the hollows of the keep, where he used his knowledge of the forbidden arts to summon the Tower's restless dead. Thus did he uncover much of the realm's history and many of the Tower's long-forgotten secrets.

"Knowing that she had done all she could to aid the Tower Lord in his plight, Elisandra returned to the wilds to live the remainder of her mortal life with her daughter. But one night, after many years, the Baron summoned the witch to the Tower a final time. She awoke inside the keep, in this very room, with no recollection of how she had come here. She tried to leave but could not, for she was bound by the Baron's magic, held captive in his ritual chamber by the ancient wards of binding. She realized then that his powers had somehow grown stronger than her own.

"The witch begged for release, but the Baron was heedless of her desires. As Elisandra gazed into his eyes she could see that the years of bleak isolation beneath the Tower's curse had taken their toll upon him. A brooding madness now welled within him, corrupting his spirit and dragging him to the depths of depravity and despair. He was no longer the peaceful priest she once knew. He was now a creature of darkness, and she was bound within his lair.

"Elisandra implored the Baron to let her return to her daughter, asking him why he had made her his prisoner. It was then that the Tower Lord revealed the tragic truth, telling Elisandra how she had come to be here. With a solemn heart, he explained that she had fallen victim to a devastating illness and lapsed into a fevered sleep from which she never awoke, succumbing at last to Death's summoning knell.

"But the Baron's tale did not end with Elisandra's death. He then revealed that after her burial ceremony he ventured to Raven's Hollow to retrieve her earthly remains. He brought her bones here, to this very room, where he carefully assembled them upon his ritual altar and then used them to conjure her spirit.

"The truth of his words settled upon her, and Elisandra knew that she was no longer among the realm of the living. She gazed upon the skeletal form that lay atop the altar, woefully realizing that the bones were hers. The Baron had summoned her spirit to fill the emptiness of his days in an attempt to stay his growing madness and calm the bloodlust that welled within him. His mind had been twisted by a torment few could endure. He felt his will slipping and feared he would no longer be able to control the monstrous demon that raged inside of him.

"Elisandra vowed to help him, if only by lending him solace in his darkest hours. And so, her spirit remained here, to ease the Baron's loneliness and pain and console his troubled mind, in turn securing the safety of all she held dear in life. The Baron could not escape the Tower's insufferable curse, but he found sanctuary deep within its walls. Only here, with Elisandra's spirit to comfort him, could he find the strength to suppress the unceasing thirst that drove him to the brink of mindless frenzy. Only then could he regain his sense of reason and maintain some semblance of humanity.

"But they had only prolonged the inevitable. As the years passed, the Baron slipped further from the virtuous man he once was, sinking deeper into the darkness that would be his eventual ruin. Elisandra knew his spirit was at its limit, and his life, such as it was, neared its end. She beseeched him to persevere through the long, trying nights until fate delivered a successor to take his place as Lord of the Tower.

"And, so it came to pass. Destiny brought another to the Tower and the Baron's vigil ended. The priest passed along his curse before surrendering his life, but he also passed along his journals of chronicled knowledge, so that his successor might glean wisdom from his words.

"As for the witch, Elisandra's bones lie here still, in this desolate chamber, sealed away behind stone walls. The Baron kept this final secret hidden from all, taking it with him to the grave."

Adrian's eyes shifted between the bones on the altar and the cloaked figure beyond. "If he told this tale to no one, how then did it come to be known by you?"

"Elisandra's spirit remained here after the Baron's death, silently watching from the shadows, offering whispers of help and guidance to the new Tower Lord." The storyteller turned her hooded head toward Brom, saying, "Surely you have heard the murmur of spirits and followed their subtle sway during your time here."

Brom remained silent, studying the shrouded figure, detecting a slight smile upon her lips.

She continued, "Elisandra guarded the Necromancer's secret, vowing to reveal it only to the blood of her own blood. And that time has now come."

While Adrian pondered her words, he heard the approach of soft footsteps behind him. He turned to see another figure entering the chamber. As the shadowy form drew closer, the candle glow revealed a familiar face.

It was Daria.

"How can this be?" Adrian stammered in disbelief, turning back toward the storyteller. "What sorcery is this?"

Daria slowly stepped between Brom and Adrian, staring at the mysterious figure beyond the altar. The cloaked form raised its head and drew back its hood. Daria stared into a face that might have been her own, recognizing it as the face of her mother, the witch Elisandra.

"Mother," Daria whispered, breathless and awestruck.

"Yes, my beautiful child." The spirit's eyes shone with a gentle look of love.

"Why... why are you here?" Daria asked.

Elisandra's face grew somber. "There is much I wish to tell you, but now is not the time. An ancient evil has been awakened. Soon, it shall rise from the depths to wreak havoc upon the world. You must be strong, my love. The Tower Lords have sacrificed their lives for us, but this battle is not theirs alone. You must lend your help however you can."

Elisandra gestured to the skeleton on the altar. "The final mystery has come to light and all that was hidden has been revealed. Now my tale must come to its end." She returned her gaze to Brom. "Knowing that his mind lacked the clarity to comprehend all he had discovered, the Baron chronicled his gathered knowledge with the hopes that it might be better understood by the next Tower Lord. His legacy was one of cryptic wisdom and veiled revelation. The answers you seek have been within your grasp all along, Lord Brom. They lie within the pages of the Baron's journals. You need only unravel the truth."

With that, Elisandra's ghost slowly faded from sight as if it were little more than dust disturbed by a subtle breeze.

Brom, Adrian and Daria stared at the altar in humble silence. Daria lowered her gaze to the skeleton before her.

"Your mother's bones," Brom said quietly. "She guided the Baron and lent him solace, even beyond death. All of Vasaria is in her debt, as am I."

Daria smiled, her eyes wet with tears. "When all this has ended and the Tower's curse is lifted, I shall return her remains to Raven's Hollow, so her spirit may find peace and rest alongside our ancestors."

Brom clenched his jaw. "Yes," he said, "when all this has ended."

Brom and Adrian took their leave, while Daria remained behind in the desolate chamber. And as the icy caress of darkness swept over her, she welcomed it without fear. For she knew she was not alone in the shadows, nor would she ever be again.

Seers and witches foretell of an age of enlightenment—a time when this curse shall end. I have heard their prophecies and researched countless ancient texts to uncover the spell of which they speak—the ritual to purge the vile taint from my blood—but, if it ever truly existed, it is nowhere to be found.

Revelations

JOSEPH VARGO

Leonidas walked along the unhallowed corridors of the Dark Tower, plagued by thoughts of demons and the restless dead. No sound or light penetrated the heavy walls. The ancient bricks seemed to trap time itself. Here, deep within the confines of stone and shadows, countless secrets remained hidden. The elder came to an archway flanked by sculpted angels of death. The winged skeletons stood eternal guard at the door of Brom's inner sanctum. Leonidas' eyes lingered on the inscription above the arch. *Noctem Aeternus*—a fitting epitaph, he thought, for one cursed to dwell in eternal night.

Inside the chamber, the Tower Lord sat at a table, lost in rumination. Leonidas entered and took a seat across from Brom. A single candle rested between them, casting a small halo of flickering light that struggled against the room's oppressive darkness. Several volumes of age-worn journals lay strewn across the table. One of the books lay open before Brom. The Tower Lord's eyes darted back and forth across the archaic, handwritten script.

Brom looked up from his book. "The Baron wrote these for my benefit," he said quietly. "He sought to shed light upon the Tower's mysteries, though many of his thoughts are difficult to decipher. At first his writings seemed beyond comprehension, but as I read them more and more, I began to grasp the messages he so desperately sought to convey. His revelations stand as a testament to his troubled mind."

Brom's eyes returned to the page before him and he began to read aloud. *"I am lost. The scant periods of clarity come less frequently with the passage of time. It is now, during one of my fleeting moments of reason, that I find opportunity to chronicle my thoughts.*

"Darkness has taken firm hold in my heart. It grows ever stronger with each passing day, eroding my will to resist. My time grows short. I know I shall not be able to uncover all the secrets the Tower holds. I have succumbed to the vile essence of sin that resides in the blood of my victims—tis a venom that corrupts my soul, dragging me further into the abyss. I can bear this burden no longer. I must find a successor, one of fresh untainted blood, to carry on this vigil. I shall pass on my legacy and guide him through my writings, granting him the wisdom of my discoveries and warning him of the pitfalls I have encountered."

Brom looked away. "The Baron spoke to me through these books. He shared his thoughts and philosophies, his passions and fears. I felt his pain as my own and have come to understand the man he was. Tis a sad and terrible fate he suffered. I have always resisted my urges to feed upon the blood of humans, though the hunger is consuming. The result of submission is horrific. I witnessed it in the Baron's final hours. He struggled to maintain his own will, but it slowly crumbled away, collapsing beneath the burden he bore."

Leonidas' eyes washed over the pile of worn journals. "Yes," he said. "The Baron was once was a man of high morals who cherished life, but even he succumbed to his irresistible lusts, losing more and more of his humanity throughout the long years. In the end he had become the very monster he sought to protect us from."

"Did you know him?"

The old man's eyes held a faraway gaze. "Only once did our paths cross, but I shall never forget the fateful encounter. It was the first time I came to the Tower—long before I became an elder. I was very young. We knew the tales of the Baron. He was said to be an ancient creature that once protected our village. According to lore, his undying spirit yet dwelled within the mountain keep. It was strictly forbidden to venture there, for those who did seldom returned." Leonidas stared into the candle's glow and began his tale.

When I was a boy of nine summers, the autumn winds brought with them an air of darkness and tragedy. Something sinister lurked in our midst. Children went missing from the neighboring villages. Only their bones were found. Rumors spread throughout the land. While some blamed the savage beasts of the wilderness, others accused the Baron. Though he was said to be the guardian of the realm, tales told of his thirst for human blood and his ravenous hunger for the flesh of young children. Other stories depicted him as a dark sorcerer who bewitched all who laid eyes upon him. It was said he commanded the wolves and ravens of the forest to devour anyone who became lost in the night or foolishly wandered into his domain. Such tales, though terrifying to most, only fed my youthful curiosity.

One early evening as I explored the deep woods, I met an old gypsy woman camped near a cave in the forest. She greeted me kindly as I approached, so I sat by her fire and engaged her in conversation. Wrapped in her thin shawls, huddling close to her fire, she seemed so alone and helpless that I feared for her. I tried to warn her of the dangers that lurked in the night.

She laughed at my tales, and as she did, I saw her teeth

were sharpened to fangs. I rose to my feet, but before I could leave, the hag's claw-like hand clamped onto my arm. Though she had seemed ancient and frail, her grip was unnaturally strong. As I struggled to free myself from her grasp, she turned toward the cave and shouted words in a strange language. Two hulking men emerged from the cavern in answer to her call.

"I have found us a morsel for our stew," she said. "What a tasty feast we shall have this night."

The men were foul and monstrously huge like the ogres of lore. Long tangled hair hung from beneath horned helmets that covered all but their fanged mouths. The twin brutes each carried heavy axes. They responded to the hag in coarse, speechless growls.

As frightful as their appearance was, the grisly patchwork that comprised their tunics filled my heart with sheer terror. They were cloaked in the skins of children. In the center of one of their macabre garments I could see a young face, its eyes and mouth sewn shut but still evoking an agony beyond reckoning.

Before the beastly men could reach me, I plucked a burning branch from the fire and thrust it against the crone's hand. Her stony grip loosened and I wrested my arm free. I ran from them as fast as I could. I heard the old woman cackle and issue commands to her brutish minions, and the creatures stomped clumsily after me. I fled into the deep forest in a desperate attempt to lose my pursuers, crossing the stream to sever my trail.

I ran as fast as my feet would carry me until my young heart pounded near the verge of bursting. I could not return home, for at every turn the hag and her creatures blocked my path to the village. I dared not scream for help. I dared make no sound at all for fear that the ghoulish horde would find me.

Darkness had begun to descend upon the woodlands,

and I feared becoming lost in the night. My only path of escape was up the mountain to the Tower. I thought I would be safe hiding there, for no one would be fool enough to venture to the Baron's keep beyond nightfall. But I was wrong. I soon spied torches approaching through the forest, following my trail. I was being hunted.

When I reached the summit, I hid behind the gate ruins just beyond the edge of the forest. A row of ravens sat perched atop the ancient archway. Their cold eyes, gleaming in the light of the early risen moon, studied me for a moment, and then the grim birds began to caw, betraying my hiding place. As the torches drew nearer, I ran to the castle.

I had never seen the Tower so close before. As my young eyes beheld it, I halted in place, for the sight struck me with awe. The keep's black spires loomed high above me, soaring upward into the night sky. I gazed in terror at the fearsome stone creatures, half man and half beast, that clung to the castle's facade and stood guard along the battlements. The monstrous sculptures seemed to stir beneath the spell of moonlight.

The ravens at the gate took to wing, following me to the keep. The birds perched above the castle entryway, croaking wildly before falling suddenly silent once more. A moment later, the Tower's massive doors groaned open and a man emerged from the shadows. His head was completely shaven and his eyes were dark and piercing. A lifetime of sadness was etched upon his face. He wore the black robes of a priest and a tarnished crucifix hung from a chain around his neck. I stood petrified as he approached me, for I knew only one person who dwelt within the Tower. It was the Baron.

"This is a forbidden place." His voice was low and hoarse.

"Please," I pleaded, "help me."

His black eyes held me transfixed beneath their gaze. "Do you know who I am?"

"You are the Baron," I said, then added, "our protector." My words seemed to stir a distant memory in the Tower Lord's mind.

He studied me for a long moment then held out a hand white as bone and said, "Come."

I was unable to resist his command. I ascended the Tower steps to stand beside him. He looked out toward the forest where the torches drew near, then gazed deep into my eyes, seeing the panic that swelled there. "Have no fear, child," he said softly, taking my hand in his.

His flesh was cold as winter ice, yet I felt a sense of comfort.

A moment later my pursuers emerged from the forest path. The crone and her ghoulish servants approached the Tower, unaware of the danger it held. The fiends held their place at the base of the steps, setting their torches into the ground around them.

The hag stepped forward. "Give us the boy," she demanded.

The Baron remained unmoved by her words. "I have granted him sanctuary here."

The old gypsy moved closer, brandishing long knives in each hand. "There will be no sanctuary for him. He is ours."

"Do you know who I am?" The Baron's voice was calm, yet now it carried a chilling tone.

"We care not who you are. My knives shall slice through your flesh just as easily as the child's, though your meat may not be as tender."

"I am the Baron of these lands, guardian of the Tower and protector of Vasaria. As such, I shall allow no harm to befall those in my charge."

"Guardian? Protector?" The hag cackled in mad defiance, revealing her razor-sharp teeth. She held out her arms in great sweeping gestures. "This forest is ours. All who cross our path have met grim fates at our hands." She pointed the blade of one of her knives at the Baron. "There shall be two meals for us tonight." She whispered a command and the beastly men lumbered forward, raising their axes.

The Baron cast his gaze upon the men, halting them in their tracks. Their axes clattered uselessly to the ground. The air itself seemed to change around us, becoming uncomfortably cold and charged with a strange power that even the dull, animal-like mind of the old woman could not ignore. The gypsy woman's eyes widened in fear. The ravens began to shriek and croak, drawing the hag's attention up toward the heights of the Tower where the monstrous gargoyles glared down upon her. Her minions remained motionless, as if frozen in time.

The Baron spoke again, still holding the loathsome men in his gaze. "All who have crossed my path have met grim fates as well. But I am no merciless savage. For those who show no mercy shall be judged without mercy—they shall be consumed in the fires of eternal damnation and their flesh shall be seared from their bones." The Baron's voice grew deeper. "I shall spare you this night if you vow to repent of your sins."

The hag fell to her knees, bowing before the Baron, "Please, I beg of you, forgive us, my lord. We dare not incur your wrath. We shall never again encroach upon your domain. We shall harm no one—this I swear upon my own blood." She laid her knives in the dirt before her and kept her head lowered in submission.

The Baron seemed to weigh the old woman's words intently before deciding her fate. At last he said, "Leave these lands and do not return. For if you do, you shall know suffering far beyond the pains of death." The dark lord released the ghouls from his hypnotic stare and the creatures gulped for breath.

The hag uttered a command and her beastly minions groveled in retreat, but as the three turned to leave, the Baron's gaze fell upon the skins of their young victims draped across their backs. In that moment, something changed within him.

"Close your eyes, child," he whispered.

I shut my eyes and clenched them tight. I felt the Baron's hand leave mine and heard the screams of men. A moment later, silence prevailed once more. When I opened my eyes, the ghouls lay sprawled at the Baron's feet. The hag lay face down beside them, her own blades protruding from her back.

The Baron knelt over one of the ghouls. At first, I thought he was praying, but as the moon emerged from behind the clouds, I saw him holding the brute's torn throat to his mouth. The creature's eyes pleaded with me as the Baron drained him of his life.

The Baron raised his head and turned his blood-gorged face toward me. "Go," he commanded, "and never return here. Tell the elders what you have witnessed. Tell them..." He stopped, as if about to speak a truth he did not want to face, then finally went on, "Tell them I am lost."

I could see the anguish in his eyes as he struggled against his dark desires to slake his thirst upon me as well. Even then, I felt compelled to stay. I felt pity for him and wanted to repay him for saving my life, to ease his sorrow, to comfort his terrible loneliness. But I ran.

When I passed the gate ruins, I heard another scream. I stopped and looked back toward the Tower, concealing myself behind the gate. The hag was still alive. She gasped for breath and tried to crawl, but was held in place by the blades that staked her to the ground. The Baron plucked the impaling daggers from her back and hoisted her to her feet amidst a torrent of screams and curses.

The Baron held the shrieking crone against a tree. He drove a knife through each of her wrists, forcing the blades deep into the tree's outstretched limbs. He then picked up a torch and lowered the flame to her dress. The hag screamed in agony as the fire met her flesh. I stood petrified and aghast by the horrific scene. The quiet man that had rescued me was now a cruel fiend who reveled in wickedness. The Baron stood staring at the writhing hag as flames engulfed her body, the firelight revealing a sadistic smile upon his face.

I turned away. As I descended the mountain, the sickly auburn light of the blaze illuminated my trail.

Leonidas looked away from the firelight, his eyes moist and glistening. "In the years that followed, the elders had little contact with the Baron. He became known as a fearsome wraith that stalked the night. As more time passed, the dark legend grew. While some maintained the Baron was our savior, others said he was a monstrous fiend, heartless and cruel. I knew he was both, for I had witnessed his compassion and his fierce wrath. The sorrowful truth was that he was merely a man, tortured and twisted by darkness and surrounded by a corrosive wickedness that consumed his heart. But even though he languished in torment, he remained our protector to the end."

Brom turned his gaze to the flame that danced upon the candle. "I met the Baron but once as well. As you know, the encounter changed the course of my destiny. Had it not been for his chronicled wisdom, I too would have been lost. Though I struggled and suffered many years with this curse, I came to accept the dark nature of my mission. Tis strange that I now feel a sense of serenity. I know the end of my vigil is approaching and I welcome my fate. I readily await the final battle, for I feel it is my life's true purpose."

Brom set aside the journal he had been reading and opened another. He had read every volume many times throughout the years, and though he had painstakingly reassembled much of the fragmented knowledge they contained, the final pieces of the puzzle eluded him still. He leafed through the pages, his eyes washing over the words, intently studying the cryptic writing, searching the familiar passages again for some hidden clue to aid him in his plight.

Brom lingered on a page, sweeping his clawed finger over the written words. After a short while his eyes grew wide. "Is Brother Adrian still here in the Tower?"

"Yes," Leonidas replied. "He keeps vigil in the chapel."

"I need to see him," Brom said. "Alone."

Leonidas nodded and left the chamber. After a short while, Adrian entered the sanctum. The monk's eyes glowed with the fires of fascination as he beheld the library of arcane books. Brom stood before a hearth at the far end of the room.

"I have found something in the Baron's writings," Brom said. "A revelation."

Adrian stepped closer.

Brom opened the tattered volume and held it before him, reading aloud like a lector delivering a sermon. *"The flesh of dead beasts revolts me. I consume not food, as I once did, yet my hunger is fathomless. I drink not water, nor wine—I hath no need, yet my thirst is unquenchable. My soul has been damned and, as such, I fear the instruments of salvation are lost to me. The holy sacraments are now my bane. Never again can I partake of the chalice of everlasting life. I dread the slightest touch of the sacred goblet, for fear it would sear my lips and tongue—that its blessed contents would scald my throat. My spirit hath fallen into darkness, plummeting further into the abyss with each passing day. I am forever lost."*

"The chalice of everlasting life," Brom repeated. "The prophecy mentions this as well."

Adrian looked at him with deep interest. "I should like to hear this prophecy in its entirety."

Brom nodded. "Yes, later."

Adrian stepped to the Tower Lord's side and read the journal passage to himself. "The Baron is referring to the sacrament of holy communion," Adrian said quietly. "But what does it mean?"

"I believe it is the answer he so desperately sought. It was within his grasp all along, yet it eluded him." Brom's eyes conveyed a wistful sadness. "The Baron thought himself unworthy of the sacraments because of the darkness residing within him. He never pursued the idea that these blessed acts might offer him salvation. He feared they would only cause his demise."

"And you think otherwise?" Adrian asked, a trace of unease in his voice.

"I do."

"Why?"

"The girl, Serena—she dreamt of a ritual—a ceremony upon an altar. In her vision, a man in dark robes held a chalice filled with blood and uttered an ancient invocation to cleanse it."

"The blood of the sacred," Adrian said, "transformed from consecrated wine."

"According to the girl's dream, it will nourish me and allow me to withstand the sun's light. Can you perform this ritual?"

"Yes," Adrian said hesitantly, "but the rites of communion cannot be performed until after the sacraments of baptism and confession have been ministered. Only then can the wine become the blood of everlasting life." Adrian paused, studying Brom for a moment. "Forgive me for asking, but were you baptized?"

A trace of a smile touched Brom's lips. "Yes, long ago."

"Then only one other rite remains," Adrian said. "The sacrament of holy communion is powerless without a sincere act of contrition, a declaration of sorrow for your transgressions. You must confess your sins to unburden your soul."

"Very well," Brom said.

Adrian left the sanctum and returned shortly, carrying his saddlebag and a parcel bound in a velvet cloth. He untied the twine bindings and carefully unwrapped the soft velvet to unveil a gleaming longsword. The pommel and hilt were fashioned in the likeness of two intertwined serpents and the blade was adorned with ornate filigree surrounding an inscription which read *Furor meus inimicus meis.*

"I used this in the Holy Land," Adrian said. "It is a remnant of my former life. Once I chose the path of peace, I no longer had need of it. I kept it only as a reminder of my past, but I feel it may now be of use once more."

Adrian offered the weapon to Brom and said, "May it serve you well."

Brom took the sword and held it up to inspect the blade closely. "My enemies shall feel my wrath," he whispered, translating the Latin inscription. "'Tis a fine weapon," he said, sliding the sword beneath his belt. "Let us pray it withstands the steel of Dravek's blade."

Adrian opened his pack and withdrew a chalice and a bottle of wine and set them on the table. He pulled out a long strip of purple cloth fringed in gold, kissed it, and draped it around his shoulders. "Let us begin," he said.

Brom knelt before Adrian. The Tower Lord lowered his head and began his confession. "I have taken the lives of men—more than I can remember. I succumbed to the temptations of the flesh and have brought a woman into darkness, damning her soul." Brom hesitated.

"You must confess all your transgressions," Adrian said softly, "no matter how small."

"I have stolen." Brom paused for a long moment before continuing. "I took the scroll from the priory." He raised his head to face Adrian, saying, "Forgive me, but it was vital to my quest, and it had brought nothing but tragedy to the monastery."

Adrian nodded. "It seems it was destined for you all along."

Brom lowered his head again. "That is all," he whispered.

"Very well. The Lord has heard your admission of guilt and he absolves you of your sins."

Adrian opened the bottle of wine and set it beside a chalice. He made the sign of the cross and poured the wine, filling the goblet with the blood-red liquid. The monk recited a prayer over the chalice then raised it over his head, saying, "*Deus det tibi vitam aeternam*—May God grant you his eternal life."

He lowered the chalice to Brom's lips.

Brom felt strangely at ease. A familiar aroma wafted from the goblet. The sweet scent was reminiscent of the watcher's blood he had tasted in the priory catacombs. He closed his eyes and drank his fill from the chalice.

Brom began to shudder and gasp, as if he had swallowed poison. He clutched his throat and threw his head back, choking. His body spasmed and he fell lifelessly to the floor. A swirling wind rose and swept through the sanctum, scattering papers and extinguishing the lone candle, engulfing the room in howling darkness.

The wind died as quickly as it had risen. Brom lay silent and deathly still. Adrian shook him and called out to him but received no response. In desperation, Adrian left Brom's side to seek help. He staggered through the lightless chamber and out into the hallway, feeling his way along the twisting corridors to the entrance hall where the dim glow of the setting sun offered meager light. He bounded up the staircase, yelling to the others. Leonidas and Daria ran to meet him on the balcony landing.

"What is it?" Leonidas asked.

"Something has happened to Brom," Adrian replied breathlessly. "Come quickly!"

Leonidas lit a lantern to guide them through the shadowed corridors and the three hastened back toward Brom's sanctum. As they crossed the threshold, Leonidas held his lantern high, illuminating the chamber, but the room was now empty. Brom was nowhere to be found.

The three set out to search the Tower, soon discovering Brom in the chapel across the hall. He stood in the center of the room, bathed in the amber glow of dusk, surrounded by watchful statues of saints and angels. The Tower Lord's eyes remained fixed on the altar ahead, where the last rays of sunlight came to rest.

Brom stepped slowly and deliberately toward the circle of light, saying, "I have walked in the shadows amidst demons and ghosts far too long." As he continued to move forward, he reached out toward the golden beams that fell upon the altar, immersing his hand in the sunlight. Brom felt no pain or burning fire, as he once would have. His flesh remained unscathed. He stopped and stared at his trembling hand in disbelief, stretching his fingers wide to catch the sun's warmth.

"At last I shall emerge from the darkness that has held me bound," he whispered.

The Tower Lord turned to face the others, a glow of vitality shining in his eyes. "The final battle draws near," he said, holding Adrian's sword before him, "and I now stand fully ready to meet my fate." Brom turned back to the altar and stepped into the halo of sunlight and for the first time in countless years, he basked in its radiant aura.

Beyond the Veil

Joseph Vargo

Brom stood in the chapel of the Dark Tower as the last rays of sunlight washed over his body, caressing the flesh of his hands and face. The light of day, which had once been scorching and deadly to the Tower Lord, now had no effect upon him. As Brom basked in the sun's radiance, the golden beams slowly faded to a fiery crimson glow, casting a macabre tint over the hallowed sanctuary. Adrian, Leonidas and Daria looked on speechlessly, seemingly unable to comprehend what they had just witnessed.

Brom descended the altar steps to stand before the others. "I have transcended the final boundaries of mortality." Though he spoke quietly, the Tower Lord's voice resonated with a vibrant power, reverberating through the chapel like the roar of a lion.

Adrian's face bore a look of grave concern. "You lapsed into a listless state after drinking from the chalice. I feared the ritual had brought you to the threshold of death."

Brom's eyes shimmered with an unearthly glow. "The sensation was overwhelming, casting me into darkness. When I awoke, I felt a new vitality take hold. Its energy coursed through my body, purging the dark taint from my blood like a ravaging wildfire. In the next instant, I became charged with life. My senses became heightened, surpassing even my own immortal limits. I now realize things beyond all imagining." Brom stared at the stained glass windows, as if he were gazing through them and peering deep into the twilight beyond. "A realm of boundless beauty exists beyond the mortal veil—a vast spectrum of colors unseen and sensations unknown."

"And what of the torments that burdened you?" Adrian asked.

"My strength is replenished and my spirit has been rekindled. My hunger is gone—my endless thirst quenched. The maddening desire has left me—for how long, I dare not say."

"And if it returns?" Leonidas asked.

"I shall partake of the chalice once more."

Adrian smiled. "I shall require more wine to perform the ritual again."

"There is none in the Tower," Brom said.

"Then I must return to the village. If I leave now—"

"No," Brom said. "The sun is setting. It is no longer safe to venture out. Remain here until the day breaks."

"Very well," Adrian said. "I shall rest, then leave at dawn."

Brom nodded. "Before you go, I require a moment with you alone."

The sunset's crimson brilliance faded, and darkness crept across the room, covering the surrounding icons in shadows. Brom escorted Leonidas and Daria to the exit and closed the doors behind them, sealing himself in the chapel with Adrian. The Tower Lord then turned his attention to a weathered fresco adorning the rear wall of the sanctuary. The cracked and faded painting depicted three angels high atop a mountain summit, their stern gazes cast downward upon a group of penitent sinners who bowed and knelt before them. Brom studied the image for a long moment as if searching for some secret message hidden within the brushstrokes. At last he turned to Adrian and asked, "You are well-versed in the teachings of your faith, are you not?"

"Yes," Adrian said.

"Tell me then, what do you know of angels inhabiting the earth?"

Adrian's eyes washed over the surrounding statues and murals, seeing all manner of heavenly creatures. "According to ancient scripture, there are several angelic orders. Of these, only the Nephilim are bound to earth." The monk's eyes fell upon one of the stained glass windows where diabolic beasts danced with winged skeletons. "They were said to be fierce creatures with monstrous powers who trod the earth when mankind was young. Some sacred texts claim they were the offspring of angels, while others say they are the children of the demon queen Lilith. They are believed to dwell with the Fallen Ones in a realm of lightless shadow, deep beneath the earth. They plague humanity with the temptations of sin and revel in mankind's downfall. Our legends call them the Dark Brood."

"And what of the Seraphim?" Brom asked. "Are they angels or demons?"

"By some accounts, they are fiery serpents, while others say they are the Lord's most exalted subjects—his chosen children." Adrian looked at him curiously. "Why do you ask?"

"The prophecy speaks of them, proclaiming they are destined to rule the earth."

"The prophecy of the scroll?" Adrian asked.

Brom's eyes narrowed. "What do you know of it?"

"Only that it exists, nothing more."

Brom looked away. "The spirit in the monastery said it was the decree of the Almighty and that I was somehow part of it. Serena's father translated it, and she in turn related its message to me. I have given the words much thought, but I have yet to unravel their true meaning. In Castle Rankorr, Dravek's warlord interpreted the prophecy as a dark omen foretelling of Mara's rise and conquest of humanity. He seemed convinced of this, yet I remain uncertain."

"Perhaps I can help," Adrian said.

"Perhaps," Brom whispered. "I have transcribed the words to reflect upon them, yet each time I do, I arrive at new conclusions—none of which satisfy the entire prophecy." He handed Adrian a piece of parchment with a handwritten passage. The monk's eyes scanned the page as he read the words to himself.

> *In the time of great darkness,*
> *There shall come one, born of mortal flesh,*
> *But endowed with the blood of immortals,*
> *Both creator and destroyer,*
> *Destined to grant both life and death.*
> *Upon discovering the mysteries of the trinity*
> *And the chalice of eternal life,*
> *The destined one shall gain sublime wisdom,*
> *And bear judgment as to mankind's fate.*
> *For it is the Lord's supreme will*
> *That the Seraphim shall inhabit the Earth*
> *And hold dominion here till the end of days.*

Adrian stared at the transcribed words, pondering their meaning. "If it is an omen, it seems to foretell a grim fate for mankind. Perhaps it does relate to Mara's reign. If Dravek resurrects his queen, then indeed a time of great darkness shall be upon us. It may be a warning of the end of days, or possibly a proclamation of a new era of enlightenment—I cannot say." Adrian shook his head. "Allow me some time to consider this."

Brom nodded and Adrian slipped the parchment into the pocket of his robe.

"There is one last matter I wish to discuss," Brom said. "Come."

The Tower Lord strode back toward the front of the chapel, leading Adrian to the side of the altar. Brom gestured to a stone plaque on the wall depicting the battle between angels and demons.

"Good and evil." Brom's words echoed through the hallowed chamber like ghostly whispers. "These opposing forces have clashed since the dawn of man, yet they remain in constant balance. It seems one cannot exist without the other, yet the lines between them are often blurred. I have spent countless hours wondering what truly separates good from evil in the hearts of men."

"And what have you found?" Adrian asked.

"This battle wages within each of us." Brom's gaze dropped to the sculpted devil's head that adorned the bottom of the plaque. "I have sacrificed much for the benefit of others, yet I am not without sin. I have taken men's lives and consorted with dark powers, yet I justify my actions, telling myself I have done so for a greater good. Still I wonder, is this how evil manifests itself—by gaining a small foothold, then spreading like a disease, slowly claiming more and more of one's soul with each new transgression?"

Adrian moved closer to stand beside Brom. He studied the sculpted plaque, noticing the delicate balance that existed between the two warring factions. After a moment of silent reflection, Adrian said, "The philosophers of ancient Greece professed that virtue was the ultimate pinnacle of logic and that evil was the rejection of reason—a vile aberration that led only to destruction and loathing. They maintained that knowledge granted men the wisdom to hold virtue above vice and that it was in every man's best interest to live in accordance with nature."

Adrian rested a consoling hand on Brom's shoulder and said, "We each have the capacity to follow the virtuous path or the path of vice, for the Lord has given his mortal children free will to act howsoever they choose in this life. The consequences of our earthly actions determine how we shall spend eternity."

"And what fate do you think awaits me?"

Adrian turned to face Brom. "When I first came to the Tower, I thought you were no better than the devils that haunted this place. But I was wrong. The man I have come to know is compassionate and wise. You possess great virtue, Lord Brom, despite your trying circumstances. I have faith that you shall conquer whatever evil you may encounter—for our sake as well as your own."

Brom's face lightened with the trace of a smile. "Let us pray you are right." As the chapel grew dim, the vigil light above the altar shone like a solitary ray of hope in the dark.

Within the confines of the Tower above, Serena sat beside an open window, watching the setting sun as it sank into the forest like a dying ember. She and the others had taken lodgings in the Tower's bedchambers while Brom maintained his vigil in the keep below. She now waited by herself, tending watch over the castle grounds and surrounding woodlands from her lofty vantage. The shadows of swaying trees stretched up along the Tower walls, climbing higher and higher until at last they reached her window, obscuring all light. When darkness claimed the room, Serena lit a candle.

Thunder rumbled in the distance, announcing an approaching storm. A moment later, an unnatural chill gripped the air and a strange sensation crept over Serena, making her feel uneasy, as if she were no longer alone. The sound of whispered laughter echoed around her, alerting her to someone concealed in the shadows of the chamber.

"Who is there?" Serena demanded, clutching her candle tightly in her small hands as if it were a ward against whatever watched from the darkness.

"Have no fear, young one," a voice whispered. "I mean you no harm. I am but a lone spirit—a mere shadow among the ruins."

"Show yourself," Serena said, holding the candle out before her. The flame's glow faded before reaching the far side of the chamber where a figure loomed behind a row of stone columns.

"I cannot," the voice replied. "I am condemned to darkness. I must remain in the embrace of shadows."

"Such is the fate of the demons that haunt this place," Serena said.

"Demon?" The echo of low laughter filled the room, then the voice spoke again. "Nay, sweet child. I am like you—a desolate soul, abandoned and stripped of all I once cherished. Long ago, I stood against a mighty king—a vengeful and cruel lord. He wrought an unspeakable curse upon my brethren and I, dooming us to forever wander this realm with no hope of release. We now dwell among the restless spirits that inhabit this place, eternally bound to the Tower's forsaken halls, surrounding the living, yet lurking unseen." As the figure spoke, its eyes lit the darkness like scarlet coals.

Serena's heart raced in her chest as fear settled upon her. She took a step back, slowly retreating toward the door.

"Wait," the voice pleaded. "Hear my words. I mean only to help you."

"How?"

"I know of your terrible loneliness and the feelings you harbor. Once, long ago, I counseled another such as you. She too felt unwanted and neglected by those who professed to love her. I helped her break free of her mortal bonds and showed her the way to true salvation, guiding her through the darkness." The figure's voice was calm and soothing. "Tell me child, what is it you desire most in this world? Surely there is something... or someone you long for."

Serena cast her gaze downward, averting her eyes from the shadow's burning stare. "We all have secret desires deep inside our hearts," she said.

"How true. And such feelings must not be denied. There is no greater tragedy than a life unfulfilled—no greater sin than a desire unexplored." The shadow's hypnotic voice remained low and soft. "Come, child, close your eyes."

Serena was unable to resist the command. She took a step forward and shut her eyes. A moment later, she felt a hand gently stroking her hair. She leaned her head back and felt the sensation of sharp fingernails lightly brushing across her skin, wandering delicately over her neck and shoulders, sending a chill down her spine.

As Serena stood rapt, a vision appeared in her mind. She saw herself in the embrace of a dark angel—the same creature she had seen countless times in her dreams. He took her in his arms, lifting her off her feet, wrapping his bat-like wings around her. She too had wings, but hers consisted of feathers, soft and ivory white. As she stared into the angel's steely gaze, she was once again reminded of Brom, though his chiseled features now appeared somehow younger and his demeanor seemed less somber. Their faces drew close and their lips met, pressing softly together in a long, tender kiss.

The vision faded and Serena opened her eyes, seeing only darkness before her.

Again the voice spoke to her. "You desire him—the dark

angel of your visions. I can help you attain your wishes. I have watched him throughout the years. He wallows in sadness, alone and forsaken, yearning for someone to share his nights."

Serena shook her head. "It is not possible. We exist in different worlds, separated by an unbreachable barrier."

"It does not have to remain so. I can make you as he is—a creature of immortal power."

A hand pale and thin reached from the shadows, offering a tarnished goblet inscribed with ornate knotwork. "Behold," the voice whispered.

Warily, Serena stepped closer, keeping her focus on the red eyes that peered from the darkness. As she stared into the depths of the shadows before her, she seemed to discern a face white as bone, painted with a leering harlequin smile. Averting her eyes from the macabre visage, Serena cast her gaze down into the chalice, noticing a black liquid within.

"Drink from this and he shall be yours," the voice said.

Serena hesitated. "What harm shall come from this?"

"Harm? How can love harm someone? It shall ease your suffering and comfort your grief. It shall join your hearts together, and neither you nor he shall ever again know the torments of solitude."

Serena's hand trembled as she took hold of the goblet. "Such a gift does not come without a price. What do you want from me?"

"I require nothing in return, sweet child. My only wish is to spare you a lifetime of loneliness—to manifest your earthly desires and allow you to see the hidden wonders that surround you."

Serena closed her eyes and raised the goblet. She fought the urge to drink from the chalice, but found it impossible to resist. Her will was no longer her own. A sweet aroma wafted from the dark liquid—an intoxicating fragrance that emptied her mind of all worries and cares. But as she inhaled deeply, an invisible force seized her. Serena felt as if a giant hand took hold of her, constricting her chest and stopping the air from entering her lungs. Though her eyes remained closed, she saw a vision of three cloaked forms hovering in the darkness before her, encircling her within a ring of writhing shadows. They reached out, guiding her hand, forcing her to bring the chalice to her lips.

Serena gasped for breath. "No!" she cried, throwing the goblet to the floor.

Black rivulets wriggled forth from the chalice, slithering along the floorboards toward Serena. As the oily liquid crept closer, Serena stumbled back, retreating into an adjoining room. She slammed the door behind her and pressed her weight against it, holding it shut. Her heart pounded furiously as she squinted into the darkness of the windowless room, desperately seeking some other way out. As her eyes adjusted to the dim candlelight, she could see another door at the far end of the chamber. But something loomed between her and the exit. A dark, hulking figure sat crouched upon a pedestal, concealed in the shadows of an arched alcove. It remained silent and lifelessly still, like a wolf lying in wait to pounce upon unwary prey.

A hissing sound drew Serena's attention to the floor beneath her. The black liquid had crept beneath the door to encircle her feet like a ring of snakes. Serena bounded toward the exit at the far side of the chamber, dropping her candle in her haste. She reached the door, only to find it sealed shut. She pulled against the handle with all her might, but the latch had been thrown from the other side. She was trapped.

Serena pounded her fists against the door and cried for help as the black fluid snaked toward her, circumventing the candle that lay on the floor. The candlelight flickered and the flame dwindled, threatening to abandon her in total darkness. The serpentine tendrils inched ever closer, but before they could reach her, the door behind her burst open, and a blinding light shone forth. Lorand stood in the doorway, brandishing a blazing torch. He charged into the room, sweeping the flame over the floor, sending the hellish serpents slithering back into the shadows.

"Are you hurt?" he asked.

"No," Serena said, keeping her voice a whisper, "but something dwells in the shadows." She pointed toward the darkened alcove. "There."

Lorand held his torch out before him and stepped slowly toward the archway. A large gargoyle sat perched upon a pedestal within the shadowed recess. The sculpture resembled a skeletal man with the wings of a bat. Long claws protruded from its hands and feet and its head hung downward, facing the floor, as if bowed in submission to whatever dark master had created it.

Lorand watched in horror as the black serpents crept up through the pedestal, intertwining around the macabre sculpture and melting into it like water. The sound of stone grinding against stone reverberated throughout the chamber as the creature slowly raised its head. The gargoyle's eyes burned with scarlet fire as the darkness took hold, imbuing the monstrous statue with unearthly life. Its claws broke free of its perch in a shower of crumbling rock, and the stone demon stepped forth from the alcove.

Lorand and Serena fled into the hall, bolting the door behind them, sealing the hellish creature within the room. The monster's thunderous footfalls shook the floor beneath them, then the gargoyle crashed through the door, splintering the heavy wood like a battering ram. Serena screamed. Her shrill cry echoed throughout the corridor as the living statue lumbered forth. Its massive wings spanned the hall, blocking the only path of escape.

Lorand shielded Serena with his body and swept his torch through the air before him to hold the creature at bay as if it were a wild animal, but the gargoyle stepped steadily toward them, backing them toward a balcony window at the hall's end. With a swift swipe, the monstrous statue wrenched the torch from Lorand's grip and threw it aside, sending sparks and fire down the corridor. As the flames illuminated the hallway behind the creature, two cloaked forms appeared at the corridor's far end. Brom and Brother Adrian had come in answer to Serena's cry.

The Tower Lord raced forward, ramming his body against the living nightmare, sending it crashing into the wall. Brom wrapped his arms around the gargoyle's neck, holding the monster pinned against the bricks. "Run!" he shouted.

Lorand pulled Serena to her feet and they fled down the corridor, passing Brother Adrian who rushed toward the fray. The gargoyle pushed itself away from the wall then whirled swiftly, tossing Brom aside. The diabolic statue lunged forward, clamping its stone talons around Brom's wrists, driving him back over the balcony rail. The monster's jaws gaped wide then snapped shut, its stone fangs coming within inches of Brom's throat.

As Brom struggled with the creature, Adrian cast holy water into its face, shouting, "I banish thee, spirit of darkness!"

The stone smoldered and cracked beneath the water's touch and black smoke hissed from the monster's mouth. Brom tore free of the gargoyle's deadly grip and leapt to the side. Once more, Adrian doused the living nightmare with sanctified water.

The blessed droplets sizzled against the stone, dissolving it like acid, sending fissures through the gargoyle's torso to reveal the creature's molten core. As the monster reached for Adrian, Brom grabbed the creature's arm, pounding the crumbling stone with his fists, smashing it to rubble. The gargoyle's shattered arm broke loose from its shoulder, breaking to pieces as it hit the floor.

A network of fiery cracks covered the monster as it staggered back against the balcony rail. Brom leapt toward the creature, bashing against it with all his might, sending the stone demon toppling over the railing and out into the night. The monstrous statue plummeted toward the cliffs below, crashing against the castle wall along its way. The gargoyle hit the cliffs with a thunderous impact, smashing to pieces, sending a shower of stones down into a craggy ravine that split the mountainside. A wisp of dust and hellish smoke was all that remained of the creature, and even that trace was quickly carried away by the evening breeze.

Brom stood at the balcony's edge, looking down upon the cliffs below. After a moment of silence, he turned his attention to the shattered remnants of the statue's arm that lay upon the floor. Black smoke rose from the charred fragments. Brom crouched and swept his fingers across the smoldering shards. The stone crumbled to ashes beneath his touch.

"The ancient darkness has awakened," Brom said. "The hour of reckoning is upon us." He turned to Adrian and whispered, "They are coming."

Unleashed

Joseph Vargo

Night descended swiftly upon the Dark Tower, like a gigantic spider closing in on its prey. A sense of dread hung in the air, adding an ominous aura to the surrounding gloom. In the chapel, Brom waited, alert and vigilant, his fingers tightly clenched around the hilt of his sword as he stared at the bronze door behind the altar. Three nights had passed since Dravek had entered the catacombs in search of Mara's tomb and there was still no sign of his return. Brom tried to ease his troubled mind, thinking that Dravek might remain forever lost in the labyrinth. But Brom knew his enemy was relentless. He would surely face the White Wolf once more.

Brom closed his eyes to focus his thoughts. In the distance he heard the muffled cry of ravens, then the sound of thunder rumbled through the Tower, rattling the ancient stones of the keep. Brom glanced up at the chapel windows, expecting to see the stained glass illuminated by lightning, but all remained dark. A moment later, another crashing sound reverberated through the castle, shaking the floor beneath his feet like a tremor. Brother Adrian entered the chapel, his eyes wide with fear.

Before the monk could utter a word, Brom said, "Stay here, and keep the others inside." With that, the Tower Lord rushed from the sanctuary to investigate the source of the clamor.

Brom emerged in the graveyard, casting his gaze to the

heavens. The sky was black and still. No lightning streaked across the clouds, nor did any tempest rage. Another series of tremors drew his attention to a gated mausoleum built into the northern wall of the cemetery. The chiseled stones that sealed the tomb heaved outward with each thunderous pulse, fracturing and crumbling from within, until they came crashing forward through the bars of the gate, spilling out into the graveyard in a tumble of broken stone and dust.

As the cloud of debris settled, Dravek's white hair and ashen face emerged from the shadows of the crypt. Behind him, a figure loomed—a menacing form that seemed no more than a skeleton, shrouded in a pillar of black smoke. Dravek lashed out with the relic sword, the unearthly blade slicing through the cross that sealed the mausoleum gate. The iron bars yielded in a shower of sparks, leaving the ruined crypt gaping open.

Dravek stepped forth into the cemetery mists. He looked up toward the moon, tilting his head far back to bask in its glow, then turned his gaze to Brom. The distant cry of ravens dropped to a hush and an eerie silence befell the cemetery.

Brom stood his ground, blocking the way to the Tower. "Turn back, demon," he commanded, his voice deep and forbidding. "This path leads only to your death and the Hell that awaits beyond."

Dravek laughed mockingly. He pointed his sword toward Brom and said, "The torments of Hell are naught in compare with the fate you shall soon suffer. Your days are at an end, crusader. Before the dawn breaks, I shall stand as lord of the Tower and my queen shall rule these lands once more." Dravek looked back to the shadows behind him where the black cloud loomed. The skeletal silhouette that stood within the smoke remained still, silently watching.

"You are no lord," Brom said. "You are but a lowly

servant, tending your master's beck and call."

Dravek's eyes narrowed in anger. "She is my savior," he said. "Before she took me into her fold, I had neither desire nor reason to live."

Though Brom stood poised for battle, his voice remained calm. "She gave your life purpose, but at what cost? She has enslaved you. She twisted your devotion until her desires became yours. She fed your hatred of your fellow man until you could bear your own humanity no longer. She is not your savior, she is your damnation."

"She is all I know!" Dravek's voice trembled with rage. "She gave me this life and I have sworn to serve her. I am bound to her till my death."

Dravek stepped forward to stand within striking distance of his foe. "Now you shall feel the wrath of the Fallen." Raising his arms, he called out to the night, "Lords of darkness, heed my call. I beseech you—rise up to smite this infidel!"

An icy chill crept through the air and the ground mists began to stir. The wind slowly rose to a mournful wail as dark, hulking shapes lumbered forth from the surrounding night to stand among the monuments and graves. The sound of low growling drew Brom's attention to a horned creature that sat perched upon a tall monument beside him. Great leathery wings wrapped around the tombstone and a serpentine tail slithered over the graven cross beneath it. Brom's eyes scanned the fog-shrouded cemetery, seeing figures looming all around him. The creatures remained at a distance, surrounding Brom and Dravek like curious spectators awaiting the inevitable battle to begin.

"You walk upon hallowed ground," Brom said. "The demons you summon are powerless here. If you dare stand against me, you shall have to do so alone."

Dravek raised the relic sword. "I possess all I need to send you to your grave."

The Tower Lord lifted his arm from beneath his cloak, revealing the sword in his own hand. "We shall see," Brom said.

Dravek's eyes came to rest on the blade. "So, you have scavenged a new weapon. But it shall do you little good."

Brom said nothing. He knew his sword was no match for the sacred blade Dravek wielded. But he could see that fate had dealt his enemy a crippling blow. Dravek's hollow eyes betrayed his hunger. While Brom had accustomed himself to surviving without human blood, Dravek indulged his bloodlust at every opportunity, only deepening his need. His days without nourishment in the catacombs had left him weakened. Still, Brom knew Dravek was a formidable adversary, cunning and ruthless. Brom knew he would have to act with equal guile and savagery to defeat him.

Without warning, Dravek lunged forward, thrusting his sword toward Brom's head. The Tower Lord reacted with lightning speed, ducking beneath the attack and parrying Dravek's blade with his own. The White Wolf unleashed a fierce assault, driving Brom backward, forcing him away from the Tower path. Dravek swung the sword wildly and Brom dodged every strike, retreating into the mist-covered field of graves.

Although Brom's sword was a sturdy weapon, he knew his blade could not withstand a direct strike from the relic sword. Each time Dravek stabbed his sword forward, Brom leapt to the side, narrowly escaping the blade's razor-sharp edge. The shadow creatures watched the duel with great interest, but they made no attempt to interfere with the fight.

Dravek's onslaught grew more furious, but Brom deftly defended himself, parrying each thrust and swing. The White Wolf battled forward, lashing out with violent sweeping strokes, driving the Tower Lord back against the base of a tombstone. As Brom glanced up, his eyes met the burning gaze of a demon perched upon the monument. The creature loomed over him like the shadow of death, baring its fangs in a grotesque smile.

Dravek sprang forth like a savage beast, grabbing the Tower Lord's throat in a choking grip, digging his claws beneath Brom's skin. Dravek's lips drew back in a feral snarl and his fangs grew long. He raised the relic sword overhead and plunged it down toward Brom, but the Tower Lord caught the blade in his free hand, stopping it inches from piercing his chest. Brom broke free of Dravek's grasp, throwing him aside, sending him crashing against a tree.

Taking the offensive, Brom leapt forward, swinging his blade toward Dravek's head, but Dravek deflected the strike and kicked Brom away. Dravek still matched Brom's speed, but his strength had begun to wane. As the White Wolf staggered to his feet, Brom charged forth, thrusting his sword toward Dravek's heart. Dravek slashed his sword outward to meet Brom's attack, shattering the Tower Lord's blade.

Dravek's eyes glistened with a lust for blood. He lunged toward Brom like a frenzied demon, swinging his sword with wild fury. Brom clung to the remnant of his sword, less than half the blade left, and continued to hold it between them as he dodged Dravek's relentless strikes. The Tower Lord fell back against the statue of an angel, finding his retreat blocked by the sculpture's outstretched wings.

Dravek thrust his blade forward, but Brom rolled to the side. Dravek's sword bit into the statue's chest, burying itself deep in the chiseled stone. The White Wolf strained to free the sword, but it remained firmly wedged, as if the angel itself would not relinquish its grip upon the blade. As Dravek struggled to wrest his weapon loose, Brom leapt toward him, wielding his broken sword like a battle axe. The Tower Lord brought the shattered blade down with all his might on Dravek's sword arm, tearing through flesh and bone, lopping his hand from his wrist.

As Dravek fell back, shrieking in agony, Brom claimed the relic sword from his foe's severed hand, yanking it free from the statue. Brom whirled swiftly around, swinging the sword in a wide arc. The blade sliced through the air, meeting Dravek's neck with little resistance, sending a shower of blood beneath it. Dravek's head tumbled to the ground, followed by his body. His eyes gaped wide in an expression of shock and anguish before they settled into an empty stare. His body lay lifeless at the base of the angel statue. The White Wolf was dead.

Brom raised the relic sword above him in victory, defying the dark angels that surrounded him. The bloodstained blade radiated a shimmering aura as it caught the gleam of moonlight. The distant cry of wolves broke the silence of the cemetery and the shadow watchers silently faded back into the mist, becoming one with the night.

Yet one final threat remained. Brom raced to the open mausoleum gate and peered into the gaping crypt, seeing only empty darkness. The sinister wraith that had followed Dravek was gone. Looking overhead, Brom saw a trail of dark smoke rising along the sheer face of the castle wall, entering an open balcony window. Brom slid the relic sword beneath his belt and leapt up onto the wall, digging his claws into the stones. He climbed upward, swiftly scaling the Tower to follow the elusive entity.

Brom entered the castle through the open balcony and quickly scanned the hallway. The black cloud was nowhere to be seen, but an ominous taint permeated the corridor. The Tower Lord peered into the darkness, silently surveying his

surroundings. He detected no sound or movement, but the foul scent of decay hung thick all around him and a dank chill filled the air.

Brom resumed his pursuit, allowing his senses to guide him up the Tower stairwell. At the next balcony landing, he came upon the monstrous gargoyle that stared out over the forest. Brom studied the stone demon, making sure it had not been bewitched to life by any dark sorcery. The gargoyle remained deathly still, yet it seemed to leer with perverse pleasure as it held fast to the skull of the ancient king who sired Mara.

A dead raven lay on the floor near the base of the statue. Brom noticed the carcass but gave it little thought. He quickly returned his attention to his search, sprinting up the stone staircase in pursuit of the dark spirit. Brom followed the entity's trail down a long corridor to Mara's bedchamber. The door which had been sealed shut now stood wide open. Slowly and warily, he stepped inside.

Brom's eyes searched the room, seeking signs of the intruder, but there were none to be found. Still, he felt a looming sense of foreboding, as if some malevolent force lurked nearby. Black velvet drapes fluttered at the far side of the chamber, drawing the Tower Lord's attention to an open window. On the floor beneath the window ledge, Brom discovered two more dead ravens. Their bodies lay mangled, as if they had been torn apart by some savage animal, yet no trace of blood was visible. Something had fed upon them, draining them of their life's essence.

Beside the window, an ornate mirror hung in shattered ruins, as if smashed by some violent force. The broken shards cast a distorted reflection of the opposite wall where ghostly masks peered out from beneath a thick layer of cobwebs. The lifeless faces stared woefully into the darkness, like grim specters, silently watching Brom's every move.

A lavish canopy bed dominated one end of the chamber. Tall wardrobe cabinets carved from black wood lined the walls on each side of the cobweb-draped bed. One of the cabinets had been pushed to the side, revealing a hidden passage in the chamber wall. Beyond the narrow opening, a stone staircase spiraled upward. The smell of death clung to the passage walls like a rancid, rotting mold.

Brom entered the secret passage, climbing the twisting stairs as they wound upward to the Tower's heights where he came at last to an iron door. He pushed it slowly open and emerged into the night atop the castle's peak. The Tower Lord scanned his surroundings, searching for the elusive entity that led him to this point. A dark figure stood among the gargoyles at the edge of the battlements, enveloped in black smoke. As Brom stepped closer, he could sense the Dark Queen's vile spirit. An oppressive feeling encompassed him, like a storm gathering around him. It was as if he were standing in the path of an oncoming tempest that would soon erupt with raging fury.

For the first time during his long reign as Tower Lord, Brom was in Mara's presence. Throughout the years, he had felt her spirit, seen her in visions and heard her bewitching call, but now she loomed before him in all her sinister glory. Mara was no longer the enticing succubus that had visited him in his dreams. The centuries in the crypt had eaten away her beauty, reducing her to a skeletal corpse—a grotesque, frail form bathed in writhing shadows. A crown of ebon spikes rested upon her head and an alabaster mask covered her face. As she stood atop the battlements, her black hair and tattered gown billowed in the wind behind her.

Mara whispered an incantation, summoning the powers of darkness, and Brom felt as if he had been engulfed by a ravaging tide. An invisible force enveloped him, assaulting his senses like a choking poison and crushing his spirit. The air around him grew heavy and thick, slowing his actions to a crawl. He stepped sluggishly forward, as if he were moving underwater. As he drew closer, the crippling effect of the Dark Queen's spell grew more devastating. Brom now realized Mara had not fled through the Tower in an attempt to escape him—she had lured him here, far away from the hallowed ground of the graveyard.

Mara gazed out over the forest, paying little heed to the Tower Lord. "Once, long ago, I ruled these lands," her raspy voice croaked. "Those who followed my path were bestowed with the powers of darkness. And in turn, they worshiped me."

Brom moved forward. "You think yourself a god?"

"Who could think otherwise?" Mara's voice sent a chill through the air. "I granted my children eternal life and strengths beyond mere mortal frailty. I am the reason they walk the earth. How could they not revere me as their divine master?"

"Your words are heresy. There is only one true God."

"God," Mara cackled. "So great and limitless is His power that He could smite us all with a mere thought. If He so desired, we would cease to be, yet He allows us to live here as long as we abide by his decree. Long ago, He granted my ancient kindred the sanctuary of this realm, to do as we wish within the borders of our earthly domain." Mara turned her head to face Brom. The crimson lips of her mask seemed to form a wicked smile. "Your god cannot help you here."

Brom's eyes narrowed. "How can this be? What god would allow his children to suffer at the hands of ones banished by him? How can He allow you to prey upon the innocent?"

"He has given mortals free will to choose their own destinies. But these creatures are weak and so easily manipulated. When they cross the threshold into our domain, they are ours, but killing them has little value in this arena. Seducing them into darkness serves our purposes far better. This shall lead to their ultimate destruction when the Black Dawn rises."

"There is purpose and order to everything. We all play a part in the grand scheme. I will not believe that this—this dark blasphemy—is the Lord's fated destiny for mankind."

Mara gazed down toward the village at the base of the mountain. "He has given them free will, and they have chosen the path of downfall."

"You have little faith in them, while I have witnessed their virtue. They are not all as weak as you think them to be. Your arrogance shall be your undoing."

"No," Mara said, "I am eternal. Have you learned nothing during your stay here?"

Brom's hand slowly reached for the sword in his belt. "I have uncovered much about the history of the Tower during my vigil. I discovered the origins of the standing stones and the boundaries they once imposed."

Mara's black eyes scanned the forest. "The ancient monoliths were toppled long ago, by my father's decree."

"The villagers set them upright once more. You shall not break free of the Tower without incurring the wrath of the sentinel angels. You are bound here."

Mara turned her gaze upward, fixing her eyes on the bell tower. Behind her, scores of bats left the belfry to descend upon the creatures of the forest. Mara raised her hand and the swarm veered toward the village. But as soon as they crossed the boundary of the standing stone, her spell was broken. The bats dispersed, flying in all directions. In her rage, Mara summoned the creatures back to her. As the bats swarmed around her, she plucked them from the air, one by one, tearing into them with her claws and drinking their blood to quench her own savage hunger.

Brom took a step closer, raising his sword. Mara peered into the Tower Lord's eyes and he could feel her entering his mind. As Mara's thoughts probed his own, Brom felt the sensation of cold fingers sliding along the inside his skull, their freezing touch seeping deeper into the core of his mind like needles of ice.

"Surrender," her thoughts commanded.

Brom lowered his blade. Resistance was nearly impossible, yet he fought the urge to submit, forcing himself to pull away. The black smoke that encompassed Mara slowly crept toward Brom.

Mara ran her claws along the wing of a gargoyle looming beside her, the solid stone eroding at her touch. "You are strong of will, but in time you shall succumb to me, as all men do."

"Never."

"You cannot hide your thoughts. The strongest feelings are the most difficult to conceal. Your deepest secrets announce themselves to me like a raven's cry. I sense the passion stirring within you for the things you cherish most. A woman, long dead... and the child she bore you."

Dread gripped Brom's heart like the claws of a tormenting demon. The black smoke encircled him in its grasp.

"Yes," Mara whispered, "your son. I visited him while he kept your vigil. Such a sweet child. I held him in my power and recognized his familiar spirit."

Brom's muscles tensed as he strained to reach Mara, but her spell held him at bay. "I will have your head, witch."

"You shall bow before me, or I shall claim the boy—body and soul." Mara floated down from the battlements to hover before Brom. "On your knees," she whispered.

Brom fought to defy Mara's command, but her will was

too strong. He felt his legs buckling beneath him. His body shook as he struggled to resist, but he was powerless against the Dark Queen's magic. Brom's head dropped to a humbled bow and he fell to his knees.

The Dark Queen stood triumphant before her fallen foe. She placed her skeletal hand upon his head and gently stroked his hair. "In time, you shall come to worship me as your queen and master."

Rage flooded Brom's mind, but he no longer controlled his own actions. He had guarded the keep with his life and had sworn to vanquish Mara at any cost, but it now seemed he could do nothing to stop her. Desperately, he drew up the last free vestige of his will and focused his thoughts, sending them out into the night, summoning the ravens of the forest. For a breathless moment all was silent, then a ghastly croaking filled the air along with the sound of fluttering wings. A host of ravens rose from the trees below, soaring up into the night like a legion of demons, blotting the moon from the sky. The black birds swooped toward Mara, ripping into her flesh with their talons and beaks, driving her back against the Tower wall. The ghoulish queen lashed out against the winged assault, swatting at the birds with her claws and hissing like a savage beast.

Brom felt Mara's spell relinquish, releasing him from her mind's grasp. He turned and staggered back to the stairwell, slamming the heavy door and bolting it behind him. He quickly retraced his path, escaping down the twisting staircase, retreating back into the confines of the Tower's dark embrace. But he knew there was no longer any safe haven to be found in the castle—no sanctuary from the Dark Queen's horrific powers. Like a plague, the ancient evil had been unleashed upon the world, and once its black shadow began to spread, it would surely consume all of mankind.

Crimson Thirst

Joseph Vargo and Joseph Iorillo

The chapel door opened with a shrill squeal, startling Leonidas, Adrian and Daria from their silent vigil in the hallowed sanctuary. Brom stood in the doorway, no more than a thin silhouette against a backdrop of shadows. The Tower Lord threw back his cloak to reveal the relic sword clutched in his pale hand. Dark blood stained the blade.

"The White Wolf is dead," Brom said.

Daria shut her eyes, and Leonidas and Adrian exchanged looks of relief.

"And what of Mara?" Leonidas asked.

Brom stepped forward into the candlelight. His face conveyed an expression of utter hopelessness, as if he had witnessed a horror beyond all comprehension. "The Dark Queen has been resurrected," he said. "She lurks in the Tower above." He stared at the red votive candle burning above the altar for a long moment, then said, "Her hatred sustained her evil spirit during her century of imprisonment, festering and fueling the fires of vengeance seething within her. Her magic is now far stronger than it once was."

Daria's voice shook as she spoke. "Mara exists between the worlds of the living and the dead. If she feeds, her foothold in this realm shall become more stable. I fear that her powers shall only continue to grow."

"You must leave here now," Brom said. He glanced around the chapel but did not see Lorand or Serena. "Where are the others?" he asked, a tone of urgency in his voice.

In the cold emptiness of the entrance hall, Lorand kept guard near the Tower's immense doors, crouched in the shadows like one of the ancient gargoyles that adorned the keep. Though waves of weariness threatened to drown him in sleep, he sensed a tension in the air, a foreboding that seemed akin to the coming of a terrible storm. Would the storm come from within the keep or without? For some reason he felt the need to guard the main entrance. It seemed foolhardy to leave the Tower doors unprotected while Leonidas and the others huddled inside the castle's gloomy chambers.

Lorand struggled to remain alert, but the long hours had worn on him. As he drifted near the threshold of sleep, a faint sound caught his attention—a distant murmur that seemed to carry a haunting melody, like the voice of a woman softly singing. Lorand strained to hear the indistinct words, but he could make no sense of them. The ache of weariness and fatigue dissipated, replaced by curiosity and something else—an irresistible compulsion to follow the enchanting voice. Part of his mind fought this desire, knowing the dangers that loomed in the keep, but very quickly all reason succumbed to the bewitching call. Soon he could find no objection to seeking out the mysterious voice, for it held such gentleness and beguiling warmth, like the voice of a loving mother lulling her babe to sleep. Yes, he told himself, there were sinister spirits and dread horrors trapped in the Tower, but he knew that there were also beings of beauty and otherworldly kindness.

Lorand followed the mesmerizing song up the grand staircase to the second floor. He reached the landing and crossed the balcony toward the grand hall, drawn deep into the shadows by the eerie melody. The voice slowly faded to a hypnotic whisper that seemed to call his name, summoning him further into the darkness. He entered the grand hall, staggering forth as if half-asleep until another voice shattered his reverie, waking him from his trance.

"Lorand!"

Drowsily, Lorand turned and saw Serena holding a candle, her eyes wide in alarm. Lorand felt momentarily disoriented. He gazed around him at the pool of shadows that encompassed him, unsure of where he was.

Serena touched his arm and said, "I saw you come up here. Are you all right? You seemed not yourself."

"There was a voice," he said. "It... it called to me. Did you not hear it?"

Serena's grip on Lorand's arm grew stronger. "We must leave," she whispered. "Now."

But before they could turn, sinister laughter echoed from the recesses of the chamber—a throaty, ancient rasp that seemed to evoke menacing power.

Lorand took the candle from Serena's hand and held it before him, moving slowly forward and squinting into the gloom. An ebon cloud churned upon a dais at the far end of the chamber. The black mist slowly settled to reveal a dark form sitting upon the room's tall throne. A crown of spikes adorned the shadow's head and a pale porcelain mask covered its face. A deathly chill crept over Lorand as he sensed Mara's malevolent presence.

"Come forth, my children," the raspy voice whispered. "Your queen awaits."

Mara rose and drifted toward them, black smoke billowing around her like a storm. She raised her arm and dozens of bats burst forth from the darkness in a screeching, raucous flurry, swooping past her and swirling madly toward Lorand and Serena.

Lorand took Serena's hand and they fled, racing back down the stone stairs toward the Tower's entrance with the ravenous bats in close pursuit. Cackling laughter echoed around them as the Dark Queen followed their trail.

In the hall below, a shadow moved swiftly toward the staircase. As it rounded the banister, Lorand could see it was Brom racing toward them, charging upward with his sword drawn. The Tower Lord bounded past Lorand and Serena to take a stand in the midst of the staircase.

Brom glanced back at Lorand and shouted, "Leave the Tower, now!"

Before Brom could turn his head, the bats overtook him, swarming around him in a deafening cacophony of thunderous wings and high, piercing cries, tearing at him with their claws. Brom slashed his sword through the air, the ancient blade a gleaming blur that the eye could scarcely follow, fending off the winged attackers, leaving those that ventured too close in bloody pieces on the stairs.

On the balcony above, the Dark Queen's shrouded form emerged from a cloud of swirling smoke. Her ghostly porcelain mask hung suspended in the darkness like the moon in the night sky. Mara tilted her head to the side and gestured with open hands at Brom. In response to her silent command, the black mist around her rushed toward the Tower Lord, blinding him and smothering him. Serpentine shadows coiled around his torso, tightening to a crushing grip. As Brom struggled to wrest himself free of the constricting tendrils of smoke and shadow, Mara turned her attention to the terrified mortals scurrying through the hall beneath her.

Adrian and Daria rushed toward the castle doorway with Leonidas trailing behind. Mara nodded toward the open archway and the immense doors slammed shut, nearly crushing Adrian as he leapt between them. Daria strained to pull the doors open but could not. Lorand and Serena reached the bottom of the grand staircase and crossed the hall, and they too struggled with the Tower's doors, unable to budge them. Leonidas stood in the center of the hall, seemingly torn between fleeing and going to the Tower Lord's aid.

Realizing their only path of escape was now blocked, Daria reached into her pack and withdrew a handful of red powder, casting it in a circle on the floor around her. "Here," she shouted, "quickly!"

Lorand and Serena rushed to her side, and Daria lowered her torch to the floor, igniting the ring of powder that surrounded them. The Dark Queen remained on the balcony, overlooking the scene. Leonidas ran toward the others but before he could cross the circle's edge, Mara waved her hand in his direction. The old man flew across the chamber, crashing against the far wall like a child's doll. The others who stood within the safety of Daria's mystic circle remained untouched by the queen's spell.

Mara floated down into the hall, hovering near the burning circle. She gestured toward the flames and the ring of fire flickered briefly, but the Dark Queen's magic had no effect on the three mortals within its confines. Mara drew closer but stopped at the circle's edge, unable to cross the magical barrier.

The queen's masked face slowly turned toward Daria. "Fear not, sister," Mara's soft voice purred. "I mean you no harm. Release the boy unto me and I shall allow you to leave."

"Be gone, demon," Daria said, clutching the pendant around her neck. She raised the ancient amulet and held it forth as if it were a sacred ward against evil.

Mara's eyes narrowed behind the ghostly mask as she studied the amulet. The black smoke crept around the circle, encompassing the ring of fire.

"Once I fully regain my powers," Mara said, "your magic shall be useless against me. We shall meet again, witch. This I assure you. And when we do, I shall drain your heart dry." The queen's words echoed menacingly through the hall.

In the far corner of the chamber, Leonidas staggered clumsily to his feet. Mara cast her black eyes upon him, raising her hand again, but before she could unleash another spell, Brom leapt toward her, swinging his sword. A cloud of smoke enveloped Mara and Brom's blade sliced through the black mist, finding no solid target. The smoke dissipated into the darkness and Mara was nowhere to be found.

Brom turned his attention to the Tower's doors and pulled against them with all his might. With the sound of squealing hinges and groaning timbers, the massive doors heaved open. Leonidas and the others stumbled out into the night, fleeing the keep and its infernal queen. Lorand paused and looked back toward the Tower Lord, but the stern expression on Brom's face told the boy that this was a battle Brom would have to fight alone.

"Go!" Brom yelled.

Adrian and Leonidas led the others down away from the Tower toward the trees where their horses were tethered. A bloodcurdling shriek cut the cold air, startling Leonidas and the others and drawing their attention to the Tower's heights. Mara now stood upon the battlements amidst a legion of hellish gargoyles and swarming bats.

The Dark Queen glared down at Leonidas and the others as they struggled to untie their horses. She held out her arms, as if bestowing a benediction upon them or welcoming them into her embrace. Suddenly, the horses began to kick and rear wildly, their eyes rolling back in their heads as Mara's magic took hold upon their minds. Daria and Serena soothed their horses and brought them under control, but Adrian's steed ran amok, galloping straight for the edge of the plateau. Adrian cried out and pulled back on the reins, but the frenzied animal heedlessly charged forward. Adrian leapt from the saddle and tumbled to the rock-strewn ground, and he watched in horror as the bewitched horse continued on without him at full stride, plunging headlong over the cliff's edge. A moment later the horrendous shriek of the animal meeting its violent end on the jagged rocks below arose from the chasm.

Mara's voice cut through the night like a poisoned arrow. "None can escape me," she hissed.

The sky behind the Dark Tower lightened to a somber grey, heralding the approach of dawn. The bats encircling the Dark Queen scattered into the shadows, seeking refuge from the forthcoming light.

"Reflect upon your lives," Mara said, her voice rising with the wind, "for this day shall be your last. When darkness falls again, the night shall offer no sanctuary." With those words, the black column of smoke arose like a thunderhead around her skeletal form in a vast swirling billow that was caught in the wind and driven into wispy tendrils of ebon mist.

Leonidas helped Adrian onto his own horse, and the others hurried their steeds down the path away from the Tower. Lorand cast a glance backward, seeing Brom standing alone in the Tower's doorway.

"We cannot abandon him," Lorand said.

"He is the Tower Lord," Leonidas replied, keeping his eyes on the path before him. "He has commanded us to leave and we must abide by his decree."

Brom watched as Lorand and the others passed the gate ruins and disappeared down the forest path. Once they were safely out of sight, he turned to the darkness of the castle's cold interior, a darkness he knew all too well from his long years of solemn vigil here. Though the shadows had always provided him with an eerie sort of comfort, tonight that comfort had vanished, for the blackness all around him was charged with an evil intensity that it had never before held. The villagers called him the Tower Lord, but the keep had been Mara's domain decades before he had even been born and it was hers again.

He strode forth into the Tower, seeking Mara, but she was nowhere to be seen. Her presence, however, seemed to emanate from every stone of the keep. Brom stalked the halls, searching each chamber with his sword drawn and ready, but he was met with nothing more than the weak flickering of the candles left behind by Leonidas and the others. Several times the cool air was split by echoes of Mara's mocking laughter somewhere in the distance, but when Brom followed the sounds he found only empty darkness. Mara's elusive spirit remained hidden in the Tower, cloaked in blackest shadow.

As the huts and hovels of Vasaria grew closer and the smell of hearthfires became more intense, Leonidas felt more at ease. His old body still ached from Mara's brutal attack but aside from bruises there was no lasting damage. At Daria's hut, their procession halted, and Daria leapt from her saddle to embrace her young daughter Annika, who greeted her at the door. An old woman who had been minding the girl hugged Daria and eagerly gestured Leonidas and the others into the hut. The old woman gave them water and pieces of bread. Leonidas was surprised by his hunger. Brother Adrian ate little, preferring to sit by the fire, staring into the flames as if searching for answers there. Lorand paced restlessly, looking both angry and terrified.

The old woman left to tend to her own family, and Lorand finally spoke. "We must go back. Lord Brom cannot be left to face the Dark Queen alone."

"Are you mad?" Adrian snapped. "Did you not witness her power? She will kill us all with a mere glance."

Daria's voice was calm and measured. "Mara's powers are not without limit. She is still restrained by the confines of daylight and the standing stones. She is free to roam the Tower and the forest, but she does not yet possess her full strength. My spells can thwart her for the moment, but with each passing night I fear she shall only grow stronger." She moved to a window that looked out into the forest. Though full daylight was upon Vasaria now, the woodlands were still rich with shadows. Daria drew the curtain. "The Dark Queen can see through her familiars' eyes while she is bound within the Tower. She watches us, aware of all that transpires here. We must be cautious as we consider our next move."

Adrian shook his head in disgust. "There is little we can do." He stood. "We are powerless against this creature of darkness. Our only hope lies with Lord Brom." Adrian's face reflected his despair as he left the hut.

Leonidas rose from his seat by the hearth. "I will speak to him." He patted Lorand's shoulder and briefly touched Serena's cheek. "For now, we must all rest."

Outside the hut, Leonidas found Brother Adrian looming near the edge of the woods, gazing up toward the Tower. The elder stood beside his friend and stared off at the citadel that crested the mountaintop. "The Tower Lord is our protector," Leonidas said softly. "Our fate rests in his hands, as it always has."

Adrian nodded. "Let us pray he can vanquish this daughter of demons."

Leonidas remained silent and turned his gaze to the sky overhead. What would the coming night bring them, he wondered with dread. He and Brother Adrian were men of God, but God felt very far away from them right now.

As night claimed the land once again, Mara crept from the keep and stole away into the forest beneath the light of the rising moon. She came to a small clearing amongst the withered trees and gazed down upon Vasaria. Closing her black eyes, Mara began to chant an invocation in a language long-forgotten by the living. The blasphemous magic of the words sent her spirit into the dreams of the villagers. Adults stirred uneasily in their sleep, unsettled by the vision that beckoned seductively, while the young of the village were far more receptive to the Dark Queen's whispering call.

In a short time, two young men and a young woman found themselves outside their families' huts, silently staring off toward the impenetrable darkness of the forest. In their minds, Mara's irresistible summons grew louder and more insistent, and they hurried along the path that led into the woods, passing beyond the threshold of the standing stone that marked the boundary between the safety of Vasaria and the realm of the Dark Queen. The three raced up the mountain trail, undeterred by the treacherous path or the fearsome shadows of the night, driven by blind, uncontrollable desire to reach the beckoning voice.

At last they came to a stony clearing surrounded by barren trees, misshapen and twisted by some ancient blight. In the distance, a shadowed form stood dark against the moonlit fog. The figure drifted silently toward them through the mist like a raven gliding in the night and hovered before them. The three villagers stood spellbound as they gazed in awe upon the terrible majesty of the Dark Queen. Mara's ebon gown was shrouded in smoke and writhing shadows that undulated beneath her. Her face was covered by a mask of ivory white and a crown of tall, thorny spikes rested upon her head.

Mara held out her arms in a gesture of gentle welcome and the woman and one of the men approached. The other young man, however, faltered, blinking steadily at the strange masked being, a sobering awareness quickly driving away the dull glaze in his eyes. He stepped backward, gasping, trying to find his voice to warn the others, but Mara's penetrating gaze held him fast. Though her mask was flawlessly sculpted to depict the face of immortal beauty, the steely eyes behind it were full of unfathomable hatred and cruelty. The young man came fully out of his trance, but it was too late, for Mara was upon him like a swift bird of prey.

"Your blood will be a sacrifice to my rebirth," Mara whispered, clutching the man's neck in her clawed hands.

The Dark Queen pulled back her mask, revealing her withered face, its dry, leathern skin stretched taut over the bones. Her soulless black eyes locked on him and he stared in helpless horror at the very image of death itself. Mara's shriveled lips drew back, and her fangs tore into his throat, sending warm blood spurting over her tongue. Stricken with terror and pain, the young man struggled to break free of Mara's unearthly grasp, but her hold was unrelenting. The queen drank her fill from his pulsing neck, draining him of his life's essence.

Mara released her victim from her grip and his body dropped lifelessly to the ground. As she slid the mask back over her face, she could feel her strength returning. Drifting before the two remaining villagers, Mara raised her skeletal hand and stroked the girl's head, running her clawed fingers through her long, auburn locks. She lifted the girl's chin and the young woman stared raptly into the mask's hollow eyes.

"What is thy name, my dear?" Mara asked softly.

"Veronika," the girl whispered.

"What a lovely child you are," Mara said. "You shall serve me well."

The girl closed her eyes and leaned her head back, offering her naked throat to the Dark Queen.

"No," Mara whispered. "Though your offering pleases me, I have other needs of you this night." Sweeping a sharp nail across her own arm, Mara opened a vein in her wrist. "The blood of the Fallen shall bind us," she said.

Mara raised her wounded wrist to Veronika's mouth and held it there, allowing the girl to partake of her dark gift. Veronika's body spasmed as she tasted the Dark Queen's immortal essence. The girl's eyes became pools of deep scarlet and her flesh paled to ghastly white. Mara lowered her wrist and stared affectionately at her creation, as if admiring a beautiful work of art.

The Dark Queen then turned to the young man, locking her black eyes upon him. "And what is thy name?" she asked.

"I am Kristoff," he whispered.

As she held him in her spellbinding gaze, Mara bestowed the same fate upon him, sharing her blood with him and delivering his soul unto darkness.

Moments later, Veronika and Kristoff stood rapt before their deathly mistress, hers in mind and spirit. The Dark Queen addressed her newfound subjects. "Serve me well, and you shall have blood enough to slake your crimson thirst," Mara's voice purred softly. "Tell me now, my hungry pets, do you know where the witch dwells?"

"Mother," Annika whispered.

With a start, Daria awoke and saw her young daughter standing beside her bed. Daria's heart raced as her eyes searched the confines of the hut. The hearthfire had dwindled to reddish embers, the soft glow lying over the figures of Serena and Lorand sleeping before the fire, each wrapped tightly in rough-hewn blankets. Their gentle breathing and the lulling chirp of crickets outside gave the impression of a peaceful night in the cold hour before dawn, yet her daughter's knowing eyes were wide with alarm.

"What is it, my darling?" Daria asked. "A bad dream?"

Annika nodded. "The Dark Queen sends her hungry children. They are coming."

Before Daria could respond, the crickets fell silent and the sharp snap of twigs echoed outside the hut. Lorand sat up suddenly, breathing heavily, his eyes fixed upon the door. The meager light from the hearth glinted off the silver dagger he held in his trembling hand.

Daria took her daughter's hand and pushed her under the bed. "Stay here, my love. Do not move."

The crude latch on the door rattled softly. Serena stirred and lifted her head from her blankets. Daria reached for her satchel of powders and potions but suddenly the door crashed inward in a shower of splinters. Serena, now fully awake, screamed, and Lorand leapt to his feet, brandishing the dagger. Daria squinted through the darkness to see two shadowed forms looming in the doorway. The figures stepped forward, crossing the threshold, hesitantly stepping into the dim firelight. Daria saw their pale, distorted faces and the scarlet glint in their eyes and knew they had fallen beneath the Dark Queen's spell.

Recognizing Veronica and Kristoff, Lorand called his friends' names. But they gave no response.

"They are lost," Daria whispered, "bewitched by Mara's sinister magic. They are now her servants."

Veronika remained near the doorway while Kristoff lurched into the room, his eyes filled with an animalistic ferocity. Lorand held his dagger out to fend Kristoff away, but Mara's minion lumbered steadily forward.

"Stay back," Lorand warned.

Veronika's eyes darted back and forth, madly searching the room until at last her gaze fell upon Daria and the amulet that hung from her necklace. The possessed woman stalked forward like a hungry wolf, backing Daria into a corner. Before Daria could react Veronika thrust a clawed hand outward and grasped the pendant. In the next instant, a fiery flash lit the room and Veronika erupted in a blaze of flames. She spun wildly, revealing a burning arrow piercing her back. Outside the shattered doorway of the hut, Falon stood with his bow.

Veronika shrieked and flailed, her hair and dress engulfed in flame. She struggled to pull the arrow from her back, but she could not reach it, her body twisting in a grotesque dance of flame and shadow that spun madly across the room. Her face blistered and contorted in fury as she turned to confront her attacker. She bared her fangs at Falon and before he could ready a second arrow, Veronika leapt toward him like a pouncing demon. The huntsman grabbed his axe from his belt and in one deft swing, cleaved the girl's head from her body. Blood spurted from Veronika's gaping neck, spraying the room like a grisly fountain. Her headless body dropped to its knees then toppled to the floor in flames. Her arms and legs trembled and twitched with the last vestiges of life as her severed head looked on.

Kristoff, his eyes glistening with beastly rage, snarled and snapped his jaws at Lorand, who held him at bay with the silver dagger. As the monstrous fiend focused on his prey, Falon lunged toward him from behind, his axe raised overhead. But before the huntsman could land the blow, Kristoff spun swiftly, catching Falon's arm in one hand and seizing him by the throat with the other. Falon fought to free himself but the creature's unearthly strength was overwhelming. As Kristoff's stranglehold tightened, Lorand leapt into the fray, plunging his silver blade deep into the ghoul's back. Lorand wrenched his dagger free and readied to strike again, but Kristoff whirled round wildly, throwing Falon across the room, sending him crashing on top of Lorand.

Before Lorand could rise to his feet, Kristoff sprang over him and grabbed hold of Serena. The girl screamed and struggled, but could not escape the creature's grasp. Kristoff swept her up in his arms, tossing her over his shoulder as if she weighed nothing. Lorand staggered toward them, but he could only watch helplessly as the fiend leapt out the door, stealing away into the shadows with Serena. The girl's wail of terror faded into the night as she was spirited deep into the forest.

Falon sat up dazed, and Lorand put a hand on his shoulder. "Remain here," Lorand said. "Watch over them." He glanced at Daria, who clutched her daughter tightly, covering her eyes to prevent her from seeing the horror that had invaded their home. Lorand stuck the dagger in his belt, and turned toward the gaping doorway, staring out into the gloom-shrouded woodlands.

"Wait!" Daria screamed. But her cry went unheeded. Lorand charged from the hut and sprinted after Serena, disappearing into the black of night.

The forest was a maelstrom of darkness and obstacles. Gnarled tree branches full of thorns tore at Lorand's clothes and unseen roots sent him tumbling to the ground more than once. He would have been lost in the maze of tree and shadow, but

Serena's cries guided him through the dark.

The forest path wound upward toward the Tower, and several times Lorand caught sight of Kristoff ahead of him, dragging Serena along with him, carrying her at some points when the terrain grew too rough. Soon the trees thinned and the ground grew rockier, and then the gate ruins loomed ahead. Stumbling and gasping, Lorand willed himself to run faster, closing the distance between himself and Kristoff. As he crossed a small clearing, Kristoff stopped and turned to face his pursuer, tossing Serena to the ground.

Lorand lunged toward the creature, thrusting his dagger forward, but Kristoff reacted with inhuman speed, swatting the silver blade from Lorand's hand, sending it off into the shadows. He took Lorand by the throat and lifted him into the air, throwing him back against an upthrust boulder. The ghoulish creature leapt on top of his victim, hissing and baring his fangs like a rabid wolf. Kristoff held his hand high then swept it swiftly downward, slicing his claws through Lorand's shirt, drawing thin lines of blood across his flesh.

"No!" A shrill voice split the night.

As the word echoed throughout the forest, Kristoff was pulled away by some unseen force and hurled across the clearing where he crashed against the gate ruins.

Mara drifted from the shadows, saying, "He is mine!"

Kristoff rose to his feet, glaring defiantly at Mara. "You promised me blood, and I shall have it," he growled, his voice low and guttural.

Mara raised her hand and Kristoff clutched his throat, then rose up into the air to hover above the ground. Mara gestured again, beckoning him forth, and he floated toward her.

Kristoff tried to scream, but Mara's invisible grasp choked his voice. His head and arms stretched backward, as if bound by unseen shackles. He struggled like a fly caught in a spider's web, but he was unable to break free of Mara's spell.

"I have no need for disobedient pets," the Dark Queen said.

Kristoff hung suspended in the air before Mara, his eyes gazing in horror upon the eerie mask that stared coldly back.

"But your blood shall serve me well," she whispered. The Dark Queen tore the mask from her face and cast it aside. Her black eyes glistened in the moonlight as she lowered her mouth to Kristoff's throat. Mara sunk her sharp fangs into Kristoff's neck, quenching her blasphemous thirst upon his blood. The ebon smoke that encompassed the demon queen rose to consume Kristoff and the two stood entwined in churning shadows as Mara drank his life. Kristoff's flesh shriveled and his body collapsed until all that was left of him was a withered skeletal form. The Dark Queen raised her head and the drained husk of Kristoff's body fell to the ground at her feet.

Mara felt an energy coursing through her with an intensity she had not known for many generations. She gazed down at her hands, which were now white and smooth like those of a porcelain doll. She leaned her head far back to bask in the moonlight and laughed, then turned toward Lorand. Mara's face, now restored to its legendary, hypnotic beauty, held the boy rapt. Lorand forced himself to look away to keep from falling victim to her bewitching gaze.

The Dark Queen drifted toward Serena, who cowered by the gate ruins. "Such a pretty girl," Mara purred. "How sweet you must taste."

Lorand stepped into the queen's path, shielding Serena with his battered body. "Leave her," he shouted. "Take me!"

Mara laughed as she grabbed hold of the tattered remains of Lorand's shirt, pulling him to her. She locked her black eyes upon him and Lorand became lost in her mesmerizing stare, unable to move.

The cry of ravens broke the surrounding silence, alerting Mara to another presence nearby. A moment later, the Tower Lord's gaunt face emerged from the shadows of the forest.

"Let him go," Brom demanded, stepping forth into the clearing.

Mara moved behind Lorand, her arms wrapping around him in a sultry embrace, her clawed fingers clutching the boy's jaw. "You have felt my immortal power, yet you still dare stand against me? What horrors must you witness before you learn your place? How much blood must be spilled?"

The Tower Lord remained silent, his unblinking gaze fixed upon the beautiful, unearthly creature that held his son.

"We each strive to leave a legacy, Lord Brom," Mara said, her fingers sliding down around Lorand's young neck. "Would you see me put an end to yours, here and now?"

Brom's eyes filled with seething fury. "Harm him and you shall know my wrath. This I swear. No magic shall protect you."

Mara's grip tightened around Lorand's throat. Her sharp nails bit into the boy's flesh, causing a small trickle of blood to run down his neck to his chest. "Listen well," Mara said. "The witch possesses a trinket I desire—an amulet that once belonged to my mother. Bring it to me before the next sun rises, or the boy shall die."

Brom took a step forward.

Mara's eyes narrowed like a wolf smelling blood. "Dare not defy me, or I shall claim all you hold dear. This *I* swear."

Serena turned to Brom, her face full of terror and pleading, but as she was about to move toward him, Mara's hand gently held her in place by the shoulder. "Come, child," Mara said.

With Lorand still in her clutches, Mara retreated back into the shadows, Serena reluctantly following. The trio ascended the castle steps into the Tower and the doors closed behind them. Brom strode up the stone steps but paused halfway, contemplating the choices before him. Though the blood in the amulet could destroy Mara forever, it came at far too high a cost.

He stared up at the faint stars in the heavens, as if some answer lay there. But he already knew what must be done. He gazed down the slope toward Vasaria in the dawning light. Ravens perched on branches throughout the forest, and Brom knew that Mara watched through their eyes. Though he could now venture forth beneath the sun's light, Brom dared not test the limits of his newfound powers, nor allow Mara to know of them. Only one course of action would allow him to save his son. When the night returned, he would set forth to the village to do the Dark Queen's bidding.

Slaves to Darkness

JOSEPH VARGO

A thunderous echo resounded throughout the entrance hall as the Tower doors slammed shut, sealing Lorand and Serena inside the ancient citadel of darkness. A numbing cold encompassed them—a bitter chill born of the Dark Queen's vile sorcery. The icy sensation slowly crept over their bodies, constricting around them like the coils of a serpent. Mara loomed in the shadows before them, her spellbinding gaze fixed upon her young victims, holding them captive against their own wills. Their minds screamed to flee, to somehow escape the grim fortress and its resurrected monarch, but their bodies were frozen in place. Lorand and Serena stood entranced—aware, yet unable to move, as if trapped in a terrible nightmare. The accursed keep was now their prison.

The faint glow of dawn filtered down from windows high above, only to be smothered by the castle's consuming darkness. Rows of sentinel gargoyles on the ledges above watched in lifeless silence as Mara crossed the hall, heedlessly treading upon the crimson sigil emblazoned on the floor.

Mara's black eyes glistened like jewels in the murky gloom. "Come," she said, commanding her captives to follow her as she ascended the staircase that twisted upward around the hall.

Though their minds struggled to resist Mara's summons, Lorand and Serena ambled helplessly forth, bewitched by their master's call. The Dark Queen seemed to hover upon the air as she drifted up the staircase. Her ebon shroud flowed behind her like a train of shadows and black smoke billowed in her wake. As she reached the balcony landing, Mara veered toward the archway that marked the threshold of the grand hall. Her spellbound prisoners followed close behind, unable to stray from their course, as if tethered with unseen leashes.

The Dark Queen entered the hall, leading Lorand and Serena past rows of tall columns toward the dais that supported her throne. The surrounding shadows seemed to stir and writhe, as if hungry spirits were looming restlessly in the darkness. The Tower's sinister aura was overwhelming. With each step, Mara's young prisoners felt their spirits sinking further into the depths of despair.

Mara drifted past the black throne and stopped before a relief of twin dragons carved into the dark stone of the wall behind the dais. The queen's eyes washed over the image, studying every part of the design intently. Her clawed fingers swept the dust from the engraving, coming to rest upon a shield carved into the stone between the dragons. Mara pressed the sculpted crest and it receded into the wall. With a grinding sound, the chiseled panel split in two, opening to reveal a secret passageway.

Mara proceeded into the passage and down a narrow staircase, leading her prisoners into the hidden recesses of her domain. Lorand and Serena staggered along the twisting stairwell that descended into the castle's forgotten depths until at last they emerged in a dim chamber far beneath the keep. The air was damp and thick with the smell of mildew and decay. Heavy, rusted chains hung from the stone walls and sconces held long-dead torches between broad columns. Mara waved her hand through the air before her and the torches around the room burst into flames.

The flickering light bathed the dim chamber in an auburn glow, allowing Mara's captives to see their surroundings clearly. Skeletal remains littered the floor, their gaping mouths frozen in screams of anguish. Lorand and Serena gazed in horror upon the final resting place of those who dared stand against the Dark Queen during her reign.

Mara stepped to the edge of a circular pit that dominated the center of the room. She picked up a jawless skull and stared into its hollow eyes, seemingly lost in morbid reminiscence. Her black nails caressed the top of the death's head tenderly as her gaze returned to her captives. "If the Tower Lord does not do as I have commanded, this shall be your final resting place." The queen's voice sent ghostly echoes around the chamber. "Your screams shall go unheard in the darkness. The rats shall feast upon your flesh and your spirits shall remain forever trapped within these walls, doomed to wander amongst the Tower's shadows for all time." She dug her nails into the skull, leaving jagged claw marks across the bone. "There is no hope of escape from this place." Mara cast the scarred skull into the pit and it disappeared into the darkness. The dull splash that resounded from the well was followed by the hissing of serpents.

The Dark Queen turned and drifted back up the stairs, and the stone doors slammed shut behind her. As the crashing sound reverberated through the dungeon, Mara's spell subsided and Lorand and Serena regained their own wills. Their eyes searched the dismal chamber, desperately seeking a means of escape from their nightmarish dilemma, but there was none to be found. Skittering sounds echoed around them as rats scurried along the bones and skulls of the Dark Queen's forgotten prisoners. Lorand stepped cautiously to the edge of the pit and stared down into the gaping well. The torchlight strained to reach the shaft's murky depths where thick, serpentine forms slithered between mossy stones. Slowly and quietly, Lorand backed away from the edge and returned to Serena's side.

"Are you all right?" Lorand's words formed a mist upon the frigid air.

Serena nodded, staring worriedly at Lorand. "'Tis you who are injured," she said, noticing blood on his tattered shirt.

Lorand lifted the torn garment, revealing four long gashes across his abdomen. Wiping the blood away, he said, "The Queen's minion left its mark upon me. 'Tis nothing."

Serena inspected Lorand's injuries. A stream of crimson slowly seeped from the wounds. "The cuts are not deep, but the bleeding must be stopped," she said. Serena quickly tore several strips from the bottom of her skirt to clean and dress Lorand's injuries. As she wrapped the cloth around his waist, her fingertips lingered upon Lorand's lean muscles.

Lorand took her hand in his. "Thank you," he whispered, staring deeply into her eyes for a brief moment before shyness made him look away.

Serena shook her head. "'Tis I who should thank you. Twice now you have rescued me from the grasp of darkness, risking your own life for mine." Her face brightened with the hint of a smile. "It seems you are destined to be my protector."

Lorand gently brushed her hair away from her cheek and said, "I shall allow no harm to befall you."

Serena leaned forward and pressed her lips against his. Lorand returned her innocent gesture with a passionate kiss. He pulled her close and Serena shut her eyes, feeling as if she were at last in the embrace of the dark angel of her dreams. As Lorand held her tight in his arms, he could feel her heart race in her chest and sensed with certainty that his love was returned. Her flesh was soft and warm, her lips moist and tender, yielding to his again and again as the two stood lost in their own desires.

Their moment of passion offered each other a small bit of consolation in the dread of their prison. "Lord Brom will come for us," Lorand whispered into her ear, "and when he does the queen shall suffer for her vile acts."

Lorand cleared the bones from a dry alcove and he and Serena sat, resting against the stone wall. They soon succumbed to weariness, drifting to sleep in each other's arms.

Hours later, the low, grinding sound of the stone doors sliding open announced the Dark Queen's return. Mara descended into the dungeon. The torchlight flickered above her, casting long, writhing shadows down upon her prisoners. As she drifted before them, Lorand and Serena rose slowly to their feet. They stood facing Mara but kept their eyes lowered, fearful of the queen's hypnotic gaze.

Mara's crimson lips formed a sinister smile, revealing her glistening fangs. "Night is almost upon us," she said. "Your fate shall soon be decided."

"We have done nothing wrong," Serena said, tears welling in her eyes.

The Dark Queen stared at her coldly. "Save your words and tears, child. Neither shall sway me to spare you. If the Tower Lord does not do as I have commanded, you shall die."

Angered by Mara's cruelty, Lorand could stay silent no longer. "Do no vestiges of humanity yet linger in your black heart?"

"Humanity," Mara hissed. "I shed my mortal life long ago, much like a serpent sheds its dying skin. Tis a decision I have never regretted. I have no desire to cling to any remnants of my former life. The world of man shall soon crumble and fall beneath the Black Dawn's shadow and a new dynasty shall rise from the ruins, heralding an era of blissful darkness."

At the risk of incurring Mara's wrath, Serena questioned her further. "Why do you harbor such disdain for all men? What spawned such bitter hatred?"

A look of disgust crossed Mara's face. "Men are wretched creatures—selfish and cruel. They are the lowest of animals. They are petty and lustful, coveting all they see, warring amongst themselves over squabbles of land. They inflict unspeakable atrocities upon one another, then beg their god's forgiveness for their terrible deeds. They offer only one thing of worth—the blood in their veins." Mara stroked Serena's head, inhaling her scent in the air. "And I shall taste yours soon enough."

Serena pulled away. "Brom shall let no harm come to us."

Mara's eyes narrowed. "The Tower Lord is no valiant savior. He and I share the same dark hungers. We are kindred spirits—the blood of the Fallen runs through his veins, as it does mine. We are as one."

Anger sparked in Lorand's eyes. "Lord Brom is nothing like you. He has done everything in his power to protect this realm from your dark forces. He has made great sacrifices for us all."

Mara's gaze shifted back toward the boy. "How can you speak in his defense? The Tower Lord is no noble champion. You know this better than anyone. He bestowed a terrible fate upon your mother, unleashing his desires and slaking his own savage thirsts upon her, heedless of the terrible consequences. He feasted upon her blood and delivered her into darkness, damning her soul for all eternity. Unable to bear the result of his own monstrous deeds, he took her life. She died at the end of his blade."

"Still your tongue!" Lorand barked.

"Is this true?" Serena asked, unable to believe Mara's words.

"Did you not know this?" The queen's voice was fraught with wicked delight. "The Tower Lord sired a son with a village wench, then murdered her without the slightest shred of remorse. Brom abandoned his child, leaving him in the care of strangers. But when the boy grew to discover the truth, he came to the Tower, seeking vengeance for his mother." Mara gestured toward Lorand and said, "Behold Lord Brom's bastard spawn."

Lorand fought to control his emotions. He turned toward Serena and said, "She twists the truth, weaving a tapestry of lies and deceit. I am the Tower Lord's son. I do not deny my heritage. But Brom loved my mother. He took her life to spare her soul from damnation only after she was possessed of this demon's vile spirit."

Mara cackled. "And yet I live, while she lies dead and forgotten."

"She has not been forgotten," Lorand said, "not by Lord Brom, nor I."

The Dark Queen looked around her, as if searching the surrounding shadows. "And where is Brom now? It seems he has abandoned you once again."

Though Mara's words stoked the fires of rage within Lorand, the boy remained silent.

Serena stepped forward to face Mara. "Brom shall come for us, and when he does, you shall meet your reckoning."

The queen laid a chilling hand upon Serena's shoulder, brushing the girl's hair away from her throat. The vein in Serena's neck pulsed with each beat of her heart.

Mara's fingers sprawled over the girl's skin and crept lightly across her flesh like the legs of a spider. "If the Tower Lord does not return with the amulet, I shall wrest your heart from your chest."

Serena stood unmoved by the queen's grisly threat.

"Does the thought of death not frighten you?" Mara asked. "Perhaps you welcome Azrael's embrace to free you from this cruel and dismal world. I assure you, I can bestow fates far worse—endless torments beyond your mind's imagining."

Serena maintained her unyielding facade. "Lord Brom has vowed to protect me and I trust his word. He shall let no harm befall us."

The queen's black eyes held Serena in their icy stare. "You are but a simple child," Mara said. "You know nothing of life. The innocence of youth is blinding to the true ways of the world. Do not rest your faith or trust in anyone, for no promise made by mortal lips has ever remained unbroken." The Dark Queen leaned closer and her voice grew softer. "Be loyal and loving only to thine own self. This world is harsh and without mercy. Like a wild beast, it preys upon the blood of the innocent. Its hungers are ravenous."

Serena's defiant glare softened to a look of pity. "How sad that you see no virtue or beauty in this world. Have you never known love?"

"Love," Mara cackled. "Never has there been a creature more dangerous. Its teeth are sharper than a wolf's, its claws stronger than an eagle's. Beware of love, child, for once you have fallen beneath its spell, there is no escape from its clutches. You shall serve its whims, becoming a slave to uncontrollable desires. Love is hurtful—fickle and cruel beyond reason. Never has a man been so vulnerable as when he exposes his own heart."

Serena lowered her head, averting her gaze from Mara. "When I was held captive in Castle Rankorr, I spent many years in painful seclusion, suffering the torments of solitude. Alone and shut away, I yearned for companionship. Each night I dreamt of a winged rescuer, a dark angel that came to carry me from my prison, taking me in his arms to soar through the heavens, together as one." Serena glanced toward Lorand, realizing how closely he resembled the angel of her vision. "This dream gave me hope, restoring my will to endure my life of isolation."

"Love and hope." Mara spat the words as if they were venom upon her lips. "Do not waste your life in the pursuit of such things. They are simple, childish notions, conjured by dreamers and fools." Turning toward the torchlight, Mara stared into the flickering flame and said, "Let me tell you a tale of love and hope."

The glow of the fire reflected in the queen's dark eyes.

"Long ago, there was a young maiden who lived a lonely life in a small village—much like the paltry hamlet that dwells beneath the Tower's shadow. One cool autumn day, a handsome gypsy found his way to her door. Upon first sight, the rogue and lass were drawn to one another by a force neither could control or resist. They soon found themselves caught in love's unrelenting grasp.

"Spellbound by love's sorcery, they spent one night in blissful togetherness. The girl promised to love the gypsy forever and he returned her vow, but in the morning, the spell was broken and he was gone. Each day thereafter, from dawn till dusk, the girl watched at her window, waiting for her beloved gypsy, but he never returned. Years passed, and the maiden yet waited, denying all other suitors as she declared, 'I have but one true love, and I am promised to him.'

"The years mounted, until at last her youth was gone and she was alone, left only with a faded memory and a broken promise. Forlorn and tormented by sadness, she climbed the highest cliff, intending to end her grief by throwing herself to the rocks below. But as she stood upon the mountain summit, she saw a gypsy caravan heading toward her village and hope took root in her heart once more. She rushed down from the cliff to meet the wagons, seeking her beloved gypsy. But as she desperately searched the faces of the men, his was not among them.

"Heartbroken, she traveled back to her home. As she walked along the stony path near the edge of a cliff, tears filled her eyes, causing her to step blindly and lose her footing. She tumbled down into a deep crevice, landing on the rocky ledges far below. She tried to climb back to the top of the cliff, but her aged and broken body no longer possessed the strength. As she lay helpless at the bottom of the forest ravine, a wolf came upon her. 'I shall soon die and you shall eat my flesh,' the old woman said, 'but, I beg of you, leave my heart, for it belongs to another.' With that, she drew her final breath and died out in the cold."

Mara turned to face Serena. "Do you now see the foolishness of such notions? Had the girl never fallen beneath love's cruel spell, she would have lived a life free of suffering. Had she not kept her hope alive, she would have thrown herself from the cliff and spared herself the pains of a broken heart and a torturous death."

Serena shook her head. "Surely you have never felt love, for if you had, you would know that a single day beneath its spell is worth a lifetime of hardship. The bonds of love are stronger than the hardest steel and the time we share with the ones we hold dear are the most cherished days of life. A world without love would be unbearable to me."

"Foolish, foolish child," Mara said, shaking her head in disgust. "If you live long enough to see the world as it truly is, you shall understand the folly of your words. But rest your faith in hope, and let us see if you live beyond this night." Mara's words echoed around the chamber as she left the dungeon once more.

As dusk settled upon the land, Brom stepped beyond the Tower doors. The surrounding woodlands were quiet and deathly still. Misty clouds stretched across the waning moon like restless ghosts wandering the night sky. The Tower Lord descended the castle steps and slowly made his way toward the forest path but stopped beside the gate ruins. Sensing a familiar presence nearby, he closed his eyes and waited. A moment later, he felt a tender caress on his cheek, as subtle and light as the evening breeze.

A soft voice whispered, "Ease your mind, my love. I am here with you."

Opening his eyes, Brom saw Rianna before him. He said nothing for a long moment as he gazed upon her visage. Her lily-white flesh held a soft, radiant glow. Her eyes stared longingly into his and her lips formed a melancholic smile. Her beauty never faded, even beyond death. She lifted her hand toward his face, but her spectral fingers passed through his flesh. Brom longed to hold her in his arms, but he was unable. They stood inches from one another, yet they existed in two different worlds.

Rianna looked toward the forest trail then returned her gaze to Brom. "You are troubled by the choice that lies before you—unsure of which path of action to pursue."

"I have made my decision." Brom stared off toward the village, glimpsing the distant flicker of torchlight between the trees. "What I do this night, I do for our son."

The spirit's eyes conveyed deep sorrow. "You cannot doom humanity for the sake of one soul, no matter how important he is to you... to us."

Brom hung his head. "He is all I have in this world. My legacy rests with him. I mean only to spare him death and damnation at Mara's hand. When he is safe, I shall deal with the Dark Queen."

"You dare risk the fate of mankind to spare him? I understand your grief and your desire to protect our son, but the Dark Queen poses a threat to all men. I beg of you, destroy this demon while you possess the power to do so."

"I know what must be done," Brom said gruffly. "Mara's

dark magic protects her from my sword. If she is to be slain, I must wield magic against her. If there is no other way to vanquish her and I am forced to choose between Lorand and the lot of mankind, then I shall do what I must for the sake of humanity. I shall not fail our son, nor you."

Rianna drifted back into the mist, saying, "I do not doubt you. Your heart is strong, my love."

"Tis eternally bound to yours, and yours alone," Brom said. "We shall soon be together once more."

"Yes," she whispered, "soon." For one brief moment, the sadness left Rianna's eyes, then she faded into the fog-shrouded night. Brom stood alone once again, reflecting upon the memory of his beloved. After a moment, the shrill caw of a raven roused him from his reverie. Peering deep into the black woods, Brom set out along the path to Vasaria.

The creatures of the woodlands remained silent as Brom traversed the forest trail. The surrounding trees appeared as sinister specters in the mist, their thorny limbs stretching outward, as if to ensnare travelers in their inhuman grasp. Roots, gnarled and tangled, covered the cobblestone path and vine-strangled branches loomed menacingly overhead. It was as though the Tower's curse had transformed the woodlands into a landscape of twisted, frightening forms that mimicked the ancient horrors buried deep in the earth below.

At the foot of the mountain, Brom came to the clearing of the standing stone. The moss that covered the ancient monolith had been cleared away, revealing the arcane inscription that had remained hidden for countless years. The runic symbols were etched deeply into the boulder, as if seared into the stone by some unearthly fire. The weathered monument was all that kept Mara from breaking free of the Tower and invading the world of men.

But Mara's powers had grown in her years of captivity.

Brom knew that it was only a matter of time before she would be able to entice and compel men to serve her once more. Soon she would command them to topple the stones that held her bound, dooming humanity to her unholy reign. The dread thought made Brom quicken his pace.

The path ended at the edge of the village where Daria's hut sat nestled in trees. Firelight and candles illuminated the windows with a soft amber glow, but the subtle stench of burnt flesh and the sight of the broken door told Brom that something was terribly wrong. As Brom approached Daria's door, a gust of wind rushed down on him and the sound of great wings drew his attention to the sky overhead where a dark angel descended from the night. A halo of blue surrounded its armor-clad form, casting a shimmering radiance upon the surrounding trees. The celestial creature alighted on the ground before Brom, stretching its raven-black wings wide, blocking Brom from his destination.

"Hail, Lord Brom." The angel's crystalline eyes shone with light as it spoke. The dark knight drew his sword and bowed his head toward the Tower Lord.

A glimmer of hope settled behind Brom's eyes as he gazed upon the blade in the angel's hand. "Have you come to lend your sword to my cause—to fight this evil alongside me?" Brom asked.

"I have come only to lend thee guidance—to ensure thou doest not stray from the righteous path. Thou doest stand at the threshold of good and evil. The forces of darkness vie for thy soul, tempting thee and testing thy resolve. Thou must take heed not to follow their call."

Anger welled in Brom's heart. "Mere days ago, when I begged you for help against this darkness, you refused and abandoned me, yet now you dare scold me on virtue and vice?"

"Must I remind thee what is at stake?" The angel's eyes fell upon the sword in Brom's belt. "This is no mere skirmish.

This battle shall decide the fate of humanity."

"I know full well what hangs in the balance," Brom said, his tone harsh and defiant, "for I alone must bear this burden. If you offer nothing other than empty words, stand aside."

"Heed my warning, Lord Brom." The angel's voice lowered to a foreboding growl. "Choose thy path carefully. If thou dost align thyself with the Dark Brood, or aid Mara in any way, thou shalt become a threat to all men. My brethren and I shall have no choice but to stand against thee."

Brom's brow furrowed in disgust. "I am no servant of Mara. I have come here of my own accord, on a mission most dire." Drawing the relic sword from his belt, Brom declared, "If you will not stand with me, then be gone."

The angel's luminous eyes held Brom in their gaze as they searched the depths of his thoughts. At last he said, "Do not falter in thy quest." With that, the winged warrior raised his ebon wings and soared upward into the darkened heavens, becoming one with the night.

Brom slid his sword back beneath his belt, chiding himself for his reckless outburst. In his anger, he had exiled himself from his god. He now was truly alone in his plight. Brom stepped toward the broken entrance to the witch's abode, the smell of smoke and death much heavier in the air. Daria and Adrian met him in the doorway, their faces somber and fearful.

"What has happened?" Brom asked.

Adrian's gaze sunk to the floor. "The Dark Queen sent her minions to plague us. The huntsman killed one of them, but the other creature stole away with Serena. Lorand chased after her, but neither has returned. We fear the worst."

Brom nodded solemnly. "Mara holds them in the Tower. For the moment they are safe, but they are her prisoners, held spellbound by her sorcery."

A look of dread swept across Daria's face. "The queen shall slay them, or worse. She shall turn them into her monstrous servants."

"I will allow no harm to come to them," Brom said. "Serena's father entrusted me to protect her, and I shall."

Adrian stared at Brom curiously and said, "A father's love for his children goes beyond his love of life itself. No sacrifice is too great for the sake of one's own child. Surely Lorand's father must feel the same."

Before Brom could respond, Daria said, "The boy's father is dead."

Adrian shook his head and smiled. "I am no fool, nor am I blind." He fixed his stare on Brom. "The resemblance between you and the boy is undeniable, as is the pride that fills your eyes when you look upon him. The truth is plain to see."

Daria averted her gaze from Adrian.

"There is no longer a need for secrecy," Brom said. "Mara has discovered Lorand's true heritage. She has taken him to ensure I will not act against her. She holds him in the Tower and threatens to claim his life."

"Why have you come here?" Daria asked, sensing Brom's discomfort.

"Mara demands the amulet, in exchange for Lorand."

Daria's eyes widened with fear. "We cannot allow it to fall into her hands. The blood within it is vital for the binding spell that can destroy the Dark Queen forever. We must use its power against her."

Brom's eyes remained locked on the amulet around the witch's neck. "I dare not risk Lorand's life. I cannot doom my son."

"Think of what you say," Daria pleaded. "If you give Mara what she desires, the consequences of your actions shall doom all of humanity."

"This is my decision," Brom said tersely. "Give me the amulet, or I shall take it."

Their eyes remained locked in unspoken conflict, neither side relenting.

"Wait!" Adrian said, raising his hands between them. Reaching into the pocket of his robe, the monk withdrew the parchment Brom had given him and began to read the prophecy aloud. *"In the time of great darkness, there shall come one, born of mortal flesh, but endowed with the blood of immortals, both creator and destroyer, destined to grant both life and death. Upon discovering the mysteries of the trinity and the chalice of eternal life, the destined one shall gain sublime wisdom, and bear judgment as to mankind's fate. For it is the Lord's supreme will that the Seraphim shall inhabit the Earth and hold dominion here till the end of days."*

The monk's eyes grew wide as he looked up from the page.

"What is it?" Brom asked.

Adrian hesitated, as if seized with emotion. "The prophecy," Adrian said, "its secrets unravel. Only now does its true message come to light. We were wrong to think it was an omen of doom. I believe it is a revelation of a glorious new age." He offered the parchment to Brom.

Brom took the scroll and studied it but seemed even more perplexed by the cryptic words.

"Do you not see it?" Adrian's voice trembled and rose with excitement. "It does not foretell the rise of the Dark Queen, as we had feared. It pertains to you, Lord Brom. You are the destined one. You were once mortal, but now you are immortal. You have sown life by fathering your son and sown death in your battle against the forces of darkness. You have ventured to the three towers and discovered the secrets hidden there, thus gaining the knowledge to fulfill your destiny. You now hold the key to the final secret—the chalice of eternal life.

This power is yours, and yours alone, to be administered by your decree. It is you who shall decide the fate of mankind."

"But what of the Seraphim?" Brom asked.

A hint of a smile touched Adrian's face. "The prophecy does not foretell of humanity being conquered or destroyed by the Seraphim. I believe it foretells mankind's evolution into a higher form of being, such as yourself, Lord Brom."

"How can this be?" Brom shook his head in disbelief. "Those of my kind are creatures of darkness, cursed by the blood in our veins."

Daria stepped forward, saying, "Twas not a curse, but a gift, corrupted by the Fallen Ones. Your blood is of divine origin. Aeons ago, the Watcher angels took mortals as mates. Their offspring possessed powerful magic. For this they were feared and shunned by humans. Blind to the true depths of their power, they abandoned their god, and in doing so, they condemned themselves to eternal darkness."

Adrian spoke again. "Without the holy sacraments, they were lost. They became primitive beasts, slaking their thirsts in the most animalistic way—upon the blood of humans. Each time they surrendered to their own dark desires, their power grew, but they also became more cruel and monstrous. They regressed to wicked, bloodthirsty creatures during their decadent reign on Earth.

"They were ultimately hunted like the ravenous beasts they had become. Those who were not slain survived to seek refuge in the shadows. They slumbered deep in the earth and became nocturnal creatures, and though they ruled the realms of darkness, they eventually became vulnerable to the rays of the sun. Its light became harsh and blinding to them and its warming caress scorched their flesh. Theirs is now the blood of the damned."

Daria rested a gentle hand on Brom's forearm, saying, "Had this gift of divine blood not been misused, there would be no monsters in the night, nor the horrors of mortal sin. Mankind would have ascended to a higher state."

"The Seraphim," Brom whispered.

"Yes," Daria said, her voice excited by the possibility of what might have been—and what still could be. "If this were the fate of humanity, there would be no need for war or killing. Humans would possess extraordinary strength and heightened senses. Their lives would be more constructive—dedicated to the pursuit of arts and knowledge. There would be no sickness or death and mortal lifetimes would span millennia. Mankind could exist in the most extreme climates without need of shelter. The Earth would be a paradise of wonders."

Daria glanced apologetically at Brother Adrian, then spoke again. "The sacraments are useless to mankind. They are hollow gestures, meaningless and ceremonial only. Man does not need to drink blood to survive. These rituals were meant for the Seraphim, to sustain them."

Adrian pondered her words for a moment, weighing their logic against the teachings of his faith. "Perhaps you are right," he said at last. "However, if evil forces were ever to corrupt this newfound power and keep it from humanity, they could enslave and rule them. Once this secret is revealed, our world shall surely change, but will it be a change for the better, or for the worse? Perhaps mankind is not yet ready for this divine gift."

Brom nodded. "There is much to contemplate. The risk weighs heavily against the gain."

Daria took Brom's hand in hers. "It seems the final decision rests with you, Lord Brom."

Adrian's eyes washed over the scroll once more. "Many philosophers and sages believe that man has been granted the freedom to choose his own fate, while others contend that all occurrences in life are the unavoidable result of divine will."

Brom stared at the monk. "And what do you believe?"

After a moment, Adrian said, "I believe all events have unfolded as they were meant to."

A wistful look filled Brom's eyes as he considered his friends' words.

Turning to the table, Adrian opened a leather sack and withdrew a bottle. "I have prepared more wine, sanctifying it for communion. You will need all your strength to face Mara again."

"Very well," Brom said.

Adrian poured the blessed wine into a simple wooden goblet and gave a short benediction. Brom raised the cup to his lips and drank deeply. Once again, his body and spirit felt revitalized.

Adrian laid his hand on Brom's shoulder and said, "We shall return with you, to help you stand against the Dark Queen."

"No," Brom said quietly. "Mara will sense your presence. I must face her alone."

The Tower Lord turned to Daria and once more, his eyes falling upon the pendant that hung around her neck. "I must take the amulet," he said, slowly stepping toward her. Brom gazed deep into Daria's eyes, penetrating her mind with his thoughts. Entranced by his spell, Daria removed the pendant necklace, handing it to Brom.

The Tower Lord stared at the blood-red amulet for a long moment, considering the unholy power it held. "Now," he said, returning his gaze to the witch, "tell me of the binding spell," Brom's voice lowered to a whisper, "the spell that shall forever end the Dark Queen's reign."

I have walked in the shadows amidst souls lost and tormented, only to emerge from the abysmal depths stronger and wiser for the final battle. Darkness is no longer my master, for the beast that resides in my heart is in my thrall.

Crown of Shadows

JOSEPH VARGO

The distant rumble of thunder sounded like the roar of an angry god echoing through the darkened heavens. As the storm approached, Brom stood upon the castle ramparts, looking out over the forest and the village beyond. A lifetime of memories flooded his mind as he recalled the faces of friends and loved ones lost to the darkness that dwelled within the ancient keep. Since fate had first brought Brom to Vasaria many years ago, it had become his home. The villagers rested their faith in him, keeping him in their thoughts and prayers, and he in turn watched over them as Lord of the Tower and guardian of the realm.

Far below, a spectral mist had settled upon the woodlands, shrouding the forest like a gossamer veil. The cool autumn breeze swept through Brom's hair and the caw of ravens rose upon the wind. He could smell the smoke of hearthfires burning in Vasaria. He closed his eyes and imagined himself there, warm and safe in the confines of a simple dwelling. But the vision quickly faded. Brom opened his eyes once more and looked around him, seeing the bleak, weathered stonework of the Dark Tower. Its black spires rose high above him, encompassing him, as if clutching him in their menacing grasp.

The Tower had defied the elements for centuries,

cresting the mountaintop like a sinister monument from a long-forgotten era. The ominous castle looked exactly as it had when Brom first laid eyes upon it so many years ago, yet much had changed during his reign as Tower Lord. He had discovered the secrets of the keep and its ancient curse, defended the fortress from invaders and battled against the dark forces trapped within its walls. But his vigil had come to its end. One way or another, this would be his final day in the Tower.

In his hand, he held the vial of Endora's blood, the mystic amulet that could destroy his immortal nemesis. For a moment Brom thought to cast it down upon the cliffs below, or to use it against Mara to bring an end to her reign. But wielding the talisman's power came at too high a price—a price he was unwilling to pay. He dared not risk the life of his only son. Brom had retrieved the grisly relic to surrender it to the Dark Queen.

The Tower Lord descended the staircase that twisted down toward the grand hall. He could sense Mara's malevolent spirit somewhere in the shadows below. The feeling grew stronger with each step he took and Brom followed it like a beacon, deeper and further into the heart of the keep.

As he emerged from the winding stair onto the balcony overlooking the entrance hall, a new sensation crept over him, alerting him to another presence nearby. Brom scanned the gargoyles that surrounded the shadowed heights of the chamber. The stone guardians kept their silent vigil over the hall below, their unblinking eyes staring down toward the Tower doors and the crimson sigil that stained the floor like a spatter of blood. The grim sculptures had remained unchanged for centuries, undisturbed by the ravages of time or by any of the things that transpired beneath their watchful gazes. But now something was different. A large gargoyle, seemingly hewn from polished obsidian, crouched in an arched alcove that had once been vacant. As Brom stared at the gargoyle, the monster raised its head, its eyes burning with a scarlet glow.

"Be gone, demon," Brom said, drawing his sword, "lest I send you back to Hell."

A low, mocking laughter echoed round the hall. The creature leapt from its perch, landing heavily on the balcony to tower over Brom. The stone monstrosity spread wide its ebon wings, blocking Brom's path. Its countenance was fierce and fiendish, combining the features of a man with those of a savage animal. Brom recognized the unholy beast from a past encounter—it was the same creature that had come to him in the graveyard long ago. Brom felt the demon penetrating his thoughts, but before he could raise his sword, the creature uttered an incantation, rendering Brom spellbound. The Tower Lord stood frozen in place beneath the demon's molten gaze.

"Dare not anger me, infidel," the creature growled. "You have survived here thus far only because you have been under the watch of the sentinels of the summit, the warrior angels that guard this place. But they are no longer here to protect you. In your arrogance, you have released them from their vows. You now stand alone amidst our legions, abandoned by your god and his celestial knights."

Brom's eyes darted around the walls. The gargoyles that lined the niches and ledges circling the hall began to stir from their roosts, as if waking from a long-dormant state. Their eyes burned like smoldering coals and dark smoke spewed forth from their gaping mouths.

"Yes," Brom said, finding that he was still able to

speak. "I now stand before you, alone and forsaken, but soon you shall face armies of foes. You and your lot are the enemies of all humanity. If you wage war upon mankind, they shall unite to rise against you. They shall not allow you to destroy their world."

"This world is ours!" the demon roared. "Humanity poses no threat to us—they are but lowly animals. Those who do not serve us shall die. Should mankind foolishly rise against us or dare to engage us in war, they shall know our wrath. We shall vanquish their armies and topple their empires. We shall feast upon their blood and the blood of their children. The price of defiance shall be annihilation." The creature gestured his monstrous hand down toward the entrance hall, saying, "Behold the destiny of man."

Brom stared at the blood-red icon that dominated the floor below and watched as cracks splintered outward from the center. The crimson sigil burned bright and gaped wide, forming a fiery crevice that consumed everything around it. The floor fell away until all that was left was a molten pit. With a deafening thunder, the castle walls began to crumble and break apart. The ancient stones toppled down into the blazing chasm until nothing remained of the surrounding Tower.

Brom stood horrified and awestruck, gazing out over a burning landscape of scorched earth. Dark, churning clouds smothered the skies, blotting out the sun and keeping all light from reaching the world below. Skeletal remains of men and women lay in heaps among the ashes and smoldering ruins of forests and towns. The devastation seemed without end. The lifeless wasteland stretched as far as the eye could see. It was as if the fires of Hell had been unleashed upon the world, setting the earth ablaze. Brom looked toward the darkened heavens, searching for some glimmer of light, but there was none to be found.

"The Black Dawn has risen," a soft voice said.

Brom turned to see Mara standing beside him where the demon had been mere moments ago. Her black hair and gown shimmered like raven's feathers as they flowed in the wind behind her. A crown of ebon spikes crested her head like devilish horns and bat-like wings unfurled from her back, stretching outward into the night. Brom tried to retreat from the sinister apparition, but he felt the crushing weight of the Dark Queen's power holding him in thrall.

"What horrors have you wrought?" Brom's voice was choked with anger and sorrow. "The Earth lies in ruin."

"We shall forge a new world together," Mara said, "a realm of nocturnal bliss. Our reign shall have no limits."

"Our reign?" Brom's mind struggled to grasp the meaning of her words.

"Yes." Mara smiled, revealing sharp, wolfish fangs. "With you at my side, nothing shall stand against us." Her bone-white hand reached toward Brom and stroked his face tenderly. "We shall rule the Earth as gods. You need only surrender to me, heart and soul."

Brom stood transfixed, his eyes locked upon Mara. His mind fought to break free of her bewitching spell, but her magic was too strong. He focused his thoughts against her and forced himself to utter a single word. "No," he whispered.

Mara moved closer, her soulless, black eyes holding Brom's gaze. "You have witnessed my power, and yet you resist your own destined fate? Surrender," she said, and then again softer, "surrender."

Lost in her hypnotic gaze, Brom felt his willpower slipping. Mara leaned nearer until her face was inches from

Brom's own. He turned his head away, staring down into the fiery chasm below. His strength faded and his legs began to buckle beneath him. He struggled to maintain his balance as he teetered on the brink of the infernal abyss.

Suddenly, the clang of steel rang out. The sound reverberated in Brom's head like the tolling of a bell, waking him from his spellbound state. The hellish landscape vanished before his eyes and he stood upon the Tower balcony once more, surrounded by the keep's ancient walls. His sword lay at his feet on the staircase landing. It had slipped from his hand and the shrill sound of steel against stone had roused him from his trance, rescuing him from the cruel grasp of darkness.

Brom gazed around the chamber but found no trace of Mara or the monstrous creature. The gargoyles remained on their perches, staring lifelessly downward toward the dusty floor below. Brom wondered if madness had seized his mind. Were the demons he saw real or merely imagined? His hand trembled as he picked up his sword and slid it back beneath his belt. The nightmarish scene of the earth and humanity ravaged beneath the black dawn still lingered in his mind. The terrible vision only served to strengthen his resolve. His spirit rekindled, Brom resumed his mission and proceeded down the staircase toward the grand hall.

The castle yet held remnants of its former glory, the bygone era before Mara's reign. The tarnished crests of forgotten kings adorned the walls, their meanings lost in time. Faded tapestries of lions, gryphons, falcons and wolves hung in tattered shreds along the corridor leading to the grand hall. The once-lavish trappings had long ago been claimed by cobwebs, dust and decay. At last he came to the twin oaken doors leading to Mara's throne room. Brom sensed the Dark Queen's vile spirit nearby, felt her icy chill upon his flesh and heard her voice echoing in his head, beckoning him forth like a siren's song. She had summoned him here. He knew his fate awaited him in the room beyond.

Brom opened the heavy doors and entered the grand hall. At the far end of the chamber, Mara sat in her ebon throne. A brazier of coals burned beside her, casting an infernal red glow upon her pale flesh. On the opposite side of the dais, Lorand and Serena stood silent and still, bewitched by the queen's vile sorcery.

Brom stepped steadily forward, his eyes locked on Mara. Thunder raged outside the keep, accompanied by violent strikes of lightning. The flashing bursts illuminated the hall for brief intervals, revealing ominous shapes lurking in the furthest recesses of the chamber. A low, mournful howl filled the hall, like the wail of the restless dead. As Brom approached the dais, three monstrous forms rose from the shadows before him, halting him in his tracks. They appeared as hulking silhouettes, more bestial than human, with wings, tails and horned heads. Their arms stretched low, nearly touching the ground, their spidery fingers ending in claws long as daggers. The demonic sentinels stood blocking Brom's path, protecting their queen from her mortal enemy.

"The slumbering darkness awakens," Mara's voice sent echoes through the chamber. "Hell's children have risen from the depths." The queen gestured her hand toward the creatures and they hearkened to her silent command, receding back into the shadows. She returned her gaze to Brom and said, "Come forth."

Brom ascended the dais to stand before Mara. He could feel her thoughts probing his mind, but he resisted her with all his will. Even so, her dark allure was undeniable. Her flawless face seemed as though it had been sculpted from smooth, white marble and her sheer black gown clung to her supple form like a veil of shadows. The ebon crown upon her head designated her as royalty, but there was no air of virtue or modesty about her.

"Do you have it?" Mara's eyes glistened with anticipation.

"I have done as you commanded." Brom's voice was a husky whisper.

Mara rose and held out her hand. Brom slowly withdrew the amulet from a pocket of his cloak. He held it over Mara's waiting grasp, but kept the chain firmly clenched in his fist. He looked toward Lorand and Serena, but they remained oblivious to the events unfolding around them. They stood motionless, like living statues staring vacantly out into the gloom-shrouded void while Mara's nightmarish minions loomed menacingly in the darkness behind them.

Mara glanced toward her young prisoners, then returned her attention to the Tower Lord. "They are unharmed," she said. "If you wish them to remain so, do not test my patience."

Brom hesitated a moment longer until at last he let the chain slip through his fingers. The crimson vial dropped into Mara's palm and her hand clasped shut around it like the jaws of a hungry wolf. Keeping her eyes on Brom, Mara opened the vial and swirled it in the air beneath her porcelain face, inhaling the aroma of the blood within as if it were a fine wine. A sinister smile formed upon her lips as she recognized the scent of her own bloodline. "You have done well, Lord Brom."

"Release them," the Tower Lord growled.

Heedless of Brom's demand, the Dark Queen stepped to the burning brazier beside the throne and poured the vial's contents onto the blazing coals. As the blood sizzled, Mara crushed the amulet in her hand and tossed the broken shards into the fire, obliterating all traces of the deadly talisman. "The last vestige of my mortality," she mused. "Gone forever."

"Release them," Brom said once more, his eyes glaring fiercely.

Mara cast her gaze upon her spellbound captives and whispered a word in an unknown tongue.

Lorand and Serena roused from their entranced state, awareness returning to their eyes. They staggered toward Brom, but the Tower Lord raised his hand to stop them.

"Go," Brom said.

Lorand turned to speak.

"Go, now!" Brom commanded, "and never return here."

Tears welled in Serena's eyes as she passed Brom. She moved away reluctantly, her fingers gently brushing his cloak as if in farewell.

Without a word, Lorand and Serena left the hall. The sound of their footsteps faded in the distance and then the slam of the Tower door echoed through the keep.

Brom stood before Mara in silence.

"At last we are alone," Mara said, reclining seductively in her throne. "Have you nothing to say?"

Brom's head hung low, his eyes fixed upon the floor at Mara's feet. "I recognize your power," he said quietly. "Tis a force far greater than any man or creature I have encountered. I have resisted your will, making it my sworn duty to destroy you and your lot, thinking this was the Lord's destined plan for me. But now my path seems unclear. Perhaps my true destiny lies with you." Brom dropped to one knee, saying, "I yield before you. Spare Vasaria and I shall join you."

Mara's eyes narrowed. "I rest my faith in deeds, not hollow words. Why would I trust you?"

Brom kept his head lowered. "I have spent my life fighting forces I cannot withstand. I have lost all that was ever dear to me. I have stood faithful guard over this abysmal keep, only to be repaid with a lifetime of sorrow and pain. My god has abandoned me. His sentinel angels are gone and I cannot defeat you alone." Brom slowly slid the relic sword from his belt. "I surrender my sword to you." Brom laid the blade across his hands and offered the sacred weapon to Mara.

Mara stepped cautiously toward him. She took the sword and raised it to study the blade, seemingly entranced by the instrument that had once ended her life. As the crackle of thunder shook the chamber, Mara turned and thrust the sword into the dais beside the throne, driving the blade deep into the black stone, the steel emitting a piercing, metallic screech. Turning back toward Brom, Mara drew closer. Her sheer silken gown slithered over her curves with each step. She stood before Brom and looked down upon him, holding his gaze with her soulless, obsidian eyes.

This was not Dravek that knelt before her, offering himself unto her. Brom was no groveling servant who would obey her whims without question. He was a warrior with a wild, unbroken spirit, the heart of a lion and the strength of a dragon. The thought of commanding him, of feeling his desires and passions, roused a long-dead fire deep within her.

"Arise," Mara commanded.

Brom rose to his feet. As Mara's eyes washed over his chiseled features, his black mane, his broad shoulders and full chest, she felt lusts and urges unknown to her. She longed to satisfy her carnal hungers.

"Take me," Mara's voice echoed in Brom's mind.

Brom took her in his arms. He pulled her toward him and drew her face near his. Mara's lips were moist with desire. She slid her tongue across her fangs, and Brom felt her claws digging into the flesh of his chest, directly over his heart.

"Do not think you can deceive me," Mara whispered. "I know the true fire that burns within your heart. You yet yearn for your dead love."

Brom's eyes held a distant glaze, as if he were seeing some fragile memory in his mind's eye. "She is a spirit, while you are flesh and blood. My desires are those of a living man, not a phantom."

Mara smiled, her fangs glistening like ivory daggers. "I can show you a realm of dark wonders, but first you must prove your allegiance to me." She removed her hand from Brom's chest and slid her fingers up his neck, caressing his face like the touch of a spider.

Brom made no attempt to turn away. "I have much to offer you, my queen. I have discovered many of the Tower's secrets—a treasury of forgotten knowledge that has been buried in time. All I ask is that you spare the people of Vasaria. Do this and I shall reveal all I know."

"And what ancient mysteries have you uncovered? What wisdom have you gleaned that I do not already possess?"

"The lost knowledge of our true origins—above all, a ritual that will allow us to survive without feeding upon the blood of mortals."

Mara's black eyes grew wider. "Tell me more."

"Swear to me that no harm shall befall the village."

"Very well," Mara said. "I shall grant your wish. The villagers shall be safe for as long as you please me. But should you dare deceive me in any way, Vasaria shall suffer the full measure of my wrath."

Brom nodded. He reached into a satchel beneath his cloak and withdrew a chalice and bottle. He poured the bottle's contents into the goblet. "Sanctified wine, transformed by divine rite becomes more potent than the sweetest blood."

"And what is the cost of such a spell?" Mara's voice held a tone of mistrust.

"All that is required is a vow of faith and a sincere act of contrition. Tis a small price for absolution."

Mara's eyes narrowed. "I shall not beg for my soul."

"The Lord requires repentance in return for His divine forgiveness."

"Never," she whispered.

"I offer you salvation," the Tower Lord said, holding forth the chalice.

"You offer nothing I desire. I will serve as slave to no man or god. Here in the earthly realm I shall reign supreme."

A look of dismay swept over Brom's face. "How can you refuse redemption? All you need do is renounce the transgressions of your past before you accept this gift, and you shall be granted life anew."

Mara took the goblet from Brom's hand. "I have no regrets for the path I have followed," she said. "My spirit is older than mankind and I shall exist far beyond their days on earth. I need no divine pity or magic to thrive eternal. I have no desire to live a life of humbling servitude." Mara's voice rose with anger. "I am no simple lamb among humanity's mindless flock. I am a ravaging wolf among sheep." Mara slowly overturned the chalice, spilling its contents onto the floor. "Mine is no small, scavenged slice of quarry—I take all I desire. I am the Queen of all darkness—the master of this realm." She let the chalice drop from her hand and it clattered down the steps of the dais.

Brom shook his head and slowly backed away. "The crown you wear is but a crown of shadows, for your power is naught beneath the light of day."

Mara's black eyes simmered with rage. "You seal your fate with your insolence." She drifted steadily toward him, black smoke churning beneath her. "You have sealed the fate of Vasaria as well. Those who dwell there shall be the first to know my wrath. My slumbering brood awakens and the sentinel angels are no longer here to protect the boundaries of old. Once the standing stones are toppled, my legions shall spread across the land like a ravaging tide. Nothing shall stand against us. Armies shall perish and kingdoms shall fall. The human plague nears its end."

Brom retreated further and withdrew a leather pouch from beneath his cloak. He opened the pouch and poured its contents onto the floor at arm's length, surrounding himself in a circle of fine gray powder. He raised his hand and a small sphere of fire hovered above his fingertips. "I have given you a chance to redeem yourself, but you have chosen to wallow in hatred and vice. I cannot allow you to inflict your horrors upon mankind." Brom lowered his arm, casting the mystical flame to the ground and setting the circle ablaze.

The Dark Queen descended the steps, but stopped at the threshold of the ring of fire. "You seek safe haven through sorcery?" Mara's wicked laughter hissed through the hall. "Your pitiful spells are useless against me," she said. "My powers have grown. My magic is now far stronger than that of your witch." Mara drew closer, smiling menacingly as she stepped inside the circle of flames, unthwarted by the mystic barrier. "Your circle of protection offers no sanctuary. You cannot escape me."

The fires of wickedness burned behind Mara's gaze.

The Dark Queen was no mere demon, she was the embodiment of evil, an immortal vessel that held the sins of all men, a raging tempest on the verge of erupting with the fury of a thousand Hells. The earth would surely wither and die beneath her merciless reign.

Brom raised his head, his eyes reflecting the firelight that burned around him. "The circle was not meant to keep you away," he said coldly, "twas meant to contain you within."

Tendrils of red smoke rose from the fire, enveloping Mara, twisting upward across her body, constricting around her like slithering vipers. She tried to retreat beyond the flaming barrier, but Brom held her in place.

"Tis your fate that is sealed," Brom whispered. His eyes held a cold, piercing gaze. "You laid waste to the remnants of your mother's blood, thinking you had destroyed all vestiges of your mortal ancestry. But your father's bones held the same power."

Mara peered deep into Brom's eyes, seeing his thoughts. She beheld a vision of the monstrous gargoyle upon the balcony pedestal. She gazed upon the grim statue in horror. The gargoyle's hands were empty. The king's skull was no longer in its grasp.

Brom pulled her closer, saying, "Inside this circle you are but a powerless mortal. The pain you feel is age taking hold. The centuries shall take their toll as time claims the lost years. Your reign has come to its end."

Mara fought desperately to escape Brom's grasp. "Release me!" she screamed, a note of fear creeping into her furious, arrogant voice. "Together we shall rule the night. The mortal realm would be ours. You would be my king!"

Brom said nothing. Mara's flesh shriveled as her body began to wither and decay. She snapped at him with her teeth like a rabid dog. She dug her talons into his arms and struggled against his grip, but Brom held her fast.

A look of sheer terror filled Mara's black eyes. "I cannot be vanquished," her raspy voice croaked, "I am eternal! I shall rise again!"

"No," Brom said coldly. "When your life expires, you shall be dead for all time. You shall return to the dust from whence you came."

Brom released her from his grip and stepped outside the flaming ring. Mara remained bound within the mystic circle, held in place by the constricting, serpentine smoke.

"Your memory will fade until at last you are forgotten," Brom said. "In time, it shall be as if you never existed. If your spirit lives on, it shall know the torments of wickedness. Your essence shall be cursed to forever burn in the fires of Hell."

The Dark Queen screamed in agony. Her hair turned grey and fell from her scalp in clumps, leaving a corpse-like skull beneath it. Her head lolled back and her eyes lost their glaze. Mara's flesh cracked and flaked away like dried leaves, falling from her bones until little more than a skeleton remained.

Mara let loose a blood-chilling shriek before her voice fell silent. Her brittle bones crumbled to dust and scattered in the air like ashes from a dying fire. The black crown fell to the ground and rolled to the base of the throne. A crash of thunder sounded and a gust of wind swept through the hall, howling like the wail of a dying beast.

Mara was no more.

But Brom knew his battle was far from over. Though he had vanquished the Dark Queen, her minions still remained. He knew they would seek vengeance for their slain master. The savage horde thirsted for his blood and they would not rest until they had drained every drop from him.

A swirling black mist circled the chamber and a raucous sound rose to fill the hall with low, guttural moans. Vaporous tendrils slithered across the floor toward Brom, reaching to entangle him in their grasp. The Tower Lord leapt to the dais and bounded up the steps to the throne that yet held the relic sword. Taking firm hold of hilt, Brom yanked the sword free and whirled to face his advancing foes.

Monstrous forms rose from the mist, surrounding the dais like towering wraiths. Their bellowing voices echoed in Brom's ears like the roar of an army. A colossal beast, seemingly made of shadows, lumbered forth, ascending the stone staircase in two strides. The demon loomed before Brom, encircling him with its massive wings. The creature's eyes burned with the fires of damnation and the foul scent of brimstone filled the air.

"Lower your blade, infidel." The demon's growling voice penetrated Brom's mind, overpowering his thoughts.

Brom's arm trembled as he fought against the creature's command, but he held fast to his sword.

"You dare defy me?" The demon grabbed hold of Brom, clutching him by the throat and pulling him close.

As Brom stared into the creature's fiery gaze, he struggled to maintain his own will.

"Fool," the creature roared. "The blood in your veins commands you to serve the forces of darkness, yet you resist your true nature. Your fierce strength and powers were a divine gift from the mother of demons. She bestowed you with immortality and you sought to repay her with death. Now you shall answer for your murderous treachery!"

Brom focused his mind upon the sword in his hand. The sacred blade began to shimmer with a blue glow, radiating

JOSEPH VARGO   243

a light from its very core. Brom's body coursed with a newfound energy and he felt his strength and will return. He wrenched himself free of the creature's choking grasp.

"Yes," Brom said, "the powers of darkness dwell within me—this I cannot deny." Brom raised the sword that now shone with unearthly light and held it between them. "But I am their master."

Brom thrust the relic sword deep into the ebon fiend, driving the blade up through the creature's chest. The demon shrieked in agony as it slumped to its knees. Its scarlet eyes grew wide, then the fire within them faded. Brom pulled his sword free and the fallen beast disintegrated into smoldering embers of ash.

Shadows descended upon Brom from every side as the infernal horde closed in. He knew he had little time before the ghoulish creatures overwhelmed him. Even wielding the power of the relic sword, he knew he could not defeat an entire legion of demons. Brom looked toward the great doors at the far end of the hall, thinking to flee the chamber, but his path was thwarted by a sea of writhing shadows. In the next instant, something took hold of Brom's leg, dragging him down the steps of the dais and into the midst of chaos. The demons converged upon him, their monstrous claws reaching toward him, their fanged maws gaping wide. Brom lashed out with his sword, slashing and stabbing at the swarming brood but there were too many. The diabolic horde bore down upon him, binding his limbs with snakelike coils and taloned hands, crushing his strength and spirit.

Brom's mind and body went numb as he relinquished his fight, surrendering himself to death's embrace. At long last, he would be at rest. He hoped that his sacrifice would be enough to spare Vasaria and all of mankind from the horrors of the Black Dawn. In his mind's eye, he envisioned Rianna, awaiting him at the Tower gate beneath the light of the full moon, her arms outstretched in a gesture of loving welcome as he crossed the final threshold to eternal peace. He began to utter a prayer, but stopped when the words of an ancient invocation sparked in his memory. Closing his eyes, Brom cried out, "Sanvi, Sansavi, Semangelaf!"

As his words echoed through the hall, the sound of thunder rang out and a blinding flash lit the dark. Three angelic warriors clad in gleaming armor and flowing robes appeared atop the dais. Each wore a crown adorned with dark jewels and wielded a sword identical to the one in Brom's hand. Without a word, the angels lifted their blades and held them high. The swords began to pulse with a radiant glow, bathing the celestial knights in an unearthly blue aura. The shimmering halo grew brighter, expanding around them to fill the hall with a brilliant light, more fervent and scorching than a thousand torches. The shadow creatures wailed and shrieked as they tried to flee, but there was no escaping the fiery light. The demonic legion met their deaths where they stood. Their ebon flesh hardened and blistered until all that remained of their bodies were charred, smoldering husks that soon crumbled to cinders. Within seconds, their black ashes scattered like smoke in the wind.

The angels lowered their swords. The light faded and darkness claimed the room once more. Brom rose to his feet and stared around him at the empty hall. A tranquil hush hung over the sprawling chamber. The storm had passed. The Dark Brood had been destroyed.

Brom returned his attention to the angels upon the dais. The celestial warriors stood motionless, like flawless statues, staring down at him in silence. Their eyes seemed to convey a sense of pride and respect, and Brom felt a strange kinship with them. After a moment, two of the angelic knights spread their majestic wings and vanished in a flash of brilliant blue.

The remaining angel descended the dais stair, his black cape trailing behind him. "Hail, Lord Brom," he said. Shimmering blue light radiated from his armor, surrounding him in a luminous glow. The heavenly warrior stopped at the base of the steps where his foot came to rest beside Mara's crown.

Brom's eyes fell upon the ring of ebon spikes that lay on the floor between them. "I have vanquished the demon queen," he said.

The angel's face seemed to lighten with the trace of a smile. "Indeed. Thou hast proven thyself worthy of salvation. Thy noble deeds hath redeemed thy past transgressions and freed the souls that hath been bound here."

"And what of the soul I have fought to save?"

"She has been spared as well." The angel's eyes shone like glistening sapphires. "Thy love, Rianna awaits thee in the next world."

"The next world?" Brom's words were filled with curiosity and wonder.

"Yes, there is much that lies beyond this mortal realm, as thou shalt soon discover. Thy vigil here is over, yet one final matter remains—a matter of the greatest magnitude."

"The prophecy," Brom said.

"Yes," the angel said. "Its time has come. The key to unlocking its immortal power is now thine. But heed these words—this power, once awakened, shall surely change the course of humanity. A great decision rests with thee. Before departing this world for the next, thou must decide how to minister this gift."

"Yes." Brom nodded. "There is much to consider."

"Indeed." The angel's crystalline eyes penetrated Brom's

gaze as if searching the depths of his soul. "Thy heart is pure and just. Allow it to guide thee." Raven-black wings, lustrous and shimmering, spread out behind the heavenly knight. "Farewell, Lord Brom." With that, the angel rose up into the hall, vanishing in a flash of light.

Brom ascended the dais to rest upon the ebon throne. He looked out over the empty hall, then turned his gaze toward the brazier beside him where flames yet danced upon burning coals, casting meager light upon the surrounding darkness. The Tower Lord stared deep into the seething fire, contemplating the decision that lay before him.

In Vasaria below, the raging storm that had unleashed its fury upon the region had passed as swiftly as it had come and the night was calm once more. An eerie hush befell the creatures of the forest, and all remained still as if time had stopped. The silence was broken by a sudden cacophony of shrill screeches and caws that rose from the mountain woodlands to fill the night air. Leonidas and Adrian hurried to the edge of the village where Daria stood outside her small home, peering into the forest. Hundreds of ravens filled the trees, croaking madly as if possessed by some unearthly force.

"What does it mean?" Leonidas asked.

"I do not know," Daria said, a worried note in her voice. "I fear it may be a dark sign—perhaps an omen of death."

The sound of snapping twigs and crackling bramble alerted them to someone approaching through the trees. A moment later Lorand and Serena ran out of the woods, wild-eyed and breathless.

"What has happened?" Adrian's tone reflected the dire concern of all.

Lorand struggled to catch his breath. "Lord Brom freed

us. We returned here as fast as we could."

Daria laid a soothing hand upon the boy's shoulder. "And what of the Tower Lord?"

"We left him alone with the Dark Queen," Lorand said. "We did not want to abandon him, but he ordered us to leave."

Daria's eyes grew wide with fear. "Did he use the power of the amulet?"

Lorand shook his head as he gulped for breath. "He bestowed it upon Mara and she destroyed it. I do not know what happened next."

As the group exchanged worried glances, young Annika stepped outside the door of her home and gazed in wonder at the trees alive with the dark shimmer of black feathers.

"Go back inside, my love," Daria said quietly.

"But mother," Annika said, "the ravens sing to us."

Before Daria could respond, the great Tower bell sounded, its deep, somber rumble stilling the ravens' cries.

Annika stepped to the edge of the woods and closed her eyes, seemingly entranced by the distant tolling. After a moment, she turned to Leonidas and said, "Lord Brom summons you to the Tower."

"Brom yet lives?" The old man's eyes held a look of bewilderment. "And what of Mara?"

"The curse is ended," Annika said. "The queen is dead."

At the break of dawn, a small caravan left from Vasaria, heading along the forest path to the Tower. Leonidas, Adrian, and Daria trotted their horses up the mountain trail, while Lorand and Serena rode together behind them. Rays of the morning light penetrated the tangled canopy of vines and bramble, casting a vibrant glow upon the woodlands.

As they emerged from the forest path, the ancient keep

appeared before them, rising through the morning mists to loom among the clouds. The sense of gloom and foreboding that usually encompassed the Tower seemed to have dissipated in the daylight. A row of ravens sat perched atop the ruins of the ancient gate, silently watching the caravan as they passed. The howling wind faded to a whisper and an eerie calm settled over the summit.

The riders dismounted and tethered their horses near the base of the Tower steps. The castle's great doors stood open, as if awaiting their arrival. Nothing stirred beyond the doors, revealing no hint as to what lay within. Leonidas led the way as the others followed closely behind. Warily, they entered the keep.

Golden beams of sunlight shone down through the windows high above the entrance hall, bathing the chamber in warm shades of amber. The sun's luminous spell revealed the hall's former grandeur, allowing all eyes to see the lavish craftsmanship and decor that adorned the ancient keep. The architecture itself seemed more eloquent and regal. Colors and details that had remained hidden beneath the shadows of night were now visible to behold. The masonry surrounding the circular chamber held intricate scrollwork that echoed the designs of the finest cathedrals. Veins of deep scarlet shone forth from the black columns supporting the hall and the crimson rune that adorned the center of the floor glistened like a fiery ruby.

As they stood in humbled awe of the illuminated hall, Daria's senses alerted her to a presence nearby. A tall figure stood within the darkened archway beneath the balcony, silently watching from the shadows.

"Rest your fears," a low voice said. "The nightmare has ended." Brom emerged from the darkness, Mara's ebon crown in his bone-white hand. As he stepped into the sunlight, his black robes shimmered with deep shades of blue and purple.

Tears streaked Daria's face as she rushed toward Brom, casting her arms around him. She felt a vibrant warmth in his embrace. "You are alive," she said.

Brom smiled as he held her in his arms. "No," he whispered, "I have merely surpassed my deathly state."

Turning to Leonidas, Brom held forth the fallen queen's crown. "The darkness that once dwelled in the Tower shall plague Vasaria no more," he declared.

Leonidas stared at the ring of twisted spikes and stood speechless for a long moment. At last he said, "All of humanity is in your debt. No words are enough to thank you. I can think of no way to repay you for all you have done."

The Tower Lord placed his hand on his old friend's shoulder and smiled. Glancing toward Lorand and Serena, Brom whispered, "Watch over them."

As Brom approached Adrian, the monk smiled and said, "It would appear that all events have unfolded as they were meant to."

"Yes," Brom said. "I now know there is purpose and reason to all things. Even our darkest hours can serve to inspire us, for these times test the depths of our spirit, allowing us to discover the true measure of our strength." The Tower Lord cast his gaze upon the crimson sigil emblazoned upon the floor. "Twas no accident that our paths intertwined. Do you recall what first brought you to the Tower?" Brom gestured his hand toward the scarlet icon beneath his feet. "It was this symbol that drew us together. The spirit I encountered in the priory called it the sign of the Seraphim. It has marked this place as their domain for centuries, and so it shall continue to stand as a symbol of hope."

Leaving Adrian's side, Brom stepped before Lorand. "My vigil has come to its end," Brom said quietly. "Now I must go." The Tower Lord's words held the bitter tinge of remorse. "My greatest regret is that we did not have more time to share." Reaching beneath his cloak, Brom withdrew a leather-bound journal and placed it in Lorand's hand. "I have chronicled my tale herein."

Lorand threw his arms around Brom, clinging to him tightly. "I have learned much during our short time together," Lorand whispered, his voice thick with emotion. "I shall cherish those memories the rest of my life."

Brom closed his eyes. "You have made me proud, my son." He held Lorand for a long moment before stepping back toward the shadowed archway. "The time of the prophecy is at hand." Brom's declaration rang through the ancient hall in a chorus of echoes.

All remained silent as they awaited his next words.

"You have each risen to a noble cause, selflessly risking your own lives for the greater good." The Tower Lord's eyes fell upon them, one by one. "You symbolize what is best about humanity. But, sadly, you do not represent all of mankind. While some men seek to follow the path of honor and virtue, there are those who are swayed toward vice. As you know, this is a grim and twisted path that leads only to misery and destruction.

"The power I hold shall change the course of mankind's destiny. Should I choose to bestow this gift upon them, it shall magnify the true nature of men, granting them immortality and allowing them to reach goals far beyond their dreams. But shall this evolution lead to humanity's enlightenment or to its downfall? Though I have witnessed much good in this world, evil and sin yet exist in the hearts of men." Brom's eyes returned to the design on the floor. He stared at the scarlet sigil for a long moment. At last, he raised his head. "No," he whispered, "humanity is not yet ready for this gift. I dare not risk its abuse.

"Though my decision may seem severe, it is not final. I have faith that someday men shall rise above sin and abandon all vice. Until that day, I shall join my love." A smile touched Brom's lips. "My transcended essence shall live on, but my body shall remain here, in deathless slumber, entombed within the mountain. My spirit shall watch over this realm from the next. When humanity has proven itself worthy, I shall return to minister this sacred gift to all mankind."

"Until that time, I shall dispense this power as I see fit, when I decree, seeking chosen ones to aid me with man's final ascension." Brom slid his sword from his belt and raised it high above his head. "The Dark Queen is dead!" his voice filled the hall with a triumphant tremor. "Go now and spread word of this throughout the land, for this day marks the beginning of a new era—an era of freedom and hope."

Serena stepped forward, her eyes welling with tears. "Shall we ever see you again?" she asked.

"Perhaps," Brom said, gently brushing a tear from her cheek. "If not in this world, then surely in the next." The Tower Lord receded back into the shadows of the archway. "Farewell," he said. The word echoed round the great room like the flutter of raven's wings, then the hall fell silent.

With that, Leonidas turned to leave, followed by Daria and Adrian. Serena took Lorand's hand in hers and gently led him away. Lorand slowly stepped toward the exit, but stopped at the Tower's immense doors. He turned back one final time and saw Brom standing beneath the archway, encircled by a halo of azure light. Another figure stood beside him, a beautiful woman shrouded in white. Recognizing his mother's spirit, Lorand smiled. Rianna's lovely specter cast her haunting gaze upon her son, returning his smile with a look of loving warmth. Great ebon wings spread out from Brom's back, wrapping themselves around the ghostly beauty, holding her in their dark embrace. The halo of blue shimmered around Brom and Rianna, engulfing them in its unearthly radiance and then they were gone. The Tower stood empty and silent at last.

In the eastern mountains of Romania, far above the region once known as Vasaria, the husk of an ancient castle yet stands, its dark stones covered in vines and bramble. Black spires stretch tall into the sky, casting long shadows over the forest below. No one ventures there, for it is believed to be a haunted place—a haven for restless spirits of the dead.

The summit is said to have been the site of an ancient battleground between the forces of light and darkness, an earthly arena where angels and demons fought to decide mankind's fate. Legends say the Tower was once the fortress of a dark and sinister queen, and that an undying evil yet slumbers in the caverns deep within the mountain below. Other tales tell of a lone guardian who dwells among the ruins—an immortal warrior who guards a divine secret and keeps eternal vigil watching over the world of man.

But these are merely legends, the fabled history of a forsaken citadel that crests the distant mountaintop like the crown of a fallen titan. Though its true name has long been forgotten, it lives on in myth and memory, forevermore known only as The Dark Tower.

— THE END —

VARGO 99

JOSEPH VARGO resides in Cleveland, Ohio where he has been conjuring fantasy artwork professionally since 1986. His gothic images open a gateway to the darkside and dare the viewer to venture within. Joseph's haunting visions of fantasy and horror have appeared in numerous publications, and his lithographs, printwear and Gothic Tarot deck are distributed worldwide. His artbook, *Born of the Night: The Gothic Fantasy Artwork of Joseph Vargo*, features a collection of over 100 paintings and illustrations spanning 20 years of his career. Joseph is also a noted composer and musician, earning worldwide acclaim with his musical project Nox Arcana. His book *The Legend of Darklore Manor and Other Tales of Terror* contains 13 sinister stories including the novella that chronicles the grim history of the haunted mansion that inspired Nox Arcana's debut album.

www.JosephVargo.com

Joseph Iorillo is a freelance writer living in Cleveland Heights, Ohio. He is a *Summa Cum Laude* graduate of John Carroll University and holds a Bachelor of Arts degree in English. As a staff writer for *Dark Realms Magazine,* Joseph contributed numerous articles on topics as diverse as secret societies, ancient Sumeria, horror cinema, haunted houses and theories of the afterlife. Joseph has written several mystery and suspense novels, including the contemporary ghost story *This House Is Empty Now, Goodnight Blackbird,* and *Psychomanteum.* He is the co-author of *The Gothic Tarot Compendium* and *The Legend of Darklore Manor and Other Tales of Terror.* Joseph holds a lifelong interest in the esoteric mysteries of the world as well as all things supernatural.

www.JosephIorillo.com

THE LEGEND OF DARKLORE MANOR AND OTHER TALES OF TERROR

Enter a dark realm of living gargoyles, sinister shadows, diabolical dolls, haunted havens and undead nightmares in this illustrated anthology of thirteen tales by Joseph Vargo and Joseph Iorillo, including the original novella inspired by Nox Arcana's haunting concept album, *Darklore Manor*.

THE DARK TOWER BOOK SERIES

The Dark Tower saga begins with thirteen illustrated tales of gothic mystery, horror and romance. Discover the origins of the sinister tower and the tragic souls cursed to forever haunt its forsaken halls.

THE DARK TOWER SOUNDTRACK BY NOX ARCANA

21 tracks of haunting melodies, ominous orchestrations and chilling sound effects provide the perfect atmosphere of mystery and menace for *The Dark Tower* book series. Composed by Joseph Vargo.

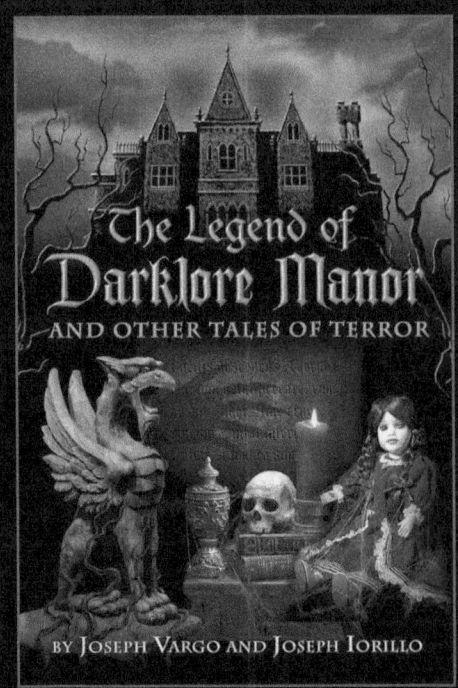

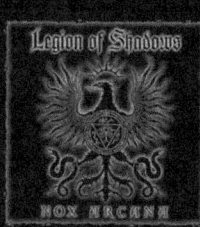

www.ingramcontent.com/pod-product-compliance
Lightning Source LLC
Chambersburg PA
CBHW051630260626
47170CB00004B/1120